Jennifer the Damned

Karen Ullo

Wiseblood Books

Bismarck

Library of Congress Cataloging-in-Publication Data
Ullo, Karen 1979—
Jennifer the Damned/ Karen Ullo;
1. Vampire fiction   2. Young adult fiction
3. Louisiana   4. Hollywood, California
5. Catholic Fiction

ISBN-10: 0692303030
ISBN-13: 9780692303030

JENNIFER THE DAMNED

I die a thousand deaths because I do not die.

— St. John of the Cross

I

THE BLACK HOLE

Vampires are supposed to be beautiful.

In novels they are always sleek and elegant, with cold but perfect ivory skin, comporting themselves with ease among the *crème de la crème,* their piercing eyes seducing victims with a glance.

In novels, vampires do not have acne — which goes to show how much novelists know.

I stood in front of the mirror staring back and forth between the great red pimple on the side of my nose and the tube of cream that claimed to be able to cure it. *Clears away dirt, oil, and bacteria,* it said, and I wondered for the millionth time whether there were, in fact, bacteria in my body. Did tiny organisms digest my food? Did microscopic colonies feed on my teeth? Was there anything about me that was *natural?*

Apparently there was something, whether bacteria or hormones or simply pores that could be clogged. Otherwise I would not have this miniature volcano growing on my face. One would think being fated for oblivion might at least exempt me from the ravages of puberty.

I squeezed the tube and rubbed the white goop onto my face just as the chime of the chapel bell summoned me to breakfast. I grabbed my books and headed to the kitchen, where the nauseating aroma of eggs washed over me. Even after all these years, I still had to work not to vomit every time I passed a kitchen. The sisters always tried to persuade me to take a balanced diet, and every morning hash browns or fruit or eggs sat as noxious complements to the rare steak — barely seared — that comprised my only sustenance. It was seared for the sisters' benefit. I would have preferred it raw.

"Morning, Jen," said Sister Diane as she slid in next to me at the table. Her humble plate carried a bagel and fruit; steak was a luxury afforded only to the oddball orphan who could eat nothing else. "Excited about the new year?" she asked.

"I guess you could say that."

"And happy birthday, too." Her eyes crinkled, almost smirking. Very little emotion ever passed through the filter of Sister Diane's blue habit, but I had learned how to read the subtle variations in the crow's feet edging her veil.

"Thank you." I took a bite of the meat.

"Good cut this morning?"

"Yes, I'll have to thank Sister Joan. Probably bought it for my birthday."

"Mmm."

This was a frequent remark upon the sore subject of my diet. On Fridays during Lent, especially, my steak sat between the sisters and me, a bleeding reminder that I could never be Catholic.

I took another bite, savoring the flavor. How long would it be before dead meat no longer satisfied? I had a feeling the sisters were going to like my new diet far less than the old.

"Good morning, Sister Theresa." Sister Diane's voice startled me out of contemplation. The half-chewed bite of steak stuck in my throat, so I chased it with water. Thank God I could drink water, or the sisters would have had me on intravenous fluids every day of my life.

"Good morning, Sister Diane," Sister Theresa replied. "Happy birthday, Jen."

"Thanks."

"Did you finish *Crime and Punishment?*"

"Yes."

"And?"

"And I don't get why the New Word would be what leads Raskolnikov astray when the themes are so obviously Christian. Wasn't Dostoevsky referring to the New Testament?"

Sister Theresa beamed. At thirty-five, she was the youngest of the nuns in our little convent and the only one who shared my habit of devouring as much fiction as the library would allow us to check out. This year, she would also be my English teacher. "I'm glad you caught that," she said. "But, no, in this case the New Word was the philosophy Raskolnikov embraced, that logic and the common good could outweigh morality."

"That makes more sense."

"I don't suppose you even glanced at your physics book this summer?" Sister Diane peered at me over the bridge of her nose.

"I wouldn't want to get too far ahead of the class."

"Right, because that's always stopped you before."

I managed a laugh as the bell chimed again, calling us to school.

Our Lady of Prompt Succor Academy was operated by the Sisters of Prompt Succor, a religious order named to honor the patroness of Louisiana. Devotion to the Virgin Mary under the title Our Lady of Prompt Succor had been common in Louisiana since the early nineteenth century, and she had even been credited with turning back the British at the Battle of New Orleans in 1815. The Sisters of Prompt Succor, however, dated back only to the 1930s. They were a small order with just two convents, their headquarters in New Orleans and this one, my little four-nun home in the heart of Baton Rouge.

I had first arrived at Prompt Succor when I was five years old, full of wonder, delighted to be among my peers for the first time in my life. I ran around the kindergarten room in ballerina-pink shoes hugging every single one of my classmates and demanding to know their names. "I'm Jennifer Carshaw," I gushed, "and this is my first day of school."

A boy with golden hair and russet-colored eyes shrugged out of my embrace and pushed me down. "Get off me! My mom says your mom is evil."

Looking back, it seems unfair that my classmates should have been better informed than I.

Of course, at the time I just stood there, not knowing what to say in the face of such an ill-mannered reception. My vigilant mother emerged from the shadows, picked me up, and gave the boy a smile that stopped him dead in his tracks. "You're Jeremy, aren't you? Dr. Higginbotham's son?"

Jeremy nodded.

"It's rude to repeat gossip, Jeremy, even gossip one hears from one's parents."

He nodded again, unable to pry his unblinking eyes from my mother's ruby mouth.

"Now, Jeremy, I want you to apologize to Jennifer."

He ground his left toe into the carpet and mumbled in its direction, "Sorry."

"It's okay," I mumbled back.

My mother nodded and then left me alone, buried alive inside a world of alphabets, Play-Doh, and friendly human smiles.

Eleven years later, I was set to begin yet another first day of school. The desks had grown, but the kids who occupied them had not changed much. Angie Carroll, wearing pink shoes and hugging a proliferation of necks, still looked and acted much as I had back on that first of first days. But my neck was not among those Angie fell upon as she greeted everyone after our long summer apart. If I tried to join the reunion, I knew she would grimace as only a teenage girl can and issue one of those biting, catty remarks I had never been able to master. I withdrew to the corner of my homeroom, pulled out my math book, and began tracing over some previous owner's margin-doodles. Matt Derwin slinked into the seat next to mine. We gave each other perfunctory nods. He was the other outcast, the kid three sizes too long and three grade levels too smart, with Harry Potter glasses and perpetually cow-licked hair. We would have been friends if he could have overcome his crippling shyness and I could have overcome the gnawing certainty that, someday, I would want to suck his blood.

"Good morning!" Mr. Valen's rotund baritone filled the room and the chatter tapered to a buzz. "Welcome to eleventh grade." He called the roll, which seemed silly, since Mr. Valen also taught tenth grade geometry and already knew every one of our names.

When he finished, he said the worst thing he could possibly say. "Jen, I understand it's your birthday today. Everybody, why don't we sing 'Happy Birthday?'"

I groaned. "It's not necessary, really . . ."

"Nonsense. Everyone?" He raised his hands like a conductor.

"Happy birthday TO you. Happy birthday TOOO YOOOU. Happy BIRTH- Day dear Jen-i-ferrrrr . . ." The mocking bellow echoed in the cramped tile blandness, the croaking tenor of Jeremy Higginbotham leading the charge. He sat there, two rows to the left of me, his golden hair flopped with an elegant nonchalance down over those glamorous russet eyes, staring at me with his nose flared as though he could smell my nerdy worthlessness. I clenched my teeth and stared right back, willing some part of the monster inside me to intimidate someone — preferably *him* — just once.

The temperature in the room seemed to drop by ten degrees. I shivered as Jeremy's eyes grew crater-wide, his croaking ceased, and for one brief instant, there was fear. I not only saw it, sensed it in all the normal ways, but I could smell it, too, wafting from his pores like musk and hickory. He turned away, but I kept sniffing, mesmerized, until everyone fell silent. I sat there, a freak with an audience, while one by one the fear spread and filled them, too, rising in a cloud of savory, tantalizing warmth.

"Er, Jennifer? Are you okay?" Mr. Valen's two-hundred-pound frame seemed somehow small as he willed his voice to speak.

"I'm fine."

"Er, happy birthday, then. Why don't we all take out our books?"

The class attempted to return to normal while I stared at my desk, trying not to breathe so I would not inhale any more of that fragrant, forbidden bouquet. My mind boggled, trying to figure out what about plain, dorky Jennifer Carshaw had suddenly caused a room full of people to stop dead in their metaphorical tracks. I couldn't wait for the bell to ring for second hour. After about five minutes of fidgeting with my pencil, I got up and darted out. I ran all the way to my room in the convent. The tube of acne cream still lay there, by the mirror. I raised my head to look.

Nothing had changed. Whatever my classmates had seen was gone. Now I would have to go back to face an entire day of whispers and stares, to be followed by a long night of nuns trying to help me through the emotional difficulties engendered by whispers and stares. But what else could I do? Cutting class was not really an option when you lived with two of your teachers and the principal.

I sat down on my bed. Clearly, my days of pretending to be human were numbered. Sixteen years had passed since I was changed, the time it takes all vampires to mature and become the bloodsucking monsters of legend. I might have a few more weeks, at most, of my charade. Or it could end tonight. The luscious smell of fear came back to me, startling yet somehow familiar, awakening primordial senses that had lain dormant throughout my long gestation. I did not know what I would be like when the instinct to kill emerged. My mother had been a master predator, a model of self-control who never left a trace. But my mother had had several millenia to hone her skills.

I lay down. Now that I had left homeroom, I might as well wait until second hour to go back. I relished the comfortable familiarity of the discount store sheets, the faded yellow quilt hand-made by a nineteenth century French nun: the thriftiness of the convent paired with the sisters' longing to shower me with good things. I looked up at the crucifix above my door and wondered whether the road to Calvary might have been easier to walk than the path that stretched before me now.

❖

I did not realize I had fallen asleep until a tapping at my door woke me. "Come in," I called, trying to remember why I was in bed in the middle of the day.

Sister Diane entered, her rubber-soled shoes squishing against the tile floor. "Mr. Valen and I both have fourth period off."

A tsunami of emotions struck me dumb as I recalled the morning's events.

"It's really not acceptable to skip the first day of school," Sister Diane went on in the same pragmatic tone she used to discuss physics, the Holy Trinity, baseball, or breast cancer. But I recognized the undertones of anxiety that only the practiced ear could discern.

"What did Mr. Valen tell you?"

"That you were radiant. In the truest sense. He and the students swore they could feel heat emanating from your body."

"So that's why they were afraid of me." My eyes glazed over as her words sank in.

A vampire's normal body temperature hovered around 97 degrees, pretty close to the human 98.6, which meant we could tolerate the same weather and touch them without drawing a comment. However, when about to kill, a vampire's temperature could rise as high as 120 degrees, often in the blink of an eye. If I was running hot, then it was time.

Sister Diane touched my forehead. "You're not running a fever."

"Of course not. That's ludicrous."

"It would be, if there hadn't been thirty witnesses." She stared me down. "Jennifer, is there something you need to tell me?"

"Like what?"

"Like the real reason you eat nothing but seared beef and refuse to have a physical exam. I've consulted doctors and nutritionists, and no one is familiar with any disorder that would require your diet to consist solely of meat. I don't know what's going on, but whatever it is, we can help you."

I gazed into her olive-green eyes, hard as nails but full of love. At any moment, I might feel the urge to kill this good woman who had been more of a mother to me than Helen Carshaw ever was.

I leaned over and kissed her cheek. "Thank you for everything, Sister Diane."

"That's hardly an answer."

"I know." I gathered my books from the floor just as the school bell clamored. "Come on. I'm in your class this hour."

She pursed her lips, letting me know she would not allow the subject to drop. I shuffled my feet and trailed behind her all the way to class.

2

Jeremy Higginbotham's unusual proclamation on the first day of kindergarten was not my first indication that I might be different from other children. I had noticed that the grocery store sold things other than raw meat, and I had also noticed that none of these things smelled edible.

"Because they're not," my mother told me when I asked.

"Then why do I see people eating them?"

"We're not the same as other people. They can eat lots of things, but you and I can only eat meat."

"You don't eat meat. You just fix it for me."

My mother pushed the grocery cart with renewed vigor and said no more.

I waited a moment, then continued, "What makes us different?"

"Our stomachs don't digest food the way others do."

"What's digest?"

She launched into a complicated scientific explanation of digestion, using my natural curiosity to distract me from the topic of my identity.

Despite a lifetime's observation and questioning, it was not until that first day of school, when Jeremy Higginbotham used the word, that I began to suspect there might be something *evil* about my peculiar family. Of course, when I asked my mother about it, she gave me a cold stare and told me not to repeat gossip. The subject did not resurface until second grade, when all of the children in my class at Prompt Succor were preparing to receive First Communion. I did not know I had never been baptized, and I could hardly wait to receive the Body and Blood of our Lord Jesus Christ, if for no other reason than because I would get to wear a new dress. My wardrobe consisted of school uniforms and a few play-clothes for after school and weekends, and that was all. I had begged my mother for such things as hair bows, frilly skirts, and ridiculous high-heeled sandals like all the other girls wore, and she had flatly refused. Such things were "impractical," a cardinal sin according to my mother's worldview. However, the beautiful white First Communion dress appeared to be part of our school uniform. My mother could hardly refuse me that. So I waited in blessed hope for the coming of the sacrament.

When she sat me down at the kitchen table one night, about a month before my class was scheduled to receive Holy Communion, I had no idea she was about to tear my world apart. My mind could not conceive of anything worse than that she was going to have to work a double shift again.

"Jennifer, you won't be receiving Communion with the rest of your class."

Tiny shards of pink crystal hope exploded inside my heart, lacerating my dreams. "Why?"

"Communion is not meant for us."

"Sister Joan says it's meant for everyone, to save our souls from the devil."

My mother smiled her crooked, perverse smile. "Jennifer, you and I . . . *we don't have souls.*"

That night, I learned that everything I had ever thought or dreamed or hoped for was a lie. I was doomed by my very nature.

I sat now in fifth hour physics, ignoring Sister Diane's introduction to Newton's laws of motion, telling myself that I could stay at Prompt Succor if I wanted, regardless of the danger to the nuns. What did it matter if I woke up one day in a frenzy of thirst and killed my friends, the holy sisters of the Lord? I was no more responsible for my hunger than a tiger or a shark or any other man-eating predator. Morality meant nothing to me. I did not have a soul.

Immortal, the legends call the vampires; ironic, since only humans can live beyond the grave. I might survive on this earth until some far-off day when meteors or gamma rays obliterated it out of the sky, but I would end, poof. Nothing of me would remain. There would be no judgment, no heaven, no hell. In the end, there would only be an end.

I felt a salty sting in my eyes and pressed my palms against them. When the bell rang, I raced down the hall to the water fountain, drinking to hide the tears.

The soft hand on my shoulder did not surprise me. I kept drinking, not wanting to face Sister Diane again.

"Hey, you okay?" A masculine voice rattled across my eardrums. I spun to find myself staring at Matt Derwin. My jaw fell open like a largemouth bass.

He looked pretty surprised himself. "Look, I'm sorry about homeroom. Valen knows what a bunch of jerks are in our class. He shouldn't have asked them to sing."

"Oh. Thanks." The breath seemed to have left my lungs.

"So, you going to be okay?"

I swatted at the last of the tears. The shock of kindness seemed to have made them stop. "Oh. Sure, I guess."

"Do you need to get the notes?"

My mind teetered backward toward the realm of academia, trying to remember what he meant. "Oh. Yeah, I guess."

"I can meet you after school. I'm in your third hour, too." He blushed crimson. "I got a syllabus for you."

"Oh. Thanks. Sure."

He smiled and walked away — and then I realized what had happened.

Matt and I had helped each other with classes before. It came with the territory, being the two smartest and least popular kids in school. However, unless I was very much mistaken, on today of all days, a human male had just shown *interest* in me. Granted, I had learned the psychology of teenage boys by watching edited-for-TV movies, but I was reasonably certain I had just been approached in a context that could be considered romantic. Which was very, very bad.

I did not know exactly how vampires reproduced. I did know that the species endured through some process of altering living humans, so vampires had no need to mate. I could never truly return the kind of affection Matt had shown; I could only twist it into a noose that would strangle us both.

I twiddled my thumbs through two more hours of lectures while the kids around me giggled, whispered, and passed notes. Apparently, word of my "radiance" had gotten around. I let them whisper. It didn't matter now. I knew what I had to do. I could not stay here to murder four nuns and Matt Derwin, too. I might never have to answer to God for my sins, but I would have to live with myself for countless ages yet to come.

As he'd promised, Matt was waiting by the door after school. "Hey." He looked almost as nervous as I felt.

"Hey," I replied. I followed him toward an outdoor bench near a statue of St. Blaise. Our classmates gawked as we sat down together, and I swelled with pride for my new friend because he ignored them entirely.

"This is the syllabus from English, although I guess you could have gotten it from Sister Theresa."

"It was still really nice of you to get it for me." I took the paper, not bothering to mention that I'd had a copy since June.

"And here's my notes from homeroom. You know Valen. He starts into the material first thing. There's even homework due tomorrow."

"Yeah, I figured." I tucked the papers into my bag, trying to decide how to end this tactfully. Instead I found myself saying, "Thank you. Really." Then I touched his hand. What was I *doing?*

He shrugged. "It's just class notes."

I willed my legs to stand, putting the bench between us. "See you tomorrow?"

"Actually, do you have to go?"

I sucked in a breath. The last thing I wanted was to hurt this poor, kind boy who had worked up quite a lot of courage to ask me this question, especially since I was aching to stay. "Yeah, I do. Sorry. It's my birthday, and the sisters have something planned . . ."

"Oh, right. Of course. I meant to tell you, happy birthday."

I rolled my eyes. "Yeah. Thanks."

He laughed. "Tomorrow, then?"

"Yeah. Thanks again." I walked away, knowing — resolving — that I would never lay eyes on him again.

❖

A well-intentioned farce of plastered smiles greeted me at home, where the four lovely women responsible for my welfare strove gallantly to ignore my disastrous first day of school. They sang a rousing chorus of "Happy Birthday" in far better tune and better taste than my classmates. I choked down one bite of cake for their benefit; it tasted like compost. They bestowed upon me a pair of cute, strappy sandals I had looked at online a few weeks back. Someone must have been tracking my browser history. A normal teenager would have been upset by this invasion of privacy, but I knew they were only trying to give me the best life they knew how.

Every one of them kissed and hugged me as they wished me good night. Even Sister Diane managed only to glare at me once, a silent promise that tomorrow the farce would end. For now, she set our conflict aside and tucked a crisp twenty-dollar bill into my hand. "Get an ice cream or something. Cool yourself off."

I packed my backpack in mournful silence while the sisters were at evening prayer, then put on my headphones and listened to Shostakovich while I waited for the right time to sneak out. The cold pursuit of pitiless brass, bows that scraped out shrieks from strings, forbidding them to soar . . . I wondered if my favorite composer had been a vampire, to know so well the colors of my pain.

The sisters returned from the chapel and went to their rooms. The fifth symphony ended. I took a deep breath and forced myself to heft my bag onto my shoulder. A minor with no driver's license, no passport, no money, and no skill at forgery did not have many options when it came to running away. I shuddered, wondering how bad my new home would smell.

In the kitchen, I found a piece of paper taped to the back door.

Dear Jen,

I pray you will never read this because if you do, it means you're sneaking out and probably running away. I won't try to stop you. You know that if there is anything we can do to help, we will move heaven and earth to do it. I know that if you're taking this drastic step, it is because there is truly nothing we can offer. I pray you will find the help you need, whatever it may be. I pray you will return to us when you can. Until that day, always remember: God loves you. I love you. You will never be alone.

Diane

The loose-leaf trembled as I tore it from the glass. I creased the paper into a tiny, hopeless square and shoved it deep into my backpack. It weighed on my shoulders like a ton of lead. I reached out, opened the door, and walked away into the darkness.

3

The moon cast ghoulish shadows as I trudged through the waterlogged night, my feet crackling on the gravel. Past the floral wrought-iron gate that gave Orchid Gardens of Memory its name, a dusty granite mausoleum loomed against the hedgerows like a coffin that had been allowed to overgrow its well-pruned neighbors. A pair of Doric columns flanked a door of solid bronze; weathered carvings on the lintel had eroded beyond shape, leaving the whole structure ready to crumble at the first sign of climbing ivy. I squinted, trying vainly to distort the stone facade into something I could call home. After a few minutes, I gave up.

I had ordered a lock-picking kit a few weeks ago in anticipation of this night. Now I retrieved it from my bag and set to work, imagining what my mother would say if she could see me now.

The greening door groaned against its own weight as I hauled it open. Inside, no windows punctuated the shadow-gray walls; no moonlit glow vied to chase away the gloom. Nothing but the harsh beam of my flashlight gave color to my new home.

I would have to invest in an economy-sized package of D batteries.

In the middle of the stone floor stood the Angel Gabriel in flowing robes, his trumpet raised in salute. I leaned against him, acclimating myself to the smell of cold antiquity, trying to banish thoughts of my toasty little convent bed. "Welcome home," I muttered aloud. I waited for confirmation – an echo, a ghost – but even Gabriel the Messenger had nothing to say. Only the click of the bolt in the lock thudded a dreary welcome.

My mother would have laughed to see me standing here. I could hear her sneer, "A cemetery, Jennifer? Are you trying to get yourself killed?"

She had told me about a time in Europe when vampires lived in cemeteries to avoid detection by humans still credulous enough to believe in our existence. When the vampires were discovered, an outright war had ensued, as a result of which the collective human psyche had forevermore linked graveyards to our kind.

I had considered this problem and decided that if humans were to find me living in a graveyard, they would not see a vampire, but a sixteen-year-old runaway with nowhere else to go. Just to be sure, I had brought along a collection of empty Coke cans and food wrappers to strew around my lair. A cemetery also solved other problems, such as where to hide the bodies of my victims. Without my mother's wisdom to suggest other possibilities, this seemed like a pretty good place to stash the evidence of my crimes. I did not think many law enforcement agencies made a habit of searching for the missing among occupied graves.

I had staked out my new abode one Saturday when the sisters thought I was at the library. I stayed for six hours and saw not a soul. The mausoleum had been closed to burials for about forty years, so most of the loved ones of those inside had since found their own way to the grave. I would not have to clean out my lair at a moment's notice for funerals, and if anyone should happen by, I could always pretend I was there to pray for Great Grandma

Alice. Yes, the plan was pretty much perfect — except that it left me sleeping on a stone floor surrounded by dead bodies, without a friend in the world.

I checked each corner for drafts, chose the windiest one — this was August, after all — and rested my head on my backpack while I waited for sleep to come. My birthday had ended, the last real birthday I would ever have. I would stop aging, frozen forever at an awkward, acne-filled sixteen. I felt along the side of my nose and sure enough, the pimple was still there. With my luck, it always would be. I would keep this exact body for as many centuries as I might endure: all angles and lines, wanting to be supple, but lacking roundness in the knees, the elbows, the breasts. Sixteen was an age of promise and potential: a stupid place to be stuck.

I tried not to think of my mother, but of course it did not work. So much for promise and potential; she'd sucked them both dry in the first screaming moments of my infant life. There in the musty blackness of my first night in the grave, the story that I wished with all my heart my mother had never told me replayed itself on an endless, nightmarish loop inside my mind.

When I was in fourth grade, my teacher assigned a project; we each had to research the news from the city of our birth during the week when we were born. By that time, I had known I was a vampire for two years — long enough to wonder about how I had actually come into being, but not long enough to work up the courage to ask. Even with the project hanging over my head, I did not dare voice the question. I only said to my mother, "I need you to bring me to the library."

She was the one who asked, "What for?"

It turned out I had been born in Cincinnati, the city where Helen Carshaw had begun her career as a labor and delivery nurse. She had chosen the profession because it provided a constant onslaught of temptation, thrilling cries of new-born life, and the heady scent of human blood. Resisting the urge to sink her teeth into her patients was just another exercise in Helen's pursuit to master her four-thousand-year-old charade of passing for a human. In those four long millenia, however, Helen had never attempted to master motherhood. Being surrounded by mothers every day finally made her curious enough to give it a try.

She took on shifts at the prenatal clinic connected to the hospital, getting to know the patients in order to carefully select her daughter. That much was certain: she wanted a girl. If Helen were going to lower herself to take on such a thoroughly human enterprise, then at least the end result should be to produce something truly sublime, namely her heir, her almost-clone. She waited three years before identifying a woman whose name she never told me, a woman beautiful, intelligent, punctual, and precise. Helen tracked her through the pregnancy, stalked her near its end, and when the woman went into labor, Helen made her move. She performed the C-section in the woman's own living room with only her teeth for a scalpel. When at last the mother lay silent, her bloodless womb spilled across the rug, Helen turned to her prize.

She kissed me and named me Jennifer. Then she made her way south, baby vampire in tow.

Sixteen years later, I lay shivering on the stone floor of the crypt, my body transforming with every breath, becoming inevitably like the monster that had created me. I told myself I would not be like her, that I would only kill out of necessity, that I would choose victims who deserved to die. I would not — could not — be the author of any scene as ghastly as my own birth. I would cling to compassion and what little goodness I might possess.

Wouldn't I?

I bit the strap of my backpack, trying not to scream, but still the sound escaped through my chattering teeth, the searing anguish of my life undone.

❖

I did not remember falling asleep, but when I awoke every muscle was locked in place. Hints of daylight peeped under the door. I pried myself from the floor and quickly checked the bolt: unlocked. Good. That meant the caretaker had not bothered to look inside when he opened it, so he was not likely to check in the future. Maybe I would not have to carry out my gruesome Plan B, which involved a pull-out coffin bed.

I stretched, letting my circulation resume. My stomach grumbled loudly. I had about fifty dollars, including the twenty Sister Diane had pressed into my hand. I hoped it would buy enough steak to keep me going until my transformation was complete.

I walked to a convenience store restroom about a block away and did what I could to make myself presentable, including rubbing in a second dose of acne cream. Then I walked another block to a grocery store to get breakfast and batteries. I ate out back, in the vacant part of the parking lot. The raw meat nearly melted on my tongue after so many years of seared beef. I looked at my watch: 10:00 a.m. The day stretched endlessly ahead of me.

What was I going to *do,* now that I was not in school and had no human contacts?

Well, I wasn't going to loiter at the Winn Dixie.

I started walking, looking through car windows at the faces of the drivers, wondering if one of them would be the first. As much as I hated the thought of killing, I had no other choice. I had read books where vampires chose to drink animal blood instead of human. My mother said she had tried it when she got a hankering to visit Antarctica. Penguins turned out to be "about as nourishing as dust," and she fled back to South America, half-starved. She tried it again when she decided to explore the Amazon, but none of the myriad creatures living in its unprobed depths could quench the fire of her thirst. If it had not been for an undiscovered tribe of natives, my mother said she would have died.

Yes, *died.* Immortality is fickle that way. Vampires are like giant sequoias: capable of withstanding ages so protracted only geologists could measure them, but a drought or a chainsaw could end that, no problem. I would either drink human blood or die. It had occurred to me that the blood bank offered a non-lethal option for sustaining my life, but they would hardly just whip up a blood smoothie, extra platelets, whenever I felt a bit peckish. I dodged a minivan on a bridge with no shoulder and thanked God that I did not have a soul. Without it, at least I would not face hell just for serving up Sunday brunch.

My feet led me to the library. Old habits die hard. I debated whether or not to go in, but I did not know where else to go, and since Tuesday was Mrs. Jones's day off, I wasn't likely to be recognized. I let myself in, found a newly published novel about the Great Depression, and settled into a sofa hidden in the stacks.

But apparently, Elma Jones had changed her schedule. I crouched behind my book as I saw her approach, pushing a cart of books to re-shelve, wearing her standard 1992-issue white oxford button-down and tapered-leg slacks. She ignored me at first, going calmly about her work, but after a moment I felt her stop moving and knew her eyes had come to rest on me. I lowered the novel.

"Jennifer, nice to see you."

"You, too, Mrs. Jones."

"Parent conference day already? Didn't school just start?"

"Yes, ma'am."

"Because nobody skips school to go to the library, right?"

"Of course not."

"Mm-hm."

I nodded and raised the novel again. She re-shelved a few more books, still watching me. "How is Sister Diane?" Elma's daughter had graduated from Prompt Succor a few years ago, so she knew the nuns.

"She's fine. I'll tell her you asked."

"And if I mention to her that I saw you here?"

"She'll be relieved. She was afraid I'd get hit walking here."

"Okay. Which book is that? *The Gin Hole* — oh, good choice."

"Thanks."

Mrs. Jones finished re-shelving and then turned down the next aisle. I returned to my story, wondering how long I had before she called the nuns. As long as I knew she was on the other side of the shelf, working her way back toward me, I was safe.

The air conditioner poured her scent into my lungs like wet cement. Muscles tensed without the aid of will. A cloud of leaden fog washed away all thought while a spring of instinct coiled, waiting, tighter. . .

I leapt . . . and crashed into the bookshelf.

The metal struck against bone, gashing my forehead. Screams issued from my prey as the shelf and all its contents collapsed on top of her. Thought reappeared, and with it the consciousness of blinding pain. The suffocating haze still clouded my sight as I ploughed through the rubble toward the door. I heard someone cry, "Stop! You're hurt!" and someone else tried to get in my way, but I threw them aside while iron bars of famine constricted every breath I could not breathe.

Past the door, the rays of blinding sun warred against the haze, a dizzy, diffuse daylight that stung my eyes with ashen tears. I raised my hand to the wound in my head, but there was no blood to staunch. Resolutely, I marched on, gasping in pollution to try to clear my lungs of human scent while the blazing August heat chilled my feverish skin. My stomach clenched, a cave of primal hunger, but my muscles defied its emptiness as they burned with a new power.

Cars honked, swerving madly, while I crossed streets without looking, cutting through parking lots and backyards, knowing that the first person whose scent wafted above the smog would die. The pain in my skull had subsided by the time I reached Orchid

Gardens, but the cement in my lungs was growing heavier, drying. I pushed past the rusting iron gates into the ordered jungle of headstones, stumbling toward the sanctuary of the mausoleum, when a breeze ensnared my senses. The gardener was here, pruning hedges along the back fence. I ran at him like a meth-head gunning for a fix.

4

He tasted like soul.

It was the epitome of everything, the summit of creation. It was to look upon the face of God and laugh.

I had been a fool.

I was whole, finished, borne aloft, Venus rising from the frothy sea. I was Nike crowned with laurels, victory with wings.

His pulse beat time with the song of my exultation. But all too soon, he was dry and I was breathless, clutched to his fading warmth, the fragrance of lilies mingling with the musk of blood. The cement prison in my lungs dissolved as cool wind rushed through me, gusts of freedom, squalls of joy.

I breathed. It was all I could do.

As utopia receded slowly into sated bliss, I searched for the remorse I knew I should feel. I knew nothing of this man, not even his name. Lying languid atop him, I did not even know the color of his eyes.

Slowly, I raised my head, daring to look on the mask of death he wore. Brown hair graying at the temples fell across a face hardened by the sun. His belly soft with beer strained against taut jeans. Olive eyes stared up at me, surprised, but not afraid. I closed each gossamer lid with a kiss. I stroked his sunburned cheek, searching myself for sorrow and regret, but finding only gratitude. This man, this stranger, had given his life to bring me to this new awareness, this existence so far from monstrous I could not remember why I had dreaded it so. I had widowed his wife, orphaned his children. I would thank them, if I could, for the gift of this dear one who would live forever now in me.

I kissed his throat once more, my lips lingering on the sweet wound through which his life had flowed into mine. Then I hefted him over my shoulders and carried him to my lair.

Back home among my Coke cans, reality slapped me, rigid and cold. I needed to pry a gravestone loose and, though I trusted my strength, a chisel or a crowbar would have been nice. Something to help dislodge the stone from the wall, preferably without bringing the whole crumbling structure down around my ears.

I locked myself in, flipped on the flashlight, and arranged the body in a corner. I sifted through my backpack until I found my pocketknife and started chipping away at the mortar. I chose the stone that seemed loosest already, but still it took half an hour of patient chiseling to access the crypt. With my hands coated in dust and the stench of stagnation creeping ever nearer, this new existence began to seem a little less sublime. It was worth it, of course; any price was worth it, to taste paradise. But I might have to rethink this business about hiding bodies in occupied graves.

The stone popped out at last, and I reached inside the crypt to pull the coffin free. It was one of those modern caskets, lined with padded satin and built to withstand nuclear attack. I could hardly believe how light it felt as I laid it effortlessly on the ground. I held my breath as I lifted the lid.

This body was different from the one I sought to hide. For one thing, I knew her name: Belinda Lewis, born April 10, 1924, died March 11, 1966. She had been embalmed, and there was little decay — just a whiff of some strange odor and the skin beginning to separate from the skull. Her colorless hair fell toward a high-necked blue dress, her hands clasped tightly over rosary beads. I wondered if she and my victim would get along.

I faced a new, unexpected problem now: how to fit two bodies into a casket built for one. I had not pondered this when I laid my plans; it had not occurred to me that the bodies in the crypt would not yet be decayed. But I knew, somehow, what I had to do. I wondered briefly if vampires could vomit. Then I bent to the corpse, put my lips to her neck, and drank.

Embalming fluid does not taste like soul.

I spat each mouthful on the ground, determined not to swallow, but it seeped into my being, the pungent horror making me long for that compost-flavored birthday cake. My stomach roiled for what seemed like hours, my mouth a blazing inferno. My lips tried to atrophy, refusing to suck, but I forced myself on, on, on, until she was dry. She deflated, a human puddle wrapped around a skeleton. I averted my eyes from her melting face and flung my victim on top, then slammed the casket shut. I collapsed with my back against it, heaving.

Stupid, stupid, stupid plan.

I could never turn back, not now that I knew. The hunt, the blood — it was food, sex, opium, and air, life itself, the summit of my existence. But it could not teach me how to bury the dead, how to find decent shelter, how to spend my days. It could not guide me through thousands of years of loneliness. It could not chase away the fear.

I was a vampire – mature, lethal, eternal – and I was curled inside a mausoleum, banging my head on a coffin, crying because I wanted my mommy.

5

Mommy.

I had never called her that. No one ever used a loving epithet for Helen Carshaw and lived to tell the tale. "Love is weakness," she always said. Helen was a spider, love the deadly pheromone she secreted on her web. Awestruck humans swarmed to her captivating eyes, two undiscovered emeralds that glowed with Vulcan flame. The angle of her cheekbones, long since skimmed from Man's genetic pool, left dropped jaws groping for adjectives. Her crimson lips danced an aeonian glissade, seducing hope with every word; and Helen's words shaped continents. Helen's words brought down kings.

Helen's words caressed my fragile ears while my seven-year-old eyes beheld an opera of gore played out upon our small TV. The very day she dashed my hopes of ever entering heaven, she subjected me to a barrage of films depicting our kind, calmly explaining the legends and filtering truth from fiction. Immortality? True, although we could still die. Super strength? True, but using it near witnesses could spell our doom. Garlic? We did not have to run from it in terror, but it did, in fact, stink worse than other human foods. Only a *very* thirsty vampire would be tempted to drink from someone who smelled of it. A stake through the heart was more deadly than some legends claimed, requiring no beheading to complete the job. Sunlight had been dangerous before the invention of sunscreen, but liberal application of SPF 35 had nullified that threat. Vampires had been nocturnal before sunscreen, too, though now it was more convenient to keep the same hours as our prey. As for that nonsense about vampires having no reflection, the physical world just does not work that way.

She skipped the scenes about crosses and holy water. That turned out to be a different can of worms altogether.

My mother taught me to perform upon the human stage, how to live as a lion without alarming the lambs. I learned to avoid public gatherings where I was expected to eat and to feign food allergies or stomachache if I could not. She taught me charm and manners suited to a queen, but also how to be aloof, to move and work and play amidst the world without allowing anyone to probe beyond the mask.

For Helen, every action, every choice, was first and foremost a disguise. She had chosen to live in Baton Rouge because it was not a place where anyone would ever think to look for vampires. New Orleans abounded with bloodsuckers, both real and fictional, its legends steeped in Voodoo and forests of above-ground graves. An hour up the road, however, the more prosaic capitol city was famed for its politics, petrochemical refineries, and college football. The world was full of such un-Gothic places, but it so happened that at the time we left Cincinnati, Baton Rouge had had an opening for a nurse at Woman's Hospital. That had sealed the deal.

My mother had been saving my lessons on the nuts-and-bolts of drinking blood until I grew closer to maturity. How to select victims, how to hunt in a large city but never be seen, how to hide the bodies; it was all on the syllabus for a later year. After all, what was the rush? My mother had plenty of time.

I was twelve when the unthinkable happened.

My mother always kept an eye on the newspapers. She did not care what laws had been passed or what Thursday's forecast might be, but three specific subjects held her interest. The first, surprisingly, was war. Helen had participated in anti-war protests around the globe and had even brokered a few treaties in centuries gone by. She explained, "A wolf does not condone the wanton slaughtering of deer," and often referred to battle as "using Dom Peringnon to water the lawn."

She also kept an eye out in case the body of one of her victims should be discovered; after all, flukes did happen. Most importantly, however, she read the papers for any sign that another vampire might be active in the area. "Some vampires are good company, but some don't take well to larvae," she said, meaning me. The terminology did wonders for my budding self-esteem.

Murders and missing persons filled the pages of the news, and I never knew how Helen expected to discover which ones resulted from vampires. I assumed she would teach me someday, perhaps when such evidence finally appeared. However, nothing in the crime section ever caught her attention until that day when I was twelve.

I was scarfing down raw steak and trying to tie my shoes at the same time. The power had gone out during the night, so my alarm clock had not rung, and I was about to miss my bus. Rather than trying to help me, my mother sat at the table, reading, as she always did. She had "worked a double shift" the night before, which I now understood to be a cover for her hunting expeditions. She had killed someone last night, and I was trying not to let it bother me, trying to remember everything for my history test instead. World War I. Archduke Franz Ferdinand, the Black Hand, the League of Nations.

She put the paper down and met my eye with a look that made me freeze, the shoelace still looped around my finger. "Jennifer, you are not going to school today."

"Okay."

She strode to the phone, placed the call to the school. Apparently, I had a bad sore throat and would be tested for mono that afternoon. I might be out for a while.

She stared me down. "You will not leave this house until I say you may."

"Yes, ma'am."

"You will not call your classmates to get your assignments."

"Yes, ma'am."

"You will not open the door for anyone, not even a police officer. You will not answer the phone if it rings."

"Yes, ma'am."

"You will not try to find me."

Her jewel-tipped eyes bored through me. I stammered, "Yes, ma'am."

I watched in mesmerized horror as she packed a bag: clean underwear, toothbrush, deodorant, wooden stake.

She patted my hair. "Don't worry. I will win." Then she was gone.

Forever.

❖

I cried until I laughed, picturing my mother's reaction if she could see me now: Helen Carshaw's hand-picked protégé, locked in a mausoleum full of spewed formaldehyde. The look on her face would have almost been worth the horror.

Finally, I hoisted myself to my feet and pushed the double-occupied coffin back inside its crypt. I had made a debacle of vampirism thus far, but I still had to get up and go on. Unfortunately, I did not have any mortar to seal the grave: one more detail overlooked in my meticulous, moronic planning. Time to foray out into the world, to test my self-control for the first time. I started to change my clothes before I noticed they were not bloodstained. I had not spilled a drop.

At least I could do one thing right.

I changed anyway, ran a comb through my hair, and hiked to the nearest bus stop. I took city buses all the time, since all of us at the convent shared one car. But as I waited, feeling the sun attempt to ignite my skin beneath its film of UV-blocking lotion, I knew that this seemingly ordinary trip could end with a mobile killing spree. I took one tentative whiff as the bus door opened . . .

Delectable.

Only a vampire could ever say that about public transportation.

Good thing I had feasted mere hours ago. Tempting as it was to rinse away embalming fluid with the liquid ecstasy of blood, the cement did not pour into my lungs, and I knew that if I took shallow breaths, I could handle this. I boarded the bus and took a seat near the rear, where the exhaust fumes were heavy and the people few.

I got off at a hardware store and asked an orange-aproned man where to find the mortar. "What's it for?" he asked with narrowed eyes.

"Service project. Habitat for Humanity." I had no idea whether Habitat volunteers would bring their own mortar. Thankfully, the clerk did not seem to know, either. He led me to the right aisle and showed me how to apply the paste, then smiled and wished me good luck. I thanked him; I was going to need it.

I stared at the pitiful contents of my wallet while the cashier counted my change. After hardware, bus fare, breakfast, and batteries, my entire life savings had dwindled to $11.66. I had no idea what life held for me past the point of re-mortaring Belinda's grave, but whatever it was, it would probably cost more than eleven bucks.

"Hey, are y'all hiring?" The question popped out before I even knew what I was thinking.

"I think so. Ask at customer service."

The lady at the service desk bubbled like uncorked champagne. "Oh, yes, we're hiring! It's a fabulous place to work." I began filling out the application while she raved about scholarship programs and paid vacation. I was wondering whether anyone would notice that 1345 North Blvd. was the address of Orchid Gardens of Memory when her prattle broke through my reverie.

"We have staff parties, and I've got so many friends. The people are great."

My hand froze mid-letter. *People*. What was I thinking, wanting to work in retail?

"Hey, are you okay?"

I raised my eyes and inhaled: dust, paint, co-dependency, music, forgetfulness. Every detail of this stranger's existence rose to me, savory and luscious. In that moment, I knew: I longed not for the taste of blood but the taste of *life*, of identity, of that one unique, unrepeatable creation pulsing under my lips. Even if the blood bank opened a smoothie shop, I would still choose to kill. So, I might as well work in retail.

Or I might as well go back to school.

My jaw fell slack with the audacity of that thought. Only yesterday I had run away, determined not to endanger the nuns. How could I even consider going back? Still, the idea taunted me, a mirage that had become an oasis.

"Seriously, are you okay?" Worry clouded the clerk's heady scent.

"I think I changed my mind."

I wandered to the bus stop in a daze. The passengers posed no temptation as my mind raced to tear down barricades that barred my pathway home. *You can't go back,* I insisted, remembering the instinct that had stolen my will. If it happened at home, the nuns would die. I wanted to kill, but I did not want to kill *them*.

I returned to the mausoleum and slathered mortar on the stone while the forbidden longing gnawed, chewing past vanity and reason to the tired, homesick core of my heart where the little orphan girl still lived. I would learn to control my hunger, but when? Could I wait it out here and go back when I had mastered self-control? No. My spine that had slept on a cold stone floor, my anorexic wallet, my ripening-by-the-hour B.O. all cried that I must leave Orchid Gardens, and soon. But what was the sense of going home only to destroy the life I loved? *"Love is weakness,"* I heard my mother's voice repeat, but even now, I could not force myself to believe her.

Inspiration struck as I wiped the stone clean. What if I ate before I got hungry?

I did not know how often that would be. My mother had hunted roughly once a month, but my newly-matured body might not take well to a strict schedule. Still, it was bound to give some sort of hint before famine derailed my senses. Even this morning's instantaneous desire had come with warning signs. If I paid careful attention and hunted preemptively . . .

Even if I could plan my feedings, there were still a million problems to solve, like where and whom to hunt and how to ditch the evidence, but I would have to face those problems no matter where I lived. The nuns would notice when I started sneaking out at night, but that was not exactly unusual behavior at my age. Could I still eat meat? If not, I would have to find something I could consume for the sake of appearances. I would need a good explanation for what had happened at the library, too. Assuming

Elma Jones had regained consciousness, she knew exactly who had been on the other side of that shelf.

They would put me in therapy. They would watch me like hawks. I would put myself in a position that demanded perfection, not only of my ability to control my thirst, but also of my ability to lead a double life. Could I do it? Was it worth it to try?

To the first question, I could muster no better answer than a tremulous "maybe." To the second, my heart thumped a resounding, undeniable "yes." I lay awake most of the night concocting lies, but I was happy underneath the fear. I was going home.

6

I awoke to the sound of someone trying to open the mausoleum door. I bolted upright, only too aware that my mortar and trowel were still in plain view — more than a little incriminating.

"Locked," said a muffled voice, and I was glad I had remembered to do at least that much. "The gardener had the keys. There's another set somewhere, but I'll have to search for them. Damn Benji, this is the third time in two weeks he's been late . . ." I listened as more than one set of footsteps retreated along the gravel path.

Benji the Gardener. Now I knew his name. Of course he had not shown up for work. Would they notice the place where the mortar was not dry? Could they trace it to me if they did?

Time to start reading the newspapers.

I waited until I could not hear the footsteps anymore, then gathered my backpack, food wrappers, Coke cans, and tools. I peeked cautiously out the door. No one in sight. I ran, surprised by my own speed, surprised that my weighty belongings did not slow me down. My lungs did not even feel tight as I pulled up alongside the dumpster behind Winn Dixie just long enough to toss the evidence.

I wanted to run all the way home. The wind brushed my skin with silky bristles while my muscles rejoiced to be free, but people did not normally run through mid-city traffic. Now was not a good time to draw attention to myself, so I found the nearest bus stop instead.

I got off at Baton Rouge High, a few blocks away from the convent, and did my best to blend in. I had come here last year to take a practice SAT, and I remembered where to find the library. I wandered in and slipped an old yearbook into my bag. One thing my mother had taught me: lies are more convincing when you bring props.

I walked the rest of the way to Prompt Succor. The convent was empty at mid-day, the sisters all at school. I went in, to my own familiar little room. My thrift store rug and recycled curtains had never seemed so beautiful. The familiar smells of candle wax and washed cotton wrapped me in their smiling arms and whispered, "Everything will be okay." The water of my shower fell, warm drops cleansing me of toil and terror. For a moment, I was just plain Jennifer again, orphan bookworm being raised by nuns.

But the person I saw in the mirror was not plain Jennifer. In fact, she looked remarkably like Helen Carshaw.

The pimple had vanished, whether because the cream had worked or not, I would never know. My complexion had softened, lightened, and an allure of green fire flecked my mud-brown eyes. A tinge of blush suffused my mouth, the lips supple now, inviting. Even my stringy hair had discovered more luster, and grown at least an inch. My body still kept its angles and lines, my figure eternally stuck in transition, but my reflection proved the novelists had been right, after all. Vampires *were* beautiful.

I shivered. Then I put on my uniform and slipped over to school just in time for fifth hour.

Sister Diane broke her chalk against the blackboard as I sneaked in. I gave her a little wave while she collected herself. "Did you check in with the office, Jennifer? Your name was on the absent list."

"Oh. Right, I forgot."

"Go do that, please."

Smart woman, that Sister Diane. She could not leave a classroom full of students to interrogate me, but she could send me to the principal, who would be more than happy to do it herself. I hunched my shoulders, trying to look nonchalant as I approached the secretary's desk.

"Checking in. Jennifer Carshaw."

The secretary narrowed her eyes and hit the intercom button on the phone. Mother Lily picked up. "Yes?"

"Jennifer Carshaw is here to check in."

An exhaled breath. "Send her in."

My legal guardian's sky-blue habit had a way of making her look starkly angelic. The face framed by that well-starched veil was young despite its wrinkles, sun-browned skin lit by an inner fire, her eyes as blue and searing as the flames of a gas-powered stove. Though it had been Sister Diane who fought the bishop and the State of Louisiana for the right to adopt me, the eventual compromise required that the head of the convent take legal charge of me. Mother Lily played her role as my adoptive mother with grace and gravity, so that even Sister Diane had as yet found no cause to complain.

"Jennifer, you're looking better than I had dared to hope." She folded her hands on top of her desk, a sure sign that I was in for a lecture.

I swallowed. "Thank you."

"Have a seat."

I took the chair across from her, hardly able to remember my lies as her scent, like balmy incense, wafted across my nose.

"I heard you were hurt," she said. "Are you?"

"Not badly. Just a bruise."

"That's good. Better than Elma Jones can say."

I angled my nostrils toward the stale coffee on her desk, hoping it would mask her succulence. "How bad is it?"

"She has a concussion, a punctured lung, and three broken ribs."

Not as bad as I had feared, but bad enough. "I'm really sorry."

"I don't suppose you'd like to explain your behavior over the last few days?"

The moment of truth. Either I could sell this story, or I would have to leave every semblance of normality forever. *So no pressure, Jen.*

"I was trying to find my father. I just thought that, whatever is wrong with me, with the hot flashes and everything, maybe it's genetic. I thought that maybe, if I could find him, he would know what's going on."

My father had been a topic of much discussion after my mother disappeared. In all probability, my biological father was alive out there somewhere, still scarred by the mysterious disappearance of his nine-month-pregnant wife, but I couldn't very well tell anyone that fact. The cover story was that Dad had abused my mother, and she ran away when she found out she was pregnant.

Mother Lily's anger cooled one degree, her folded hands relaxing at the wrists. "Where did you go to look for him?"

"My mother kept a storage locker. She paid the rent for ten years in advance and gave me a key. She told me never to go there unless she said it was okay, and never to tell anyone about it."

"Why didn't you ask one of us to go with you?"

"Because the way she treated it, I thought she must be hiding drugs or blood diamonds or something."

"But instead you found . . ."

"This." I handed her a photo torn from the old yearbook, a history teacher from the late 1980's. I prayed she had not known the man. He had taught high school just a few blocks away, after all.

She studied the photo, and when she looked at me again, I could tell she had taken the bait. "So then what?"

"Then I waited for morning and went to the library."

"Where you suddenly felt the need to attack the librarian?"

"I didn't mean to hurt her. I just . . . I searched all morning, and I was coming up empty, and I was so frustrated, I just needed to hit something. But then I heard Mrs. Jones scream, and I knew it was bad, so I ran." I hoped she couldn't hear me taking choppy, shallow breaths as her heady scent assailed me. It took all my strength not to dive across the desk and sink my teeth into her veins.

Mother Lily shook her head. "This just isn't like you, Jennifer."

"I think I had another hot flash at the same time."

She stared at me a moment, then picked up the phone.

"Who are you calling?"

"You're going to the doctor. Right now."

I bit my lip to still my terror.

Mother Lily made the appointment, then hung up and looked me in the eye. "We will leave in fifteen minutes. So, where did you go after you left the library?"

Steady, Jen. "I remembered Sister Diane had told me to get an ice cream to cool off, so I decided to try it. I went to a grocery store and bought a pint of vanilla. But it turned out to be a bad idea because after I ate it, I got really sick. I ran to the bathroom in the store and spent the next few hours throwing up. And apparently, they forgot to check it before they closed, because by the time I came out, I was locked in."

Mother Lily eyed me, clearly suspicious. I did not look like a girl who had spent last night locked in a filthy grocery store bathroom, bowing to the porcelain gods. In fact, I looked healthier than I ever had before. But I was experiencing unexplained hot flashes – hot enough for people near me to feel them – and my physical changes were too drastic for the short time they had taken to occur. Clearly, I *was* sick, all appearances to the contrary.

"Jennifer, are you pregnant?"

My eyes flew open. Of course, now that she said it, it did seem the most reasonable explanation for my symptoms. It would have been a perfect excuse if I could have somehow spent the next nine months growing a human being inside myself. However, I was pretty sure the sisters would notice when my due date passed without producing a baby, so I said, "No. Of course not."

"Well, the doctor will tell us for sure."

7

We drove in silence, the radio playing Christian pop music and commercials. Mother Lily smelled like the wedding feast of a king. I had to sit on my hands to keep them from taking hold of her neck. Thankfully, we made it to the doctor's office in two pieces: one living nun and one rapacious vampire. I breathed deeply of the disinfectant they had used to clean the lobby while Mother Lily checked me in.

The nurse called me back and took my temperature with a gizmo that registered a confident 97.2 degrees in under two seconds. She strapped a cuff on my arm and started pumping, her stethoscope pressed to the inside of my elbow. A little crease appeared between her eyes. She adjusted the cuff and pumped again. This time her brow furrowed in real earnest. Mother Lily asked, "Is everything okay?"

"I can't really say. Dr. Fielding will be along shortly." She jotted down a number on my chart and circled it three times.

Uh-oh.

I had no idea what made me physically different from humans, but I was also not eager to let our family physician find out. I tried desperately to imagine a way to leave his office without surrendering any bodily fluids, but only one person I knew could ever have managed such a feat.

Time to find out if I could be my mother's daughter, after all.

The metallic thunk of the doorknob announced the arrival of Dr. Gregory Fielding, a thin, forty-ish man with graying temples and kind eyes. "Well, the famous Jennifer," he said. "We meet at last."

He extended his hand and I took it, careful to turn so that Mother Lily could not see the invitation in my smile. "I take it you're one of the doctors Sister Diane consulted on my behalf."

"You could put it that way. I treat all the sisters, so I hear a lot about you." He dropped my hand, signaling an end to the small talk. "So, what seems to be the problem?"

A no-nonsense kind of guy. All right, I'd give it to him straight. "I'm having hot flashes so hot people near me can feel them, and I spent last night vomiting in a grocery store bathroom."

"And in the last two days, her eyes have changed color and her hair has grown about an inch," Mother Lily added, as though the information were burning a hole in her tongue.

Dr. Fielding sounded strangled as he asked, "Anything else?"

I've recently developed a taste for human blood. But I did not need to be quite that straightforward.

"She only eats meat," Mother Lily went on. "Basically raw meat. She barely allows us to sear it for her."

"Yes, Sister Diane mentioned that." He began to poke and prod, peering into my ears, my mouth, my nose. He listened to my chest and abdomen, and I leaned in ever so slightly, so that his fingers brushed my skin. I thought I heard his heart add an extra beat. Then he opened my chart, saw the thrice-encircled number screaming from the page, and turned a delicate shade of magenta.

"Have you eaten anything unusual lately?"

"A pint of ice cream, but it didn't stay in my stomach very long."

"Trauma of any sort?"

"I banged my head on a bookshelf."

He pursed his lips, made a note, then glanced furtively at Mother Lily. She gave a slight nod and left the room. He tried to be clinical as he asked, "Sexual activity?"

"Not yet." I ran my tongue along my teeth, and a bead of sweat dripped down his neck.

"It's confidential, you know. I can't tell the sisters."

"I know. I'm still a virgin."

Oops. The word seemed to throw cold water on the fire I'd been stoking. With genuine professionalism he said, "We'll do a pelvic just in case." He made another note, then gave me a very grave, doctor-y sort of look. "Jennifer, I've never even heard of anything like this. Your blood pressure alone ought to have killed you, but you don't even look sick."

If seduction did not work — which was not exactly a surprise — then I would have to take my chances with logic. "Doctor, you're not allowed to repeat anything I tell you to anybody ever, like the confessional, is that correct?"

"Yes."

I leaned forward. "I'm not sick. My body is doing exactly what it should be doing."

"I don't understand."

"My mother was the same. She was a nurse, so she knew her blood pressure was insanely high, but she was perfectly healthy. She had the hot flashes, too, but they're not dangerous. The truth is they happened when she was hungry, and it's the same with me. It's a genetic mutation, evolutionary adaptation, whatever you want to call it. In my family, we just don't work the same as other people."

"But the vomiting?"

"I made that up. I didn't come home last night and I needed an alibi. I didn't really eat a pint of ice cream, either." What the heck. I smiled and batted heavy lashes, just in case.

"That's the most absurd thing I've ever heard."

"I know, but unless you can offer some better explanation for why I'm not dead after sixteen years of living on seared beef and a blood pressure of 240 over 130, then . . . Hakim's razor. I'm telling the truth."

"Jennifer, I get that you want to get out of here, but even if your mother was like you, then it's some kind of genetic disorder and we need to treat you if we can. Didn't your mother die young?"

I wondered what he would think if he knew how old my mother really was. "Yes, but since they never found the body, I don't think genetics had much to do with it."

He cringed. "I'm sorry. I didn't know."

"Well, now you do. So, how about giving me some sugar pills to make Mother Lily happy, and we'll all go on with our lives?"

"What diagnosis am I supposed to give her?"

"You're the doctor," I crooned in a voice I had heard so many times, but never from my own lips. Finally it broke across his face, the kind of smile that a forty-something man ought not to give a sixteen-year-old girl. I returned it, my facial muscles arranging themselves into shapes they had never worn before.

Dr. Fielding shook himself and turned away. "No. It's absurd. You're clearly very ill. . ."

I reached out and touched his arm. Instantly, he melted, my hand a hot knife cutting through culture, morality, and fear. He met my gaze, longing for something so much greater than I could ever give. His arms curled around me, his lips reached for mine. It would have been so easy to fall under his violence and answer it with my own. Instead, I thought about Mother Lily waiting outside, about everything I would lose if he died, and I threw him away from me, hard. Dr. Fielding groaned as he hit the wall and I flew through the door.

Mother Lily dropped her magazine. "He tried something," I breathed, tugging her toward the car while protests sputtered through her breathless lips. I hurled myself into the passenger seat, nearly ripping the handle from the door as I slammed it shut.

Mother Lily toppled in beside me. She caught her breath while I tried to steady mine.

"Jennifer, what happened?"

Why did she have to smell like that, like manna or ambrosia or whatever it was the gods ate? I rolled down the window and stuck out my head, trying to concentrate so I could understand.

"If he hurt you, Jen, we need to press charges."

"I'm fine, just please, let's go home."

She seemed about to say something, but let it pass and started the car. We drove a few blocks before she tried again. "Did he touch you, Jen?"

"He tried to kiss me, but he missed. That's all."

"I don't understand. I've known Greg since he was twelve . . ." Her voice faded as she lost herself in thought, finally leaving me free to do the same.

My mother had taught me the importance of charm, a weapon useful both for luring prey and for smoothing over suspicion. However, Dr. Fielding's reaction had eclipsed any rational human response. Apparently, vampire charm was more than a convenience; it was a potent, irresistible drug.

That solved one problem. I now knew how to get my victims alone.

"Jennifer, whatever happened in there, it wasn't your fault. He had no right to touch you."

"I know. It's fine, really, I just want to go home."

Poor Mother Lily. She was trying so hard to comfort me, and I was trying so hard not to drink her blood. I kept the window down, gasping for clean air to cover her scent, but it was all I could do not to smile and watch her succumb.

I darted from the car as soon as it stopped, forgetting to taper my new super-speed. I hoped Mother Lily didn't notice the blur as I blazed past. Inside, I stuck my head in the sink and drank from the tap, filling my stomach with the only liquid available. Rivulets ran down the side of my face, dripping with the razor-cold edge of my escape.

Yet somehow here I was, at home, drinking water like a real human being. I had conquered a temptation greater than any I had ever imagined. Mother Lily and Dr. Fielding were both alive. I was wreaking emotional havoc left and right, but my victims were all still breathing.

I could do this. I could stay.

8

Apparently, Mother Lily knew she was not the right person to deal with Dr. Fielding's supposed assault. She left me alone in my room, though I knew the solitude would not last long. I downloaded Marilyn Manson, thinking it would be cathartic to listen to someone else scream, but after half a song I got annoyed and switched it off. I sat down on my bed and tried to slow my breathing while I waited for whatever would happen next.

"Next" came rather predictably in the form of Sister Diane. About twenty minutes later, she knocked on my door. That must have been how long it took Mother Lily to give her the rundown. I twiddled with the edge of my quilt and didn't meet her eye as I scooted to make room for her on the bed.

"Well," she said, "it's been an eventful couple of days for you, hasn't it?"

"You could say that."

"I know you got my little goodbye note. If I'd had any idea you were off on some harebrained middle-of-the-night storage raid . . ."

"Where did you think I was going?"

"To find your father, not to give up and go vomit."

Either I was much too good at this, or she was lying, too. As usual, her voice told me nothing, so I met her gaze. "Where did you really think I was going?"

"I don't know, Jen. Where did you really go?" She gazed coolly back with olive eyes: the very same olive-green as Benji's.

Remorse hurled through me like a thousand tons of bricks smashing into my skull. I could not move or speak any more than if shards of bone had sprayed like shrapnel through my brain. The living eyes denounced me, glaring like an effigy of the pair that I had closed. Had I stolen someone else's solace, someone else's Sister Diane?

"Jen? Jen, breathe. Breathe, Jen."

I tried, but found my lungs unwilling to obey. Sister Diane walked calmly to the bathroom, filled a glass with water, and dumped it over my head. That did the trick. I spluttered and gasped while my antique quilt turned to cottony mush around my drenched rear-end. Sister Diane wrapped me in her arms. How could she hold me, when I must reek of murder and lies? How could I let her, when even now, I was planning to kill again?

"Shh," she whispered. "It's going to be all right. Dr. Fielding won't hurt you again."

"He didn't hurt me. I threw him against a wall."

"Good for you."

"I lied to you."

"I forgive you."

"Why?"

"Because I love you."

Her words like giant forceps reached into my chest, clenched my heart, and twisted. "I'm not worth it."

"Of course you are. You're God's child just like the rest of us."

With that, the floodgates burst, and I dissolved.

❖

"Mother, why do people think crosses and holy water burn us?" I was eight years old when I saw a cartoon where people fended off Count Dracula with religious icons. The idea that Catholicism should be toxic to vampires confused me, to say the least. I signed myself with water from the baptismal font every week at school Mass, and crucifixes hung in every classroom. I was none the worse for wear.

"I'm glad you asked," my mother said. Did I only imagine the tension in her fingers as she took my hand? "Jennifer, what do you know about God?"

"Sister Joan says God is good and loving. That He sent His Son to die for us, and the Holy Spirit comes to help us do right." I tugged at the skirt of my uniform. "Is any of it true?"

"All of it. God loves human beings more than anyone could ever measure or understand."

"But I'm not human."

"That's right."

"So He doesn't love me?"

"No." She stroked my hair. "I put you in Catholic school for a reason, Jen. I wanted you to know the truth. I wanted you to see how cruel God is."

The legends are right, in their way, though it is not the symbols of God that repel vampires. It is God Himself, the One who created us as humans, the One who allowed us to forfeit our souls, the One who allowed our corruption to exclude us from His grace.

My mother would have sooner drunk my blood than admit she envied her weak, mortal prey. Years later, however, I understood the glimpse of her deepest psyche she had revealed that day. She had watched the faithful, the meek and the dull, partaking of the only power greater than her own, and she hated the God who raised undeserving mortals into eternal glory. She surrounded me with religion so I would know the desperate rage that smoldered through her existence, consuming the fallow emptiness that should have been a soul. But I never hated the people of God. I never believed God was wrong or cruel to exclude me from a salvation I did not deserve. I only wished with every fiber of my being that, against all odds, He might love me, too.

I cried myself to sleep in Sister Diane's arms and did not wake until the first morning bell. I knew I could get away with staying in bed after all I had been through. I had not hunted and did not know how I would react to the smells of my classmates and teachers. But I couldn't bear the idea of lying around all day pondering the essential paradox of my existence, so I got up and went to breakfast.

Every one of the sisters smelled more enticing than the seared piece of beef on my plate. I swallowed about half of it. It did not nauseate me, but it also did not nourish me. Like water, it simply took up space in my stomach, but it did nothing to meet my caloric requirements.

A knock at the door cracked our steely silence. Mother Lily rose to answer it. She returned a moment later with a letter in one hand and a very strange expression on her face. "It's from Dr. Fielding. Special courier." She handed it to me.

It was an apology. Dr. Fielding wrote that he did not know what had come over him, he'd never had such inappropriate desires before, the recent emotional trauma of divorce was no excuse, he was already seeking counseling. It was all gibberish designed to convince me not to press charges. He resigned as the nuns' physician and included a referral to a "trusted colleague" at a different office. He closed with a diagnosis that I knew was his way of trying to make amends:

As for your medical condition, it is my belief that your vomiting was caused by too much ice cream and your hot flashes are likely the result of panic attacks or generalized anxiety disorder, which would also account for your elevated blood pressure. I recommend seeking the help of a psychologist and avoiding stress whenever possible.

He was doing me a favor, trying to prevent a second doctor's visit. I handed the letter around the table for the sisters to peruse, but I did it knowing I had screwed up big time.

Any reasonable physician would have prescribed medicine for blood pressure as high as mine and insisted I see another doctor immediately. Dr. Fielding *was* a reasonable physician when not drunk on vampire charm, and presumably that had worn off by the time he wrote the letter. There was only one reason he would lie for me: he believed me. He had experienced my super strength first hand. He did not know I was a vampire, but he knew I was not exactly human. If he ever decided to tell the nuns, my life was over.

Mother Lily surveyed me over the top of the letter. "Anxiety," she said.

I shrugged. "Guess so." I had a feeling that diagnosis was going to prove prophetic.

❖

I waited until the last possible second to walk to school and slipped into homeroom just as the bell rang. I told myself the chatter fell silent because class was starting and not because I had walked in. God only knew what rumors had been flying about my absence, and of course, I now looked more like Jennifer's pretty sister than like the old Jennifer. I avoided every eye as I skulked to my desk.

While Mother Lily read the morning announcements over the intercom, I worked to acclimate myself to the smells. Even staring at the top of my desk, I could identify every one of my classmates by using my nose. Angie Carroll smelled appropriately snobbish; Kayla Richards, winner of many a singing competition, smelled like talent. Jeremy Higginbotham smelled jealous, and . . . afraid? That couldn't be right.

Matt Derwin smelled like the shiest, sweetest, most confused and humiliated person on earth. I could not help looking up.

He had been staring at me, but turned away the instant I moved my head. I kept looking, trying to get him to meet my eye, and finally he did. He glared a silent accusation, and I wondered what I had done to deserve his scorn. That is, I wondered what he thought I had done, since I doubted he knew the real reason he ought to hate me.

I turned my attention toward Mr. Valen's lecture and started taking notes, trying to ignore the not-so-subtle stares being cast in my direction. It didn't work, so I distracted myself by dreaming about how each smell would translate into taste. I savored Angie's acid tang, Mr. Valen's well-structured palate, Matt's peppery, succulent bite . . .

Mr. Valen's slanting penmanship blurred as a familiar fog crept across my vision, my chest growing heavier with every sniff of concrete air. I jerked upright, forcing myself to take steady, measured breaths. But as my self-control slowly returned, so did the weight of hostile glares and the growing consciousness that my status as a tolerated nerd had degenerated to that of first-class freak.

Rrrring — the school bell declared open season on Jennifer's self-esteem. I lingered at my desk, gripping its edge with sweaty palms, hoping my classmates would file out without bothering me. No such luck.

"We missed you, Jen. The heaters were broken."

"You should call Guinness. Sixteen must be a record for menopause."

"I feel sorry for the nuns. Hot flashes come with mood swings, too."

Mr. Valen ignored them, pretending not to hear, his rich aura tainted with cowardice. I gritted my teeth, picturing the look on Sister Diane's face if she should find me drinking blood, until the parade of taunts had filed past. Even so, it was a good thing ignobility smelled so foul, or I would have slaughtered them all.

The insults did finally come to an end, and I slowly relaxed my jaw, my hands. I opened my eyes, expecting the room to be empty, but both Matt and Jeremy were making quite a show of putting away their books. I glanced at Jeremy and steadied myself to endure the meanest insult of all, but he ignored me, his face completely obscure.

Matt, on the other hand, was waiting. I gathered my books and he followed me into the hall. "Hey," I said, feeling bad that I had fantasized about eating my only sort-of friend.

He blocked my path, hands stuffed deep in his pockets. "Look, if you already had a boyfriend, you should have just said so."

"What?" My mind battled its way back to the planes of normal high-school thought, but even then, this assertion seemed patently bizarre.

Matt suddenly got shy again and turned his face toward the ground. "I heard you were pregnant."

"Who told you that?"

"I was walking past the teachers' lounge. Mother Lily and Sister Theresa were talking."

"Oh." I was starting to catch up — starting to realize that those big, puppy-dog brown eyes might be better cast in a different sort of fantasy.

"Are you?" he asked.

"No, of course not." I inhaled, drinking the scent of his relief.

"Really?"

"Really. I've been sick, and the sisters thought that would explain my symptoms. But they were wrong."

"I'm sorry you're sick."

I shrugged. "I'm better now."

We stared at each other, a pair of mutes. The halls cleared as people made their way into second-hour classrooms. The bell clattered, declaring us officially late.

"So, I've got gym this hour," I said.

"Oh. Yeah. See you in English." He walked off, and my feet carried me, zombie-like, toward the next class, my brain a sticky lump of melted moron.

The locker room smashed against my sinuses, a wall of sweat and pheromones and blood.

"Get out of the doorway, freak."

I whirled around, snatched the owner of the voice by the arms and raised her neck to my mouth, its pale skin supple and ripe.

"Let go! Hey, *let go!*" The bratty squeal of Angie Carroll called me back from the depths of the paralyzing fog.

Oh, crap.

I blinked and held my breath, my cerebrum kicking into overdrive as I raced to form a plan. It was too late to pretend I had not intended her harm; there were witnesses. Thankfully, I had a reason to attack Angie, author of the recent jibe about menopause. My only hope was to play this as revenge. I balled my right hand into a fist and let it rip into her cute little turned-up nose.

People swarmed to gawk at the commotion, but I dropped Angie like a rag doll and took off across the football field. I managed to run at less than top speed, but still much too fast to be caught. Within seconds, I covered the three blocks to Government Street, where I found a dim little coffee house that almost certainly peddled hash out of the back room. Lava lamps of every color glowed against the iridescent walls. What little sunlight dared to penetrate the frosted slits of windows danced in shadows spun through the blades of a buzzing fan. The shop was empty except for the barista.

"What can I get you?" she asked. Her psychedelic eye shadow glittered under the black lights. She smelled like superficial happiness and mocha cream.

She tasted much, much sweeter.

Like fireworks, I launched myself across the counter, exploding into ecstasy as I sank into her arms. I gulped down glory, the fulfillment never full enough.

Then a soft voice gasped out, "Please."

I pulled back and gazed into her burnished copper eyes. Her will to live trembled next to mine. "Please," she gasped again, her violet hair glistening with sweat. I smiled and traced a tear as it traveled down her cheek. Her pain relaxed, her body yielding to the power of my touch. I watched her elfin figure breathe with openness, and I cradled her face against mine. The salty wetness touched my tongue, a song of submission that played my bones like the strings of a lithe violin. Gently, my teeth slipped through her sweet meringue of skin. Her abandon poured through me, and I succumbed. I floated, helpless. To fight would be to drown.

The last drop washed me in its emptiness. Lost, I lay and panted, a cushion of violet tresses pinned between my cheek and the cool tile floor.

Slowly, slowly, the icy ballast of that tile dragged me back down to earth. Slowly, the touch of a cotton T-shirt against my hand told me that it was not I whose lifeless body gave it shape. Slowly, my senses rent me from the realm where all was one, where both of us had lived and breathed and died and been reborn. Only I was here – but the barista was not gone.

I touched her cheek. It could not tremble now. It could only condemn me.

I rolled her body over, facedown on the ground. Then I got up, locked the door, and flipped the sign on it to "Closed."

I had watched enough crime shows to know that blood was the telltale evidence of foul play, never bleached or scoured beyond the reach of crack forensic scientists. Fortunately for me, this girl was literally bone dry. If I'd had a car, I could have thrown her in the trunk and driven her to the river without staining the upholstery. But I did not have a car.

I had a backpack. So did she; I found it stashed away under the counter. If she had been anything other than a five-foot toothpick, it would have been a ludicrous plan, but it was the only plan I had. I shoved my books into my bag's front pocket, glad I had come from gym and was not carrying much. Then I emptied her bag.

This was not going to be fun, but it beat the heck out of drinking embalming fluid.

I tested a finger first. It crackled as it tore like a breadstick, warm and dry.

I found some garbage bags and spread them underneath her to catch any excess fluids, just in case. If I could use one backpack for the torso, leaving it intact, I thought I could minimize the spills. I worked through the extremities joint by joint, gaining confidence and speed as sinew after sinew, bone after bone, crumbled and snapped with astonishing ease. I forced myself to focus only on the piece at hand, never a face, a body, a person — only a jigsaw puzzle of arms, legs, feet, and skull, compacted into one single bag-shaped piece.

By some diabolical miracle, it worked. I balled up the garbage bags and stuffed them in with the torso, barely damp. Then, one bag on each shoulder, I ran. At top speed, no one would see my face or even a girl with two backpacks, just a wash of color and a wake of wind. All I had to do was never slow down.

Government Street led me straight toward the Mighty Mississippi. I took a left and followed the footpath on top of the levee, the current ambling next to me, the muddied dregs of all America coursing toward the cleansing sea. Past the stadiums and traffic lights of LSU I ran, down to the grassy fields where generations of scientists had revolutionized Southern agriculture. With several interested cattle standing witness, I weighted the barista's backpack with gravel and tossed it into the river. It bobbed just once and then sank into the tide. My own bag, however, I needed to keep. The nuns would ask awkward questions if I came home without it. I hiked another hundred yards toward a sty full of pigs. Wondering what the change of diet would do to some poor grad student's thesis, I emptied my jigsaw puzzle into their trough. They squealed and feasted like kings.

As I watched a herd of swine devour my leftovers, I thought to myself that, whatever my mother's method of hiding bodies, it had probably been more elegant, but it could not have been more effective. A fine layer of dust at the bottom of my backpack would convict me if anyone should test it for the barista's DNA, but no one ever would. I knew I should not feel proud of the grisly morning that had just passed, but I could still taste the salt of her surrender. The rest just did not matter. Scrubbing the dishes does not ruin the decadence of the meal.

9

I returned to school halfway through third hour, but I didn't bother going to class. Instead, I headed off the inevitable and went straight to Mother Lily's office, determined that she would not mar my conquest with the stench of shame.

Of course, the barista's death was not the crime I had come here to discuss. I walked in to find Mother Lily on the phone, her brow furrowed under her habit as she tried to get a word in edgewise. "Yes, I understand . . . No, ma'am . . . That's not . . ."

She turned and saw me standing there, and dropped the phone.

Whoever was on the other end yelled so loudly, I could hear it across the desk. Mother Lily scooped up the receiver. "Mrs. Carroll, please calm down. Jennifer just walked in. I'll call you back after I deal with her."

I wilted into the visitor's chair. Mother Lily hung up, took a deep breath, folded her hands, then finally turned to face me.

"Well? What excuse have you concocted this time?"

I thought about the smell of mocha cream and arched my spine. "No excuses. Angie had it coming."

"Angie Carroll is in surgery right now. She may be permanently disfigured."

I swallowed hard, but set my jaw. "Are you going to expel me?"

Mother Lily gritted her teeth. "We will discuss your punishment after you finish telling me what I want to know. Where did you run off to after you left the locker room?"

"I got a drink at a coffee shop to cool off."

She stared me down, but I refused to blink. "Is that all?" she asked.

"Yes, ma'am."

"Jennifer Carshaw, you are grounded until further notice."

"Okay. Anything else?"

She finally broke, the angry principal giving way to the confused, frustrated guardian. "What's going on, Jen? This isn't you."

"I'm not going to apologize for standing up for myself."

"I understand that after yesterday . . ."

I had forgotten I had an actual excuse for my new tough girl persona. "That's right. Dr. Fielding didn't get the best of me, and no one else will, either."

"Jennifer, I know it must have been hard getting up this morning, trying to seem normal after everything, but I don't care what Angie said to you. Violence is not the answer."

"What was I supposed to do?"

"You could have come to me."

The compassion in her eyes invited me curl myself into her arms and loose the floodgates of my tears. I could smooth over the whole thing if I let her believe this was all the emotional backlash of yesterday's assault. But the thought of crying now, with the barista's tears still clinging to my tongue, would have felt like a betrayal. It would have felt like guilt.

"Mother Lily, this may be hard for you to understand, but violence works. Angie isn't going to tease me anymore, and I bet no one else will, either."

"That doesn't make it right."

"If right doesn't work, then I'd rather be practical."

The blood drained from her face as she groped for a response. I wondered briefly where it had gone, that sweet, pure, luscious blood . . .

The bell rang, jolting us both back to our senses. "Go to class, Jennifer. We will deal with this after school — in detention."

"Okay. See you there." I marched out, head held high, my dusty backpack sticking like a rap sheet to my shoulders.

❖

I caught up with Matt in fifth-hour physics. He gave me a mischievous smile and mimed a punch to let me know he was in on the gossip. I smiled back, but Sister Diane noticed. She stopped her lecture to glare at me.

"Jennifer, have you had your share of the principal's office for one day yet?"

I turned toward my desk and mumbled, "Yes, ma'am."

"Then wipe that smirk off your face."

"Yes, ma'am." But for once, I did not mind Sister Diane's anger. It felt too good, being sated, avenged, and having someone to share it with.

When the bell rang, Matt and I barely made it out the door before he gushed, "I can't believe I missed it. That had to be so awesome!"

I grinned. I had not felt the true satisfaction of watching Angie's face collapse because I had been blinded by thirst at the time, but the satisfaction of *this* moment was enough. "It was pretty cool. I'll be in detention the rest of my life, but it's worth it."

He reached for my hand without a blush or hesitation. Not that I was complaining, but I had known Matt for eleven years and, until this week, he'd never marshaled the courage to speak more than three words to me at a time. Maybe I was not the only person on this campus going through a monumental change.

He led me to Spanish class like a practiced suitor. "Meet me after school," he whispered, then smiled and trotted off to his own class. My hand tingled with the imprint of his warmth.

I was deep in verb conjugations before my reason returned, screaming. *You can't have a boyfriend! You're a vampire!* I should not have needed to remind myself of this, considering I could still feel the trill of the barista's pulse against my tongue. But right now, I did not feel like a vampire. I felt remarkably like a giddy teenage girl in the grips of her first crush. *Hey, Jen, you're asexual, remember?* The sensible part of my brain pleaded to no avail. Matt Derwin made me feel like a normal girl for the first time in my entire life, and I was not about to give that up. So I settled into solving a different problem, with fewer cosmic implications. How was I going to meet Matt after school and still meet Mother Lily for detention?

Two hours later, Matt was waiting by the door. I grabbed his hand and dragged him behind the school. "Hey, slow down," he panted.

I faced him, the air between us electric. "I've got detention."

"Then we'd better be quick." He wrapped me in his arms and pressed his lips against mine.

For three whole breaths, I was just a girl, putty in his hands. Then the taste of him crushed me, and in one breath more, he would have died. I ripped myself away.

I expected him to be mad or hurt or both, but he only leaned against the wall, looking dizzy. "Detention," I muttered, trying to make my response seem natural. He nodded. After a few seconds, I added, "Okay. See you tomorrow." He nodded again, and I started to go.

"Hey, Jen?"

I stopped. "Yeah?"

"Just . . . last time you said that, you didn't come back."

"I will this time. I promise."

He nodded, and I felt a grin steal across my face. It stayed there all the way to detention.

It fell off when I got there. Instead of Mother Lily, Mrs. Hargrove, the guidance counselor, was waiting for me. I had known the sisters would put me in therapy, but I had thought it would be with someone qualified.

She smiled beatifically. "Good afternoon, Jennifer."

"Hi, Mrs. Hargrove." According to some official-looking pieces of paper on her office wall, she was a real, licensed psychologist. I should have guessed this would be the result of Dr. Fielding's letter, but I always forgot she was supposed to be competent. Mrs. Hargrove's warm fuzzy approach to "guidance" offered less depth and insight than *Barney*.

"Have a seat." Her horn-rimmed glasses attempted to make her look older than twelve, but they failed. No accessory in the world could age that perky smile, those nut-brown Cherub ringlets straight from the brush of Raphael.

I slid into a desk. "So, which of my psychological problems did Mother Lily send you here to solve?"

"Take your pick. I'm sure she'd be happy with any one you choose."

"How about my sudden tendency toward violence?"

"Good choice."

And we were off into the wonderful world of Disney. I nodded and mm-hmmed until the clock finally let me go.

❖

The big guns were waiting back at home. I had not actually attended English class yet, but I knew we had a paper due next week, so I was at my computer, writing. The bell had rung for vespers, and the sisters should have all been at prayer, but Sister Diane slipped casually into my room and glanced over my shoulder.

"Homework for a class you've never been to. Well, at least that hasn't changed."

I saved my work and swiveled to face her. "Why should it?"

"Good point." She took a seat on the bed. "So, Matt Derwin, huh?"

"Yes." I managed what I hoped was an appropriate blush.

"Well, we've dodged the boyfriend bullet longer than we had any right to. He's a good kid."

I didn't answer. I didn't know what I was supposed to say.

"Angie Carroll did have it coming." One would think, after all these years, that Sister Diane would have lost the power to surprise me, but she never did.

"You're not mad?"

"I didn't say that. We've got to figure out what's causing these outbursts, Jen. If it were just today, I'd punish you and call it an end, but Mrs. Jones is still in the hospital, too. If you and Mrs. Hargrove can't make any progress, we'll get someone else. The violence has to stop."

"Yes, ma'am." Of course she was right. Even my mother would have agreed.

Sister Diane toyed with my quilt, worse for wear after its dowsing. "Jen, what's really going on?"

It's vampire puberty. Yes, that would go over well. But I had to tell her something. She would find an explanation with or without my help, and, knowing Sister Diane, she would come uncomfortably close to the truth.

"It's a genetic disorder. My mother had the hot flashes, the violent tendencies, the . . . unusual diet. There is no treatment because no one has ever studied it, and I don't want to be the guinea pig."

She stared at me, her green eyes lit with a flame that I knew boded ill for me. She let me stew for a moment, then said, "That business about searching for your father so you could find out what's wrong with you? Seems pretty unlikely if it came from your mother and you already know."

I blinked a lot, trying to keep up with the speed of her logic.

"You want to tell me where you really went Monday night?"

"No."

"Well, at least that's an honest answer."

I waited, knowing I would only get myself in more trouble if I tried to speak.

"As for this disorder of yours, I've been searching for an answer for years."

"You knew?"

"Jen, in the four years you've lived with us, you've eaten nothing but seared beef and one bite of birthday cake. Your body is obviously not normal."

"Oh." I should have realized that any explanation I could think of, Sister Diane could think of, too.

"But there's nothing about it on the Internet," she said, "and I've already told you the doctors are stumped, so you're right that no one's studied it." She took my hand, a gesture much too sappy for Sister Diane, so I knew the weight of her gravity when she asked "Is it dangerous?"

"Not to me. I won't vouch for Angie and Mrs. Jones." Or Benji Gardener or Violet Barista.

"What did your mother tell you?"

"Not much. Just not to worry about it."

"If it's nothing to worry about, why run away?"

Wow, she was good.

Sister Diane grinned; it would have been an evil grin on anyone else. "The yearbook photo was a nice touch. Shows planning, premeditation, and probably robbery, since we don't keep books that old lying around. Wherever you went, it must've been pretty bad."

I just sat there and tried to remember to breathe.

"I called Mother Celeste," she went on, and what little blood was still running through my veins froze in its course. "She gave me a message for you. I don't know what it means, but she said to tell you, 'Don't worry. I keep my promises even when ungrateful orphans don't.' She really has a way with words, doesn't she?"

I nodded.

"Should I give her a message in return?"

I shook my head no.

Sister Diane kissed my forehead. "All right, then. Sleep well. Tell Matt I've got my eye on him."

She went out and closed the door as my sluggish mind managed to think, *Poor Matt.*

10

Thunderclouds were gathering across Lake Ponchartrain as we made our way to New Orleans on that hot October morning when I was twelve. I watched from the car as yellow flashes of deadly light danced across the sky, and hoped they were too obvious to be an omen.

Five eternal weeks, my mother had been gone, and Sister Diane had decided to try to call me her own, if she could. The court battle still lay ahead, but first, we needed the permission of someone whose authority reigned above the law.

"You shouldn't worry," Sister Diane said. "If Mother Celeste decides not to let me adopt you, it will be because she sees something you and I don't, and she knows what's really best."

"She can't possibly know that. She's never even met me."

"But she has met me. You're not the only one whose life is changing here, you know."

"I don't understand why some old lady gets to decide what happens. You have as much right to adopt a child as anyone else."

"Legally, maybe, but she's the head of our Order, and part of becoming a nun is being obedient to my Mother Superior. I'm telling you, don't worry. After God, the person I trust most is Mother Celeste."

I slouched in my seat and tried not to let my face show how queasy I felt.

The sisters' convent in Baton Rouge was just an ordinary house, but the original New Orleans home of their order was an institution. A great Neoclassical façade ushered us into a rotunda complete with stained glass, gilded columns, and a triple-tiered fountain with a cherub on top. The building had originally been a bank, built in the nineteenth century to cater to the *nouveau riche* of the bustling port city. The Sisters of Prompt Succor had had the great good fortune to be founded during the Great Depression, and when this particular bank went belly-up, they picked up the building for a song.

A skinny, forty-something woman named Sister Constance led us through the rotunda to a cavernous dining room, its walls bedecked with murals of biblical scenes. I stared at Daniel bearding his lions while we ate a quiet lunch with all nine of the convent's residents. They were even kind enough to prepare my usual very-rare steak.

Mother Celeste picked at her food and did not look at me much. I cast her sidelong glances, taking in her liver-spotted hands, her stocky frame unbent despite her years, and I choked on my beef as a tide of resentment surged through my throat. Who did she think she was, to stand in the way of my happiness?

When the meal was over, one of the sisters cleared the plates, and at last Mother Celeste looked at me squarely. "Jennifer, I'd like you to follow me."

Her blue eyes, bright as spotlights, seemed to trespass through my heart. I held my breath, waiting for that stare to discover my darkest secret and expose me to the world.

"Well, come on. I haven't got all day."

I pushed my leaden feet with painful slowness down the hall. Fortunately, I was walking behind a ninety-two-year-old with a cane. She led me to a room that was unmistakably her own, a spartan apartment starkly at odds with the building's ornate architecture. The four white walls housed a metal-frame twin bed, a plain wooden desk, two simple wooden chairs, and a plethora of statues of Our Lady of Prompt Succor. The Blessed Lady in her golden gown reigned from desk and night table and shelves, the infant in her arms adorned with a crown as large and brilliant as her own. I had seen that image a thousand times at school, but suddenly the globe topped by a cross in Baby Jesus' hand — symbol of power and dominion — seemed as fraught with foreboding as the Lady's eyes were charged with hope.

Mother Celeste sat down in one chair and motioned for me to take the other. I shifted nervously, trying to find a position that agreed with my back. She waited for me to stop, and finally I did, not because I was comfortable but because I gave up.

"Jennifer." Mother Celeste rested her hands on her knees. "Let's get one thing straight. I know you aren't Catholic. That's fine. It has no bearing whatsoever on this adoption business, nor will anyone coerce you to convert if indeed our order takes you in."

"Thank you."

"But if we do — and I say *we,* because Sister Diane is part of a community and what she does affects us all — if we take you in, our first responsibility will be to save your soul." Her eyes never left mine, as if she were trying to compel me to admit that I had no soul to save. "Would you like to know what I mean by that?"

"Yes, please." I wriggled some more in my chair.

"It means we will pray for you every day. We will encourage you to pray, to ask questions about God and the Church."

"Okay."

"It also means we will not tolerate sinful behavior. You're at a delicate age when the world will present you with many temptations. You must expect to be punished if you give in."

"Okay."

Mother Celeste paused. "Jennifer, Sister Diane loves you. Mother Lily and the other sisters love you, too. Do you know that?"

"Yes. I love them, too."

"People who love each other often hurt each other."

I bit my lip, unable to keep from imagining that far-off day when I would run away to become a monster.

"I will allow them to adopt you, Jennifer. And I will make you a promise, but you must promise me something, too."

I knew she was waiting for me to ask what, but I could not force my voice to speak. I would never be able to make any promise I could actually keep.

"If you come to live with our order," she continued at last, "I promise I will be here for you as long as God permits me to remain on this earth. If the day should ever come — and I pray it never will — when you find yourself without a friend in this world, I will help you."

"What if I kill someone?" I could not stop myself from crying out as those incisive eyes drilled into the well of my sorrow.

"I will be here. You may not like the help I give, but I will give it all the same. But, Jennifer, you still have to make a promise in return."

Tears streamed down my cheeks. "What?"

"Promise that you will never knowingly break the sisters' hearts."

I hugged my knees as sobs racked through me, the horrible wooden chair resonating with my grief. What wouldn't I give for a life without heartbreak? Maybe it was not too late. Maybe I could tell the truth, and the sisters could help me find a way to survive without needing to kill. Maybe Mother Celeste could really do what she promised and stand by me despite what I was.

But my mother's disappearance still blistered inside me, oozing the poison of betrayal. If Helen Carshaw, who created me, who invested so much energy in my growth and education, who chose me from among every little girl in the world to become her replica and heir — if she could abandon me to face eternity alone, how could this stranger claim she would stay by my side? If my immortal, invincible mother could vanish, how could I trust a nonagenarian who said she would always be with me?

I looked up, my eyes falling on the Virgin, and I heard my mother laugh. "I promise," I said to the statue, because plaster could not impugn me like Mother Celeste's gaze of living love.

"All right, then," she said while I dried my tears. "Welcome to the Sisters of Prompt Succor. May God forgive us both."

❖

I lay in bed now, slaked by the barista's surrender, haunted by my careless past. *"What if I kill someone?"* Mother Celeste possessed exactly the kind of insight that might equate a four-year-old pre-crime confession with my current streak of rash behavior. I had to get up, get out, but the anchor of fear still kept me moored to the only life I knew.

At breakfast Friday morning, I sat amongst the sisters, my nostrils heavy with the smell of silent heartbreak.

When the school bell rang, I shuffled off to endure another day of salty teenage backbiting only to find myself swept up in a flash flood of goodwill. It turned out I was not the only person with reason to despise Angie Carroll, and the other victims of her acid tongue surrounded me with meek smiles. Plus, my dash across the football field had not gone unnoticed, and suddenly every member of the cross-country team wanted to become my friend. Somehow, by noon, people had replaced books as my companions at the lunch table.

"Jen, you have to tell me what you did to your hair," a girl named April gushed. "I can never get mine to shine like that."

"It's just a new shampoo." I shivered pleasantly while Matt toyed with one of my curls.

As if to prove I had stepped into some kind of alternate universe, Jeremy Higginbotham spent the day staring wistfully at me in every class we shared. He always turned away the second I noticed, but not fast enough. At first I thought he was scared I might punch him like I had Angie; he deserved it, after all. Then I remembered he had gotten some stupid medal for boxing last year, so he probably wasn't afraid of my fist. In the end, I just chalked it up to him acting like the idiot he was and tried to ignore him.

I forgot about idiots easily enough when Matt and I walked hand-in-hand through the halls, my cheek resting on his shoulder. He brushed my face with his fingertip and asked, "Is there any way I could take you on an actual date?"

"Sorry. I think I'm grounded until I graduate."

"I wish you could come over. My parents didn't believe me when I told them about you. They thought I made it up to get them off my case."

"Why would they be on your case?"

"Jen, it's not like I just woke up Monday morning and suddenly started liking you."

"Oh." I stopped in my tracks.

He laughed. "Is that what you thought?"

"Well, I do look different this year . . ."

"Jen, I like the new hairdo, but you've always been beautiful."

I stared at the ground, my heart in my throat.

"Hey, you okay?"

"I like you, too."

"Would you mind repeating that to my dad?" He grinned, then wrapped his arm around my waist and led me to class. I wondered why, in the movies, Prince Charming never wore glasses. They highlighted his eyes so well.

My "therapy" sessions with Mrs. Hargrove had been moved to my study hall, fourth hour, because she couldn't stay with me after school every day. Inexplicably, she was old enough to have children who expected to be picked up from daycare on time. Today was only the second of what looked to be an unending series of lightweight feel-good lectures, but she did actually manage to say one non-moronic thing:

"Sometimes athletics can help you channel your energy. Have you thought about joining a team?"

Of course I had thought about joining a team now that I was stronger and faster than any human being on the planet; but I had also thought about what would happen if someone were to be injured during said athletic pursuit and there was blood involved. However, I was getting better at self-control. I'd been practicing at home, forcing myself to think about my breathing, to find smells other than the people in the room, especially any time Mother Lily was with me. I had even managed to dress for gym and shower afterward, without seeing the fog creep in. Maybe now I could excel at something not-nerdy. Maybe I could feel what it was like to make other people stand up and cheer.

Maybe I could use it to my advantage, too.

I waited until Saturday, when the first shock of my lies had worn off and Mother Lily was digging in the garden, doing what she liked best. I brought her a glass of lemonade and sat on the grass, watching as she systematically ripped up weeds. After a few minutes of sunny summer silence, she pulled off her gloves, drank half the lemonade in one gulp, and said, "Shouldn't you be inside making up the work you missed?"

"I needed a break."

"Then maybe you should use it to tell me where you went Monday night."

"I can't. I'm sorry."

"Of course you can. You're choosing not to."

I let the silence agree. She tugged her gloves back on and pulled a few more weeds.

"I have a proposition for you," I said at last.

"You've got some nerve, if you think anything you say is going to get you out of being grounded."

"It's not me. It's Mrs. Hargrove."

She pivoted, wearing her most dangerous principal expression, the one that dared young miscreants to justify themselves. "All right. Let's hear it."

"Mrs. Hargrove thinks I need to socialize more. She wants me to make friends."

"This is about Matt, isn't it?"

"Yes. I mean, he is the first actual friend I ever had. But it's kind of hard to *be* friends if we never see each other outside school."

"If you think you'll be going out on dates after everything you've done this week, you're sorely mistaken."

"I'm willing to pay for the privilege."

She paused, as if debating something within herself, and finally asked, "How?"

"You know how you're always telling me to put down the books, get outside, and run around? Well, Mrs. Hargrove says you're right, that a sport might channel my energy away from violence. So, I was thinking I'd join cross-country. I'll go to all the practices and work really hard. In exchange, I get to go out with Matt one night a week."

"Cross-country isn't a penance. It's more like another way to get out of being grounded."

"Then what do you want me to do?"

She dusted a stray leaf off her gloves, and I saw her eyes brighten as a light bulb popped on above her head. My heart skipped an expectant beat. She was about to give the counter-offer. It did not matter what it was. It was *something,* and that was all I needed.

"Okay, here's the deal, take it or leave it. You will join cross-country and go to every practice, like you said. You can go out every other Friday, but you will be back by ten-thirty on the dot. You will do the dishes every night in addition to your regular chores. And you will begin attending daily Mass."

My heart crashed into my heels. "Mass?" The word stung like venom.

"I know you don't understand this, Jen, but your real problem isn't some bizarre genetic disorder. I'm not trying to trivialize the physical things you're dealing with, but the real reason you're violent and unhappy is that you don't know God."

"No offense, but if Mass were going to bring me to God, don't you think it would have worked by now?" I could not tell her what I was really thinking as my chest filled with razors.

"God works in His own time and His own way."

"Does it have to be Mass? Can I do morning or evening prayer instead? Or both?"

"No. The fact that you don't want to go to Mass tells me it is exactly what you need."

I groaned and sank my head into my hands.

"Jen? Do we have a deal?"

I pulled at my hair.

"Yes or no, Jen?"

"Yes," I breathed — the single stupidest word I had ever spoken.

❧

What happens during Mass — more specifically, during Holy Communion — is one of the most contentious issues between Catholics and Protestants. Catholics believe that, during the Eucharist, bread and wine are transformed into the actual Body and Blood of Jesus, in accordance with the words He spoke at the Last Supper. Most Protestants believe Jesus was speaking in metaphor and Communion is merely a symbol. Centuries of holy wars could have been avoided if people had just invited a vampire to Mass. If the Catholics were right — if the Eucharist was really the Blood of the Son of God — then it would send us into a frothing, rabid rage.

Which, of course, it does.

My mother had discovered this truth for herself nine hundred years ago. She was walking past a tiny, rustic church in France when a scent slammed against her olfactory nerves, so overpowering that she burst through the doors and killed six people just by throwing them out of her way. As she snatched the holy chalice from the altar, one single purple drop still glistened in the golden cup.

"I am only alive today, Jennifer," she said, "because I found the strength not to drink it. That one drop would have satisfied a thousand years of thirst — and that one drop would have killed me."

❖

I left Mother Lily in the garden and made my way inside the convent, dragging my feet over the carpet in the living room. I had known when I came home that I would have to find a way to avoid the same danger my mother had survived so long ago, the irresistible temptation to die inside the Divine. I had already asked Mr. Valen, a fellow non-Catholic, to please turn a blind eye when I sneaked out to the bathroom during Communion at weekly school Mass. The nuns would give me no such leeway.

As I turned the doorknob to my room, the static from the carpet shocked me. For a fraction of a second, my heart seemed to stop, a timely preview of the fate that awaited me. I knew I should back out of Mother Lily's deal, but I had not agreed to it for the sake of my social life. I had to have an excuse to leave home now and then or I would never be able to hunt. If my study hall had not been usurped by the human version of Jiminy Cricket, I might have been able to sneak away then. If I had not been grounded, I could have made occasional trips to "the mall" or "the library." As things stood, however, dating Matt was the only available alibi.

You cannot do this, Jen. You have to leave. Reason spoke for the umpteenth time. For the umpteenth time, I did not listen.

11

Mother Lily graciously allowed me to forego my penance for the weekend in order that I might catch up on homework, so I had a day and a half in which to talk myself out of this lunacy. Instead, I spent the weekend actually doing homework. Junior year was rich with all the best subjects: world literature had introduced me to Anton Chekov and Victor Hugo, Spanish had reached a level where we were actually reading short stories, and even physics had turned out to be surprisingly engrossing.

I also used the time to catch up on the week's newspapers. They yielded no mention of a body being found in the Orchid Gardens mausoleum, nor of pigs having eaten anything unusual at LSU. As the weekend drew to a close, however, I had no choice but to face the reality that lay ahead. My first Mass would be Monday at 6:00 a.m., and even if I managed not to kill anyone, I could not betray the slightest sign of my thirst. A curled lip, a snarl, fists balled too tightly under wild eyes . . . Humans did not have such reactions to the presence of wine transforming into Blood. I had to seem indifferent, even bored, or my house of cards would come tumbling down.

I took what few precautions I could think of. I stole a clove of garlic from the kitchen and a missal from the chapel. Then, holding my breath, I smeared the spice across the cover and many of the pages. I struck a second deal with Mother Lily, offering to scrub the chapel floors in exchange for letting me off my nightly dish duty. She agreed, and soon a toxic cloud of Pine-Sol lurked in the sanctuary. It was like a ludicrous comic book: Garlic Man and Pine-Sol Girl versus Jesus Christ. Somehow, I thought I knew how that would end.

I tried to psych myself up, silently cheering myself into willpower. Like the Little Engine That Could, I chugged through the day. *I think I can, I think I can, I think I can,* but I knew it was in vain. Sunday night, I did the only thing I could think of that might actually work. I got down on my knees and prayed.

Lord, it's Jennifer. I know you can hear me. I don't know why you allowed my mother to turn me into a vampire, but I'm trying to do the best I can under the circumstances. I know you don't want me to drink your Blood. I know that would be a profanation of everything holy. So, if you could just help me resist, I'd appreciate it, and that way we can both get what we want. Thank you.

I made the sign of the cross for good measure and climbed into bed, wondering whether my mother, in all her years of self-discipline, had ever thought to employ the simple expedient of prayer.

Monday morning, I dragged myself to the chapel like a lamb to the slaughter.

Daily Mass is usually a quick affair, with no music or fanfare and a very abbreviated sermon. I only had about fifteen minutes to collect my willpower and fill my nostrils with residual toxins before the consecration began. Sister Diane, sitting next to me, had clearly noticed my aromatic missal. She kept darting her eyes at me with a mixture of wonder and disgust. I did my best to ignore her, as well as the violent pitching of my stomach caused by the garlic. I reminded myself that I had smelled – and tasted – worse, and I had survived. With every breath, I prayed. *Just let me sit here quietly, Lord, that's all I ask.*

All too soon, Father Henry elevated the host. "This is my Body given up for you," he said, and instantly, it was. Through my Pine-Sol forest, the fragrance of flesh wafted to me, perfect and pure. Every hair on my body stood on end. My nostrils flared as if to allow temptation a freeway to my brain. Father Henry raised the cup. "This is my . . ."

In the split second before he could say, "Blood," I took a breath deeper than any I had ever breathed and held it in, my last weapon against the desire palpitating through my very pores. The microscopic particles of scent beat against the small hairs in my nose, daring me, cajoling me, imploring me to let them in. Father Henry droned on, wheezing the Lord's Prayer in slow motion while the air, ripe with poison, echoed against some primordial memory, some hint half-forgotten. I could discover it, if only I would take a breath . . .

"Lamb of God," blah blah blah, and then Father Henry ate the Body, drank the Blood. I watched because I had no will to move my eyes. With seasoned nonchalance, the essence of perfection slid down his mortal throat. The sisters lined up, waiting their turns, so calm and matter-of-fact. Did they know what they were drinking? Could they understand the gift? Why should they be chosen when it was I who thirsted, I who craved, I who could appreciate and savor?

Lights danced before my oxygen-deprived eyes, prismatic flashes of unconsciousness, a veil of oceanic blue that drenched my vision in its folds. *Don't faint!* I ordered my wavering brain, knowing that the smell of the Blood would revive me instantly, and I would leap toward the prize as surely as if I had breathed by force of will. Sister Joan was drinking from the chalice, last in line. The blue gave way to violent red, a pulsing, fiery sea. I focused the contracting tunnel of my sight toward the altar, where only the cup was visible as Father Henry wiped it dry. I hugged my burning ribs, squeezing out my last drops of resistance until his hands left the frame and I knew the vessel of my longing was safe within the sacristy once more.

Air exploded from my skull and rushed back in, nature correcting the vacuum of my lungs. Five heads swiveled to watch as I hyperventilated, but no one took a step to comfort me, no one asked what was wrong. They simply stared until I brought my breathing back under control.

Mother Lily whispered, "Jennifer?"

I nodded, still beyond speech.

"Er, may Almighty God bless you in the name of the Father, Son, and Holy Spirit," Father Henry said, and the nuns murmured, "Amen."

"The Mass is ended. Go in peace."

"Thanks be to God."

No one went in peace. They all just stood there, staring at me like my homeroom class on the first day of school. Sister Diane made as if to step toward me, but Sister Joan put out a hand and said, "Jennifer, may I have a word with you over breakfast?"

"Okay," I gasped, and followed her out of the chapel toward the kitchen. I could almost feel skin growing on my teeth, the infinitesimal film by which I had escaped yet again.

❖

Sitting in close proximity to Sister Joan never failed to make me want to cry. Prompt Succor kids sometimes called her the Saint of the Second Grade, the beatific shepherdess who herded small souls toward the sacraments. For years after I failed to receive the First Holy Communion she had made me so hungry to experience, I made a point of never meeting her eye. It was not her disappointment that made plumes of guilty fire burn through my being; it was the way her stalwart smile never gave up hope.

She slid in across from me at the breakfast table and folded her hands while I poked mindlessly at my steak. "Jen, do you know the first memory I have of you?"

I looked up, curious in spite of myself. "No. What?"

"I remember an awkward little five-year-old in a white cap and gown receiving her kindergarten diploma with no one in the church to clap for her."

I blushed. That was before I knew about vampires, and I had been heartbroken when my mother did not come.

"I can see that you remember. What you don't know is that I called your mother afterward and gave her a piece of my mind. Do you know what she said?"

"No."

"'Thank you for looking out for my daughter, sister.' Then she hung up."

One corner of my mouth twitched backward. Yes, that sounded like my mother.

"The next year, we put on a play. You remember, we hadn't built the auditorium yet, so we had to perform in the church. You were a sheep in the chorus."

"Yes, I know." I was starting to see where this was going, and I did not think I liked it.

"Your mother didn't come."

"I know that, too."

"But after we built the auditorium, when we did the talent show and you played the recorder . . ."

"She came."

"I was so happy for you. I thought maybe we had turned a corner, that she would take more of an interest in your education. But when you received your award for Outstanding English Student . . ."

"She didn't come, and it was held in the church. I see the pattern. What's your point?"

She paused, studying me, but I just continued poking at my steak. "That's a very expensive cut of beef you're destroying."

"Sorry." I popped a bite into my mouth, trying to remember what it used to taste like when it was still food.

Sister Joan sighed while I chewed. "Jennifer, is there something repulsive about our Church?" I could hear the implied capital C, and the keenness of her understanding surprised me. She was not asking about a building, but the great universal Church, Catholicism itself.

"It's part of my disorder," I answered. "My mother had a highly developed sense of smell, and now that I'm changing or the gene's been activated or whatever, I've got it, too."

"And there is something foul-smelling about our Church?"

"Yes."

"What, exactly?"

Now came the tricky part. I could not tell her it was the Blood of Christ. She might believe me, but it would mean admitting I believed the dogmas of the Church, which would rather complicate my continued non-compliance with its practices. I had to think of something that was present in a Catholic church but not in the other places of my daily life.

"It's the alcohol in the wine."

"You're telling me that your mother, a *nurse,* couldn't be around alcohol?"

Oops. I backpedaled fast. "Its just wine. Grape products in general stink pretty bad, but wine is . . . have you ever stuck your head in a sewer pipe?"

"Of course not, and neither have you." I had forgotten how literal Sister Joan could be. "And there was no wine at your graduation or at the play."

"But the church always smells like it. I know it sounds weird — it *is* weird — but it's true. We never went to restaurants, either." That much, at least, was not a lie.

She leaned forward, peering firmly into my eyes. "You want me to believe that wine smells so bad you feel it necessary to hold your breath to the point of passing out and rub garlic all over a missal in order to avoid breathing any?"

"Yes." I met her gaze, unabashed, though I wished I had been subtler with the garlic. I had not realized it was pungent to human noses, too.

"I guess it makes as much sense as anything else you've said lately."

"Do you think Mother Lily might have a little pity and let me trade my Mass penance for something else?"

"You'll have to ask her."

"Can you put in a good word?"

She looked at me once more, and there it was, that undaunted hope peering out from behind the walls of frustration. "Jen, I never had a second grader as eager to receive Holy Communion as you. I just wish you could look back through my eyes and see that little girl, the way you answered all my questions before I could call on you and corrected your classmates when they said something wrong. I wish I could talk to that little girl and tell her it's okay, that she can come to the table now. The Lord is waiting."

I stuffed a bite of steak into my mouth to avoid having to answer. In hindsight, I knew I had only been so eager because somewhere inside me the vampire lurked, ardent for blood. But I remembered what it had felt like at the time, to be invited into *communion,* to be told I could be one with someone greater than myself. I remembered because I was still that little girl. Blood or no blood, I still wanted to *belong.*

Sister Joan stood and took her plate. "I'll tell Mother Lily what you said." She sounded tired.

"Thanks." I swallowed the steak with my tears.

12

Angie Carroll returned to school with her jaw wired shut and so much plaster on her nose that no one would have known who she was if they had not witnessed her injury. My newfound friends receded into obscurity. The punch I had thrown did not seem triumphant now so much as downright mean. Even Matt looked at me differently, and when I called him on it, he said, "It's just, did you have to hit her so hard?"

"I didn't mean to shatter her jaw. I guess I don't know my own strength." I slipped an arm around his waist. "Guess what? We can go out this Friday . . . if you want," I added, hoping Angie's face had not turned him off of me permanently.

"Seriously?"

"Seriously." I filled him in about the details of my deal.

"That is so awesome! So, what do you want to do? Dinner?"

"Not dinner. Food allergies. I can't eat much they serve at restaurants."

"Oh. Okay. Movie, then?"

"Sure."

Matt turned out to be a cinema buff, so by the time he kissed me and boarded his bus after school, I had learned a great deal about terms like "film noir" and "montage." We had also formed a plan to see something called *Two-Tone Memories,* which seemed the least bad of the choices currently playing at the multiplex.

His kiss left the taste of human flesh lingering on my lips, and I was wondering whether I would be able to make it to Friday without hunting, when I felt a hand on my shoulder.

"Hey, can I talk to you?"

Jeremy's sudden appearance did not shock me as much as it should have. His recent behavior had seemed to indicate that a conversation was imminent. I put my hands on my hips and demanded, "What do you want?"

"Let's go someplace more private." He nodded toward the courtyard with a glint in his eye that my brain rejected as nonsense. Jeremy Higginbotham, my age-old arch-nemesis, could not possibly find me attractive. Then I remembered that of course it was possible, since I was an irresistible vampire. I wondered what it said about me that, of all the changes I had gone through lately, being pretty was the hardest to get used to.

"Fine. Whatever."

I followed him to the bench near the statue of St. Blaise. Jeremy set down his backpack, but neither of us sat. I wasn't exactly comfortable reclining next to the patron saint of ailments of the throat. I folded my arms across my chest, daring Jeremy to speak.

"I know you're with Matt."

"Then what is this about?"

He tucked my hair behind my ear. "You don't have to be."

I stepped back, torn between wanting to punch him, kiss him, or kill him. I settled for just getting out of his way. "I know. I choose to be."

"Jen, the guy looks like that kid in *Willy Wonka* who got caught on a taffy puller, and he hardly says three words. Admit it. You're settling."

"And you think you would be an upgrade?"

"Of course." The smell of fear rising palpably from his every pore belied his swaggering nonchalance.

"You're an arrogant jackass."

"And you're a temperamental bitch with one hell of a right hook." He moved closer, until I could feel his hot breath on my cheek. "So, what do you say?"

"If you come any closer, I'll show you what that right hook can really do."

"Come on, Jen, just give me a chance."

Why is it that horrible, egomaniacal boys always smile like movie stars? Never in my life had I thought of Jeremy as anything but a bully, yet, for some unfathomable reason, my knees were shaking.

"A chance to pretend you haven't tried to make me miserable every day of my life since kindergarten?"

He smiled wider, heightening his resemblance to a young Brad Pitt. "You know what they say. You only torture the ones you love."

That was corny enough to break the spell. I gave a fleeting thought to unleashing my balled right fist, but decided he was not worth the trouble. Besides, no matter how cocky he might pretend to be, I knew his secret. I could smell it, layering the air with its musky perfume. He was desperately afraid, tortured with a terror so real, his very life might as well have been at stake.

I prepared a more potent weapon than my fist. "Well, I guess Matt had better watch out, then, because I love*him* ."

I waited for the air to be rent with misery, but Jeremy only nodded, and the fear did not climax or change. "All right, if that's the way you want to play it." He picked up his backpack. "By the way, if you tell anyone about this, I'll tell your secret."

"What secret?"

"You know." For a split second, I thought I saw what I had always feared: the hint of recognition that named me as *other,* alien, sub-human. But Jeremy had always looked at me that way.

"You're an idiot," I scoffed, and walked away.

❖

I had no trouble forgetting about Jeremy as I dressed for my first cross-country practice, mostly because the locker room still smelled like blood. I was late and therefore alone, so I used the opportunity to practice self-control. Inhale, one-two-three; exhale, one-two-three. Every breath weighted my lungs with desire, but I enjoyed the release that came from not trying to fight. I allowed myself to appreciate the scent for what it was: a perfume, not a meal. Relaxed as I would ever be, I spritzed on an extra coat of sunscreen and joined my teammates by the bleachers.

Prompt Succor cross-country existed mostly to give the other teams someone on the schedule they knew they could beat. Students did not have to try out for the team and only had to attend two practices to be allowed to compete. People came and went, using running as a way to socialize and keep in shape, except for a core group of two girls and four boys who actually treated it as a competitive sport. Despite having seen what I did to Angie, the Core Six could not keep the smiles off their faces when I arrived.

"Hey, Jen," said April, the girl who had gushed about my hair. "Glad you made it."

"Thanks." More quietly, I asked, "So, what do we do?"

She smiled. "We run."

That was about the only thing I did know about the sport of cross-country. I followed April through the neighborhood surrounding our school and soon found myself on the track that circled the LSU Lakes. The lakes themselves were small, man-made creations, too dirty for fishing but home to plenty of ducks, geese, and pelicans. The running track hugged a portion of their grassy banks, but also meandered through old, rich neighborhoods and along busy streets, cutting across itself at several points to create routes of any desired distance.

"How far are we going?" I asked.

"A little over five miles."

"How long does that take?"

"Forty minutes or so."

If I let myself really run, that was about thirty-nine minutes more than I would need.

Normal walking did not bother me much, but once my muscles shifted into a mode that called for speed, I had to grit my teeth to hold myself to April's pace. I could have stalked out ahead, run with the boys toward the front of the pack, but I knew if I allowed myself even a tiny bit of freedom, my legs would kick into gear and run the way I was meant to run. The team fanned out around us while I trotted determinedly alongside April, feeling like a film someone was watching frame by frame. After about three minutes, I started to think that thirty-seven more would drive me insane and that maybe this whole cross-country idea was stupid. I was just about to fake a Charley horse and give up the whole pursuit when April spoke.

"Seriously, what did you do this summer?"

"What do you mean?"

"I mean, you look like you went to supermodel camp."

"Good genes, I guess. They just finally kicked in."

April rolled her eyes. "That is so not fair."

Then we were chatting affably about the things teenage girls chat about, which was a revelation to me, since most of my previous "chats" had either been with nuns or my vampire mother. April was dating a boy named Clark but thinking of ditching him for a basketball player named Tate, and the schemes she had planned to judge whether or not Tate shared her interest were as complex as the web of lies I had spun to protect my secret life as a mythical monster. Maybe my aptitude for intrigue came not from being a vampire, but from being sixteen. After a few minutes of talking to April, I decided that was probably the case. She appeared to be better at it than I was.

Two miles later, April ran out of breath to talk, but our shared silence was comfortable, rich with promise. I knew that fifteen minutes of pointless gabbing did not amount to joining the Ya-Ya Sisterhood, but there was just something about April. She had a pleasant, complicated smell, and she did not knock me senseless with desire; she was too full of contradictions, just like me. April had only started at Prompt Succor last year, so she was a blank canvas that my eleven years of nerdiness had not yet managed to stain. In defiance of every teenage social law, it seemed I might have found both a boyfriend and a friend: a universe so backward, so beautifully off-balance that it *must* topple down around my ears.

"Is Matt a good kisser?" As we walked toward the showers, April's sudden question broke the silence. I shuddered away thoughts of impending doom and reached deep inside to find the friend I had always wanted to be. However brief our friendship might be, it was still more than I had ever dared to hope for.

"Yeah." I paused, debating how my next thought would sound out loud, but I decided to let it through. "He tastes like Christmas."

"What, peppermint?"

"No. Just . . . that sort of excitement you feel when you're waiting for Santa Claus? Like that."

April shook her head. "You are one strange girl, Jen." But I could hear — and smell — the affection in her voice, ready and willing to let me in. *One day at a time,* I told myself. *Today, I have a friend.*

13

Wednesday morning, I faked having menstrual cramps to get out of going to school Mass. My lungs were not prepared to desist in their function long enough for six hundred kids to meander down the Communion aisle. I would have to get them into shape before next Wednesday, though, because I couldn't very well have cramps two weeks in a row. Once the nuns had left for school, I got out a stopwatch and started practicing holding my breath.

I had topped out around eight minutes when the phone startled me out of my exercise. I answered, "Hello?"

"Jennifer, how are you?" an aged voice croaked through the line.

"Um, I'm fine, Mother Celeste. Are you looking for Mother Lily?"

"No, I just spoke with Mother Lily. I'm looking for you."

I took a deep breath. "Okay. Here I am."

"I assume you got my message from Sister Diane?"

"Yes, ma'am."

"Good. I'm a woman of my word, even if I can think of a few unsavory names for what *you* are. Now, Mother Lily just filled me in about your new, augmented sense of smell. That wouldn't happen to be the reason your 'cramps' coincided with Mass-time today?"

"Of course not. It's just that time of the month."

"Uh-huh. Jennifer, I've seen a few things in my time. I have a little theory about your recent behavior that I'd like to put past you, face to face. Would Sunday work for you?"

I swallowed knives. "Um, sure."

"Bring Mother Lily and Sister Diane, if you don't mind. Two o'clock."

"Okay."

"And Jennifer, try not to hospitalize anyone between now and then."

"Yes, ma'am." The phone clicked as I laid it in its cradle, ominous as gunfire. A theory about my sense of smell from a woman who had spent eight decades serving desolate souls in a city that offered a guided tour of its vampires. I was screwed.

One day at a time, Jen. I checked into school after lunch and spent the rest of the day wondering whether the churning in my gut could be called "butterflies in the stomach," or whether it was really caused by tiny bats.

Wednesday passed without further incident, and when Thursday miraculously followed suit, I almost let myself be lulled by the promise of a routine. I spent my school days clutching Matt's hand, then in the afternoon trotted off to suffer through five miles of slow motion made beautiful by April's friendly chatter. By the time Friday arrived, bearing the promise of both my first date and my next meal, I'd decided the wings in my stomach were not butterflies *or* bats. They were hummingbirds, pattering blurry excitement in time with my heart.

Matt kissed me goodbye after school, his eyes glittering more brightly than the sun-drenched lenses in front of them. "I'll be back to pick you up in three hours," he promised.

"I'll be ready." My hummingbirds gave a lurch as I realized I had no idea how to make that true. How was I going to hunt? More importantly, what was I going to wear?

Thank God for April. I headed off toward the locker room to seek her advice.

"Hey," she greeted me with a smile. "You getting excited?"

"Is it that obvious?"

"You're practically wearing a neon sign. Don't worry, though, I saw him in religion. He's glowing even brighter than you."

I blushed and tried to hide it by tying my shoes.

"So, what are you going to wear?"

"I was kind of hoping you would help me with that."

She cocked her head and studied me. "Jeans for sure, and a top that's sexy, but doesn't try too hard. Those sandals you got for your birthday, definitely. And normally I'd say makeup, but your skin is so ungodly clear, and guys hate lipstick anyway. Smears all over them when you kiss. So maybe just a little something to highlight your eyes . . ."

"Could you just come over after practice and help?" I hoped I did not sound too desperate.

She smiled. "Sure."

The flurry of girlishness that followed was like hearing a favorite song for the first time; it made me want to play it on an infinite loop. I had never been a tomboy, though people often assumed I was because of my plain clothes. As a child, I had craved frilly dresses, giant hair bows, and patent-leather shoes, but my mother had never approved of such nonsense. The nuns imposed rather different restraints on my wardrobe: modesty and budget. Modesty was fine by me, but the strict convent budget had curbed any fashionable flights of fancy I might otherwise have indulged. April literally screamed when she opened my closet.

"That's it?"

I stared at the floor and mumbled, "No place to wear anything."

"The *second* you get un-grounded, we are going to the mall."

"Okay."

A tap on the door, and Sister Theresa's round face poked through. "Something wrong? I heard a scream."

"No," April answered.

I cut her off. "Yes. I don't have anything to wear tonight."

"Ah. That is a problem." Sister Theresa nudged me aside and stared thoughtfully into my closet. April gave me a look that clearly said, *What are you doing? Why'd you ask a nun?* I just smiled and waited.

I only owned three blouses that were not school uniforms. Sister Theresa proceeded to pull all three from the closet. The first was a basic blue button-down. She gave it a critical glance, then hung it back up. "Too professional." She held the others toward me with an editorial eye. "What do you think, April?"

"Depends on the accessories."

"You're right. Here, Jen. Put this one on."

I slipped into the sleeveless white tunic, and a thrill shuddered through my spine. For half an hour, I played the part of Barbie doll, allowing myself to be dressed, re-dressed, and accessorized. The tunic — flowy and free — had to compete with the charms of a more form-fitting rayon V-neck, both of which got overshadowed by the need to include my favorite jade pendant necklace. For the first five minutes, April only gawked while Sister Theresa gave shrewd, fashion-savvy advice, but then she got used to it and played along.

What April did not realize — what students at Prompt Succor never seemed to realize — was that nuns are not born nuns. April would have been shocked to see the LSU *Gumbo* yearbook from thirteen years back wherein one Jessica Theresa Linnell smiled in successive photos as the vice-president of Kappa Delta sorority and as a member of the Homecoming Court. In my opinion, she looked better now, robed in humility and joy. But no one could deny that, once upon a time, Sister Theresa had been hot.

The ex-sorority girl stepped back to admire the latest permutation of tunic, jade, and small hoop earrings. She raised her finger as an idea dawned. "Wait here." She returned a moment later with a lacy gray bolero I had never seen before that was somehow both classic and retro. April squealed as Sister Theresa draped it over my shoulders.

"Sister, *where* did you get that?"

"I wore it to my senior prom."

April's jaw fell slack as she imagined that startling image. Sister Theresa let her gape and pulled up my hair. "It needs to go back — like this — to show off your shoulders. Do you have a barrette?"

By six o'clock, I could have outshone my mother, if only because my smile was more genuine than hers had ever been. Sister Theresa hugged me and whispered, "Matt doesn't stand a chance."

Fingers of ice slipped down my spine and I closed my eyes, praying she was wrong.

April left for home around five-thirty, never knowing how her giggly departing hug made my eyes tear up in gratitude. Then, at ten after six, Matt jumped out of his dad's Suburban with a grin wider than the Mississippi. "Hey," he said as the sisters and I gathered to meet him at the front door.

"Hey." I took his arm, and he led me toward the car, then opened the back seat door. We climbed in together, fingers instantly entwined.

"Jen, this is my Dad. Dad, this is Jen."

An even taller, older version of Matt turned toward me from the driver's seat. "Hi, Jen. It's nice to finally meet you."

"You, too, Mr. Derwin."

We pulled away from the convent, and an awkward silence filled the air. I had not been so nervous in a very long time. Fearful or worried? Sure, every day. But not *nervous,* with that prickling sensation shooting up my spine, embarrassment the only thing at stake rather than life and limb. It should have been an improvement, but the novelty of it left me speechless.

"So, Jen, I hear you're an athlete." Mr. Derwin made a laudable attempt to set us all at ease.

"Yes, sir. I run cross-country."

"How'd you do in your last meet?"

"The first one's tomorrow, so I guess we'll find out."

"Oh."

Silence again. It seemed that Matt had inherited his taciturn ways. Mr. Derwin's first attempt at conversation was also his last. Fortunately, we had to go only about two miles. Before the silence had a chance to become stifling, we arrived at the theater. Mr. Derwin pulled to the curb. "Have fun. I'll be back at eight-forty."

"Thanks, Dad."

"Thanks, Mr. Derwin."

We merged into the ticket line still holding hands.

My nerves calmed a little now that the third wheel had gone. "It sucks that your curfew's so early," Matt grumbled, nuzzling my hair. I had told him I was due back at nine.

"Well, you can't break your classmate's face and expect to get a lot of leeway."

"I guess not."

I turned and kissed him, surprised by my own daring. Of course, we had been kissing every day for a week now, but never when I was preparing to hunt. I tasted his tongue, its piquant fire sending thrills through my bones. *An appetizer,* I told myself, but somehow that did not seem quite right.

"Hey," came a disgruntled voice behind us. With a jolt, we broke apart and realized it was our turn at the window.

"Sorry," I muttered as Matt stepped forward and said, "Two, please."

Something bothered me, buzzing around my mind like an elusive mosquito. Something about the kiss, but what?

One way to find out. When we reached the concession line, I threw my arms around Matt's neck and pressed my mouth to his once more. His surprise took only an instant to dissolve before his hands reached for my face, holding it gently as his lips danced across mine. The rich beauty of his joy intoxicated me, drawing me in . . .

I came up for air, and a light bulb flashed above my head. I *enjoyed* kissing Matt. It seemed the most natural thing in the world, but it did not make any sense. Why would an asexual vampire enjoy an embrace designed to foreshadow sex? There was only one logical reason: human flesh tastes good. But that could not be the true answer, or I would have killed Matt by now.

Maybe I just liked feeling normal. I had never dreamed I would be able to participate in such an ordinary teenage activity, and I was, of course, a sucker for such things. Then it would stand to reason that Matt himself did not matter. I ought to get the same satisfaction from kissing any boy who was willing to oblige.

I looked around the popcorn line and found three boys my age standing together, laughing and teasing each other, and I tried to imagine kissing each of them in turn. The first looked too much like Jeremy; I aborted that attempt. The second seemed nice enough, a little shy – like Matt – but more muscular, without the glasses. I closed my eyes . . .

"Hey, you okay?"

"Fine. I just get lost in my thoughts sometimes."

"What were you thinking about?"

Kissing other guys. For once, the truth had very little to do with being a vampire, yet somehow it still managed to be incriminating. "Kissing you," I said instead.

He smiled. "I think about kissing you all the time."

We kissed again, a little harder, a little longer, and the taste of his longing drenched me in its fragrant caress until once again the person behind us coughed and said, "You're up."

Matt ordered popcorn and drinks. I went back to pondering the other guys in line, smelling, tasting, imagining . . .

There was only one way to find out.

"You ready?" Matt asked.

"Yes." I took his hand.

We handed a wispy-looking college girl our tickets and then made our way into the hushed darkness of stadium-style armchairs. We found two empty seats fifth row center and settled in.

"I can't wait to see what Hudson's done with the set design." Matt dug into the popcorn. "Want some?"

I wrinkled my nose. "No, thanks."

The lights dimmed, and Matt turned to watch the previews while I settled my head on his shoulder, closed my eyes, and turned to the task at hand.

I had not been in a room with so many people all at once since I had matured. The luscious bouquet filled my nose, a wonderland of humankind laid out in neatly ordered rows like the aisles of some exotic bazaar. Scent by scent, I surveyed them, weighing the luster of this one's recklessness against the wiles of that one's generosity. My mouth watered at a whiff of invincibility, the confidence of a champion, and I opened my eyes to find its source. However, the man who owned the athletic body was twice my age, not at all right for the experiment I had determined to stage. I crossed him off my list — and then I realized what I was doing.

I had to choose.

I had not had to look Benji or Violet in the eye, to pluck them out like apples from a bin and name them mine. Fate, chance, luck, or even God had sent them to me. Nothing in my power could have saved them.

That would not be true this time.

Anticipation pulsed around me, ecstasy imprisoned in the fragile bonds of flesh. Every fiber of my being ached to set it free, to soar, but beneath the thin veneer of paradise, I knew the god I served: the leaden fear, the strangling cement, the unrelenting need. Ecstasy was my reward for faithful service, but I was still a slave. *You have to do this, Jen. It's them or you.* I took another long, deep breath, hoping for a sign, but only Matt's dimpled smile stood out from the crowd.

"You okay?" he asked as the last of the trailers faded to black and a choir of cellos scraped out the dark opening notes of *Two-Tone Memories'* score.

I forced myself to smile back. "Yeah. Of course." I laid my head on his shoulder and set my kissing experiment aside. I was a lion in a herd of wildebeests; surely, one of them would stumble. If I did not make a choice, then surely Darwin would.

I settled in to watch the movie, which was almost engrossing enough to distract me from the distant echo of my conscience. Determinedly, I focused every mental process on unraveling the mind-bending, time-twisting storyline, but I still didn't have it all sorted out when the lights came back on.

"So was the guy with the ponytail really Sarah's brother?" I asked as we made our way out to the lobby.

"Yeah, but I think he was that kid's father, too."

"I thought the old guy was the kid's father."

"The old guy was Sarah's father. I think."

I kept my eyes peeled as we walked, my predatory senses running on high alert. The faintest hint of stony fog insisted that I must not leave the theater without choosing a meal.

"Hey, do you mind if I run to the bathroom?" Matt asked.

"Sure. Go ahead." The hairs on my arms tingled as I watched him trot off toward the men's. *It has to be now.* I leaned against the wall by the water fountain, watching a parade of feet thud across the tacky red carpet. Loafers, high-tops, sandals, spiked heels . . . *Pick one, Jennifer . . .*

An elbow jostled me, pushing my ribs into the fountain. "Oh, crap, I'm sorry," a boy muttered as he reached to steady me. His skin connected, his hand against my arm – and, by instinct, I smiled.

His fingers curled around my bicep while his lips crept up to mirror mine. It was the boy from the popcorn line, the one who had reminded me of Matt. "Hey," he said, his pupils dilating as if he had been drugged. "Are you all right?"

I swallowed and leaned in toward his ear. "Meet me here in half an hour," I breathed, still oozing charm. I slipped out from his grasp just in time, as Matt returned.

Matt grinned his goofy, dimpled grin and took my hand. "You ready?"

"Yes."

The boy stared after us, frozen, glassy-eyed. *It's natural selection,* I reminded myself. A cobra does not mourn for the snake that it has swallowed.

14

Mr. Derwin picked us up right on time. The traffic lights on the way home all raced to turn green, as if the East Baton Rouge Parish Department of Public Works were determined to undermine my scheme. The most complicated part of my evening lay just moments ahead. My overtaxed brain had been working for a week to figure out how to make Matt and Mr. Derwin believe I had gone home while letting the nuns believe I was still on my date, and I had finally hit on the solution.

Chapel bells.

At eight o'clock, the sisters had retired to their rooms for private prayer. They would not be looking for me to return until ten thirty, so if I could turn the key at precisely nine o'clock, while the bells were ringing, odds were ten to one no one would hear. But the bells would not ring even a minute before nine, and we pulled onto my street at only eight fifty-three. I still had seven whole minutes to kill. Desperately, I started singing along with the radio. When Mr. Derwin stopped in the convent driveway, I touched his arm before he could cut the engine.

"Please let it finish. I love this song."

Matt gave me a look like I had lost my mind. The song was awful, some kind of hip hop-ballad hybrid that ended up as a nasal wail. I sang right along, watching the minutes tick by. It ended — mercifully — at eight fifty-six, and I had no choice but to let Matt walk me to the door. I dragged my feet while he asked, "Do you really like that song?"

"No. I'm just not ready for the evening to end."

"Me, either. But we'll have more nights like this."

"Better ones." Even as I said it, his kiss left me trembling with the flavor of goodbye.

Clang. I drew myself away and put the key into the door. "Thanks for everything."

"No. Thank you."

I waved from the open doorway until the Suburban was gone. Then I closed the door and stepped out into the sultry night. Back to the theater I ran, covering the miles in mere seconds. *He will not be there,* I told myself, never quite deciding whether or not I wanted it to be true. But there he was, standing by the claw machine clutching a stuffed bear. His friends from the popcorn line were with him, looking put out, clearly unconvinced by his story of a mysterious girl who would come back for him. He glimpsed me across the room and pointed.

Show time, Jen. I waved and flashed my most dazzling smile. "Hi." I shook hands with each of his friends in turn, their jaws falling slack. "I'm Nicole." No point giving the witnesses my real name.

My "date" held out the bear. "Here, this is for you."

"Thanks. That's sweet." I gave it a kiss. The touch of polyester fur against my lips reminded me of my unanswered question. I looked up at the boy, his wide brown eyes expectant and hungry.

I offered him my arm. "You ready?"

"Yeah." He ran a nervous hand through his hair, flashed an I-told-you-so grin at his friends, then laced his arm through mine. I steered him out toward the parking lot.

"I'm Martin," he said.

I winced. I did not want to know his name.

"Where do you go to school?" he asked.

"Baton Rouge High," I lied.

"Too bad. I go to McKinley." The two schools were academic rivals, always fighting for the most National Merit Scholars.

"That's okay. We all make mistakes."

He laughed and started to slip his arm around my waist, but his shyness burst into full bloom and he made a not-so-graceful recovery, scratching at an imaginary itch on his side. I reached over, took his arm, and slipped it around my waist for him. I led him through the back of the parking lot, away from crowds and streetlights.

"Where are we going?" he asked.

"I don't know yet. Somewhere." I searched for a spot dark enough, isolated enough, that no one would see us. Another minute, and I found it. The theater was just off the interstate, and we had reached the back of the sound-retaining wall, a small, otherwise useless strip of land where only highway work crews would ever have reason to come. None were out tonight.

We sat down, our backs to the cement, cars racing past us on the other side. "Weird place for a date," he said.

"Sorry. I just wanted to be alone with you."

"Not that I'm complaining or anything, but weren't you with that boy before?"

Thoughts of Matt assaulted my mind, the charm of his sweetly dimpled grin and the electric charge of his lips on mine. I crossed my fingers behind my back as if that could protect us both from the lie I was about to tell.

"He's just some guy I can't get rid of, and I didn't have anything else to do tonight. Until now." I reached out and took his hand.

The shy part of him kicked into high gear again, and he looked at the ground. "Look, Nicole, don't you at least want to get a coffee or something first?" Every word he spoke was an arrow in my armor, too sweet, too relatable. Why couldn't Fate have sent the boy who reminded me of Jeremy, instead?

"I don't drink coffee," I said.

"Is this for real? I mean, like a one-time thing, or . . ."

"Would you please just shut up and kiss me?"

He smiled. "Okay."

Lips suffused with salt and Chap Stick pressed like embers next to mine, all hint of shyness washed away by an eruption of craving. Like lava, passion poured through his veins, igniting my own. His hand lingered just on the edge of my breast, stirring an ache that answered one question definitively enough: reproduction aside, I was now pretty convinced that vampires were not asexual. I pushed his hand forward. Could I do this? And if I did, then . . . what?

"Nicole," he whispered, fumbling at my bra, "I think I love you."

I pulled away and looked at him, his tousled chestnut hair, the freckle on his left cheek, the sweat that dripped like honey down his chin. Something visceral had hardened in his eyes, something that stripped away whatever boyishness had reminded me of Matt.

Just like that, the urge I had never dreamed I could feel turned to ice inside me. He wasn't Matt.

And it *mattered*.

I pulled back, panting, screwing my eyes shut against the bewildering impact of that truth.

"I'm sorry." Harsh street lamps shone down upon Martin's wide brown eyes, illuminating his confusion. "It's cool. I mean . . ."

His warm young body exhaled desire, and all I wanted was to share it. But the word "love" hung between us, as luminous as the stars and just as far beyond our reach. We were both grasping after forgeries, tiny flashlight bulbs of brightness to replace the nuclear reaction we knew not how to ignite. All he wanted was a moment with his face turned toward the light. The girl lying next to him could not give it to him; but the vampire could.

I opened my arms and smiled with the full force of the vampire's allure. "Come here."

He crushed his lips to mine, his arms engulfing me with a will and a power all their own. I traced my tongue along his neck until I tasted the cotton of his shirt. With a flick of his wrist, he tore it off, stripping away the offensive barrier between our skins. I flipped him on his back and he smiled a wild, insatiable grin. His fingers scored my back, taut muscles quivering as I raked him with my kiss. "Oh, God," he gasped as his hips arched upward in a gesture as old as man. I kissed the skin above his navel, so softly I could just feel the small hairs standing on end. His hands fumbled for my jeans, but I pinned them to his sides and kissed that same soft skin, and then the flap of denim bulging precariously beneath.

He cried aloud, hands straining against their bonds, aching to entangle his life with mine. I lifted my right hand, giving him his left, and it curled around my waist, pulling every fiber of my body into his, raggedly inhaling the rhythm of my heart.

I bared my teeth and plunged inside him, detonating rhapsody, a savage jubilance that sprang like a geyser from his veins. He gulped the hot, wet summer air and threw his arm around my head, pulling me still further in, rapture measured by the fathom, our bodies turned to wind. As the last impassioned drops of life gurgled past my tongue, the boy who smelled of stardust groaned and smiled. Surely, if I could offer any goodness in this world, this was it. I could make the dark absolute of death arrive bathed in astral light.

I laid my head softly on his chest as it worked to find the air. The end came gradually, each tiny rise just slightly weaker than the last. When his lungs stood still, I kissed his lips once more, knowing that, for better or worse, we two had become one.

I carried him intact to the fields by the levee, the teddy bear tucked under his arm. The pigs squealed impatiently, sniffing at the feast. I laid his body on the grass and tenderly closed each eye. Then I locked away my heart and tore him limb from limb, sating the lust of the flesh-eating swine. But the head, the mouth that had thirsted for love, and the torso containing his radiant heart, I sent instead downstream.

I don't know why I made the sign of the cross over the river as it carried him away.

I sat and breathed, my mind sifting restlessly through a night too full to comprehend. Still, I knew enough to check my watch, and the angle between big hand and small kicked meditation swiftly to the curb. I scrambled to my feet and ran toward home.

I slowed down two houses from the convent, steadying my lungs and working to remember the plot of the movie I had seen only hours – it seemed like years – ago. At ten twenty-nine, I opened the front door, my breathing calm, hair and clothes appropriately smoothed, with a film synopsis duly prepared.

The sight of three nuns weeping sent shivers down my spine. Sister Diane sat across the living room from them, ashen-faced, alone.

"What happened?" My voice cracked as I imagined the worst. They knew, they must, somehow they had learned . . .

Sister Diane bit her lip and battled back her tears. It seemed at first she was going to lose, that I would be left to wonder and surmise because no one in the room could speak, but she mastered herself and found her voice.

"It's Mother Celeste. She's dead."

15

Grief swooped down on me like a bird of prey, goring my eyes with its bullet-sharp beak. *Why?* I wondered stupidly as the vanguard waters dripped, carving a canal for the inevitable flood. I had barely known Mother Celeste. A few hours ago, I had dreaded being sent to look her in the eye. Shouldn't I be relieved that she was gone?

My tears already knew what my mind was sluggishly beginning to comprehend: I had believed her, after all. Despite the screaming protest of every rational gray cell, I had trusted that Mother Celeste would never let me down. In those half-waking moments between night and dawn when I lay in bed and imagined the worst — when Mother Lily and Sister Diane allied to exorcise the Demon Jennifer from their lives — Mother Celeste would always descend in a fiery cloud to save me. Now my blazing rescuer was gone.

I sat down numbly next to Sister Diane. "What happened?"

"Heart attack."

Mother Celeste was ninety-six years old. Something in her body had been bound to fail, yet I could not bring myself to believe that it had been her heart.

"We'll go down Sunday," Sister Diane added when her voice was strong enough to speak.

"Why not tomorrow?"

She lifted her eyebrows. "Your cross-country meet."

I blinked as if trying to find the picture hidden in a pattern of dots. High school athletics could not possibly matter now.

Sister Diane read my thoughts, as she so often did, and her wonted steady timbre crept back up through the tears. "You're going to run. You've worked too hard not to."

"I . . ." *I haven't worked at all.* The admission died upon my lips.

She put an arm around my shoulders and squeezed. "I love you, Jen. I'm proud of you."

Something inside me popped like a pierced balloon. I threw my arms around her waist and sobbed, the realization dawning that someday she would leave me. This implacable thing called death would one day steal even Sister Diane. Yet here I sat, death's minion, enslaved to its cruel purpose even as I mourned. How dare I weep for the end of a woman aged and infirm when barely an hour ago I had killed a young man full of promise? The ruthless irony mocked me, demanding confession and remorse, but none would come. Even as I felt Sister Diane's arms tighten around my own, her sorrow dripping into my hair, even as I imagined that baleful day when I would weep for her, alone, I could not bring myself to equate what I had done with the tragedy that faced me now. Martin's death had gleamed with beauty, a passage from monotony into blinding wonder. Mother Celeste's death was merely death, preposterous in its finality, draining the font of her warm heart from a sere and desolate world. So I lamented unabashed, justified in my hypocrisy by the radiance of my sin.

Sometime around midnight, woeful silence reigned at last, our wounded hearts weary of tears. Mother Lily stood, wiped her hand across her face, and said, "Jennifer, you ought to get to bed. You've got to run in the morning."

I could not bring myself to cleave my body from Sister Diane, my rock, my all-too-mortal stronghold. My arms remained tied to her frame by bonds more powerful than muscle and bone.

Sister Diane rubbed my back and gently pulled me away from her. "Come on, Jen. Get some sleep. I'll be here when you wake up."

So she would, for one more day. For one more day, the game would still go on, but mortality had shredded my ace in the hole. I was playing against the House of Death, and the house would always win. As Sister Diane half-dragged my torpid body toward my bed, I said a bitter prayer. *God, if you can hear me . . . thanks a lot.*

❖

That was the night when I dreamed.

In sixteen years, never once had my mind created visions while I slept, or, if it had, I never remembered them when I awoke. My mother had said vampires *could* dream, but it did not happen very often. She herself dreamed perhaps once every ten or twelve years. Dreams usually came on momentous nights, when something frightening or important had happened, but not always. Once, she had dreamed about buying a hat, a wide-brimmed, flower-bedecked concoction wildly at odds with my mother's disdain for ornamentation. She told me this (she said) so that, when dreams should finally come to me, I would not overreact.

"I've known vampires who went mad chasing their dreams. They come so rarely, we think they must be more important than they are. Dreams are just random pieces of information reconstructed by the subconscious mind. They are not prophecies or omens or divine communications of any kind. They're just dreams. Do you understand?"

"Yes, ma'am," I said. Unknowingly, I lied.

The dream found me lying in an open casket inside the Orchid Gardens mausoleum. Above me, the stone Gabriel stood poised, wings open as if to shoo away any mourners from my side. Yet a line of people stood waiting to view my waxy corpse, wisps of shapeless color muttering amongst themselves. I strained my eyes, searching for the sisters, for April and Matt, the people who might be sorry I was gone, but I could see nothing more than misty figures made of light. Then Gabriel's robes began to billow in a non-existent breeze. He blew his trumpet, strident and long, filling my ears with a single-note dirge. I cried for him to stop, but my voice rang out in unison with his horn, so that I only sharpened the vibrations pulsing knife-like through my brain. *I'm dead,* I thought, *so why do I feel pain?*

Gabriel stopped abruptly, and stone returned to stone. From the line of those who had come to grieve, the first face now stepped forward to gaze upon my lifeless form.

Benji Gardener leaned over and laid his lips against mine.

Rising now outside myself, I watched as a blush of color rose upon my cheeks, drained from Benji's own. His face grew white, then gray, then sodden as the flesh shrank against the bone. I did nothing — for I was dead — yet his life flowed out until his skin hung loose about his skeleton, as once his deflated coffin-mate's had done. At last he pulled his mouth away — my cheeks were bright as fire — he crawled inside the casket and lay down. His body melded into mine as if he were a ghost, and he was gone.

He had given me his life, and yet I was still dead.

Violet Barista came out next, though I was not surprised to see her now. Violet had brought a violet to my grave. She laid it atop my folded hands, then plunged her teeth into my neck, savaging the skin until embalming fluid poured out through the tear. I felt nothing as she climbed atop my body, clawing, biting, and gasping weakly, "Please." Her life drained into me just as Benji's had, until she was gone and normal color returned to my skin.

I looked to the line of mourners, expecting Martin to be next, but it was Mother Celeste who came and stood above me, studying me with those trenchant blue eyes. She took the violet from my hands and swallowed it whole. A fit of coughing seized her and she bent, clutching at her stomach before she sank to her knees, heaving forth a great something from inside.

It was my soul.

An emptiness, a hole, a pool of shadow in the air, yet all that ever might have been shone brightly from within, craved by every sense I never knew I had. I could not cry out, or reach to touch, or move to make it mine. Mother Celeste, businesslike, brushed the wrinkles from my soul and hung it just above me, dangling it like laundry from Gabriel's bright horn. Then she stepped inside my coffin and vanished into me. *No,* my disembodied consciousness longed ardently to cry, *I did not take her life!* Yet it was mine. She gave it freely, and beneath my sewn-shut eyes, a flicker of motion betrayed the first signs of my return. One more life, and perhaps I would be able to reach up and take my soul.

I looked back toward the line, knowing that Martin must come, keen to let his kiss bring this unlikely princess back from her enchanted death. A footstep echoed across the stone as a boyish teenage figure came slowly into view. I relaxed, awaiting his embrace.

"Hello, Jen." *Matt's voice.* I groaned within, willing mortified flesh to move, to cry out, "Stop! You must not touch me! Go away!" The footsteps progressed ever closer. My soul hung there, taunting, just above my reach. If only I could tell Matt to hand it down, to give me *that* instead of him. . .

The wispy figure reached my casket-side. Warm hands took both of mine. No, I longed to scream, *not you, please, not you.*

His life did not flow away. My soul stayed put, just where it was.

Inside the casket, I opened my eyes.

Standing above me, brandishing a grin, stood a boy with golden hair and russet-colored eyes. Jeremy Higginbotham.

"Jen, it's time to wake up now," he said.

16

When I calmed at last — when the great, gasping sobs that woke me finally died down and I swallowed the bile that rose into my throat when I thought of what I had seen — I was grateful that Jeremy had wormed his way into my dream. Otherwise, I might have believed it meant something. I might have spent my life wondering whether my soul could still exist, whether the people I killed held the key to some unforeseen salvation. I might have gone mad, as my mother had warned, but Jeremy Higginbotham was not the stuff of mystic revelation. He was a mosquito bite, annoying but insignificant, festering harmlessly on the skin of my life. Any dream with Jeremy in it could not be more than a dream.

I forced myself to breathe, to gaze upon the phantoms of the night in the harsh new light of day. Images of angels, violets, faces, souls, all slowly dissipated in the morning's solid rays while I repeated my mother's mantra. *It was just a dream.* Still, one thing lingered that light could not efface. At the moment when I had thought Matt was about to give up his life for mine, my inmost being had wept fierce and bitter tears. I knew, now, why I kissed him. I knew why he mattered.

You're sixteen, Jen. You don't know how to be in love.

In the midst of that comforting lie, my alarm clock rang. I embraced the excuse to get up, glad that I had a cross-country meet today. Running, even at lethargic human speed, would still be a reprieve from my endless attempts to ponder, plan, and understand. I pried my weary body out of bed, sprayed on three coats of SPF 45 waterproof, slipped into my regulation Prompt Succor T-shirt and shorts, laced up my Reeboks, and headed to the car.

Sister Diane was waiting. "Here." She thrust a plate of pre-cut steak into my hands. "I knew you'd try to skip breakfast."

I had not done it on purpose. I had just forgotten to pretend to be hungry. "Thanks." I reached for the passenger seat door.

"No. Back seat."

I raised my eyebrows in a question, and she motioned toward the house. "They're coming."

"All of them?"

She nodded.

Sobs pricked my throat like swallowed thorns. They had stayed. I had thought they would leave Sister Diane to chaperone me, and the rest would go ahead to New Orleans to commiserate with their sisters. After all, how many people did it take to stand around and wait for the end of a race? But they were here, with me.

Sister Diane's eyes narrowed as she saw my eyelids tremble. "Jennifer, don't you dare cry. There will be plenty of time for that tomorrow, at the wake. Today, we're all going to soak up some sun and pretend everything is fine. Especially you."

She glared at me until I had to smile. "Okay."

"Now eat your steak before it gets cold."

I sat on the hood of the communal Volvo and nibbled my beef, determined to obey. Sister Diane was right. Neither Mother Celeste nor my over-active subconscious ought to ruin a perfectly good excuse to act like a regular kid.

We did not often pack all five of us into the Volvo. Our elbows and knees seemed to multiply when we did, but today it felt good to be smushed onto the middle back seat, soaking up Mother Lily's ambrosial scent and the nudge of shoulders on either side. Sister Joan put her arm around me, mostly to get it out of the way, and I relaxed against her, imagining that the fragrance of her pale white flesh held no power over me.

The illusion shattered as I emerged into the parking lot at Baker High. Nothing could have prepared me for the sheer volume of the odor that assaulted my nose. Hundreds of students had gathered from all across South Louisiana, plus their parents, coaches, and supporters: a human stew rich with promise. I steadied myself against the car door as the familiar river of cement gushed into my lungs. *Just breathe, Jen. One-two-three in, one-two-three out.*

"You okay?" Mother Lily came around the side of the car, her luscious single-note aroma overpowering the complex stew. Tempting as she always was, at least this was a battle I knew I could win. I inhaled and let go.

"I'm fine. Just nervous."

Sister Theresa squeezed my shoulders. "You'll be great. Just drink something, make sure you're hydrated." She handed me a sport bottle, and I gulped it down.

"Hey! Jen!" April was approaching from a nearby car with a woman who must be her mom. "How'd it go last night?"

"Good." I debated whether or not to tell her about Mother Celeste, but decided against it.

"Good how?"

"You know, just . . . good."

April was never going to let me off that easy, but Mother Lily interrupted. "Jen, have you met Ms. Willette? Monica, this is Jennifer."

I shook hands and went through the pleasantries, surprised to find that April's mom neither looked nor smelled like April. Monica Willette's overdone makeup could not compensate for her pudgy features, nor mask the downtrodden aroma of menthol cigarettes and dead dreams. Meanwhile, her daughter, dark and lean and arrogant, carried an aura of disgust that must have been directed toward her mother because I had never smelled it before. Maybe I needed to stop sapping April's friendship to make myself feel normal and actually get to know her.

"Hey! Jen!"

I jerked my head toward the unexpected voice, and my heart gave a funny lurch as my eyes landed on Matt. He waved like a maniac across the parking lot, holding a dozen roses, with his dad at his side. "Surprise!" His goofy grin grated unmercifully against the fresh revelations of my dream. "Hope you like pink."

He had gathered up the broken dreams of my childhood and glued them together in one single bouquet. "It's my favorite color," I stammered as I kissed his cheek and drank in the sweet floral fragrance that so closely mimicked his own. "You hold on to them for me while I run."

"Speaking of," April interrupted, and nodded toward the field.

I took one more breath of Matt's devotion and reluctantly let him go. With my game face pasted on, I hugged each of the nuns, and then April led me away, a knowing grin on her face.

"What?" I demanded.

"Last night, you did it, didn't you?"

"Did what?"

"Come on. The way he hugged you back there, and roses? At a cross-country meet? You totally did him."

"Of course not. It was our first date."

April smirked, unconvinced. "You two are going to be one of those sickening old couples who are like eighty-five and still making eyes at each other."

"No," I sighed. "I'll never be eighty-five."

April gave me a weird look but didn't say anything. I loved her for letting me be strange.

Coach Taylor stood a little way off, trying to corral the team and put the correct numbers on their sleeves. April, the veteran, waved to girls from other schools as we passed, occasionally stopping to give hugs and trade hellos. We fell into the circle around Coach Taylor, got our numbers, and started to stretch. Through it all, my brain worked valiantly to delete unbidden scenes of future domestic bliss, but they kept creeping resolutely back. A white silk dress with a pink rose bouquet; children with glasses and goofy grins; a Jennifer with wrinkles and gray hair . . .

I did not notice who had come up behind me until the familiar scent of fear drifted across my preoccupation. "So, Carshaw, you planning to live up to the hype? They clocked you going ninety that day you laid out Angie."

I rounded on my heel. "Jeremy, what are you doing here?"

He put his arm around a small redheaded girl I had seen at practice. "I'm with Kelly."

"Then stay with Kelly."

"What? I'm just trying to wish you luck."

"Thanks, but if I actually had any luck, you wouldn't be here."

"Ouch. I knew your fist was dangerous, but no one warned me about your tongue."

I envisioned using that fist to pummel him into the ground. Why did he work so hard to annoy me, even in my dreams?

But he hadn't been annoying in the dream. He floated back to me as he had appeared last night, the golden smile, the soft touch of his hands, the whisper, "It's time to wake up." He had been gentle in the dream, a friend, someone to stave off the loneliness of the grave . . .

Which was just more proof that it was only a dream.

I did a few vehement lunges, scratching at my stupid metaphorical mosquito bite. Jeremy hung around, catching my eye as often as he dared and flirting ostentatiously with Kelly. I balled my fists and imagined myself turning his brown eyes black, but then Coach signaled for us to start the warm-up.

Since cross-country is exactly what it sounds like, a race on natural terrain, no two courses are alike and the runners get a chance to jog the route before the meet. The whole team now headed out to warm up and explore.

"What's the deal with you and Jeremy?" April asked when we were out of his earshot.

"He's just an ass. He's been picking on me since the first day of kindergarten." *And he wanted to date me, too,* but that part still seemed like some bizarre, squeamish nightmare.

April stared.

"What?"

"Nothing. I mean, I know you like Matt, but Jeremy's hot."

"And he acts like that makes him king of the world."

April shrugged and let the subject drop. We jogged twenty yards or so before she asked, "So, what really happened last night?"

"We watched a good movie and had a good time."

"That's it?"

"Yeah."

"Then why do you seem all different today?"

"Different?"

"Yeah. Like, I don't know, you're just kind of quiet, and I can't tell if you're happy or sad."

"Well, I was kind of trying to forget about it, but Mother Celeste died last night."

April stopped in her tracks. "Oh. Really? I'm so sorry. I mean, were you close to her?" Students at Prompt Succor all knew Mother Celeste, at least by reputation, so I was spared the trouble of explaining who she was.

"I guess not. I mean, I only met her a couple of times, but the nuns are pretty broken up."

"Oh. God, that sucks."

"Yeah."

We gawked at each other, at a loss for words. Before the silence could stretch too long, two guys from our team came over. "Hey, y'all okay? Why'd you stop?"

April answered, "Mother Celeste died last night."

Kyle let out a low hiss while Brandon said, "Oh, that sucks. Jen, you okay?"

They looked at me with eyes full of real concern, and I almost started crying again. I had gone to school with these boys all my life, sharing classroom space and lunch tables, never seeing beyond our mutual apathy. Now, we were teammates, maybe even friends, and they wanted to help me if they could. I remembered my promise to Sister Diane and sniffed back the tears before they could fall.

"Yeah. I'll be fine."

April looped her arm around my waist, and the four of us finished the course together. The perfume of camaraderie helped me believe that my words might really be true.

❖

Cheering fans surrounded the two hundred girls at the starting line, some yelling, "Go Lucy," and "You can do it, Caroline," while others shouted, "Bulldogs!" or "Eagles!" I strained my ears as above the din came a small, united knot of voices chanting "Jen-ni-fer, Jen-ni-fer!" Matt cried the loudest, but other voices joined him: the nuns, Mr. Derwin, Ms. Willette, Coach Taylor, and *every boy on our team.* The girls gathered near me, patting my shoulders and bestowing smiles. Word about Mother Celeste had gotten around, and my teammates actually cared. It almost made me forget I was surrounded by two hundred young, succulent hearts pumping bright red blood.

April gave my elbow one last squeeze and turned toward the course. The starter pistol sounded, and we were off.

Until this moment, I had never planned to do anything but shadow April, just like practice, but as the chant of my name followed me into the woods, I knew what I had to do. I had to thank them, the sisters most of all, but Matt and my teammates, too. I had to win. However, I had to do it without knocking people down or disappearing into my speed, which was easier said than done.

At first, the bodies were packed so closely, I had no idea how to pass anyone. Thankfully, running at human speed always gave me the sensation of watching the world turn one frame at a time. I spotted a gap between April and Kelly, just wide enough to slip through. Then another, a tiny bit wider, just ahead. Suddenly I was swimming through a sea of girls I had never met, a wilderness of ankle socks and ponytails. Sweat, determination, and fellowship drenched the air. These girls were rivals, but they were also friends.

I was one of them. Every eye that saw me told me I belonged.

I wanted to hug every person I passed. I wanted to kiss their feet as they thudded companionably through the dirt. Even when I passed a girl with a fresh scratch on her arm and my vision threatened to cloud over with the familiar fog, I blinked until my eyes cleared. She had nothing to fear. I would have sooner killed myself than one of these, my peers.

Still I found the gaps, gaining on the field.

Bobbing and weaving in slow-motion got old pretty fast. I turned my attention to discipline, making sure my feet did not suddenly speed away. The crush of girls thinned as I reached the leading pack. The finish line called to me, the crowd just coming into view. With a measured burst of speed, I broke away. Images of victory cavorted merrily in my mind, the smiles and hugs, the trophy engraved with my name . . .

A single red T-shirt splashed against the trees like a toreador's cape, a runner who had pulled out alone long before I reached the front. She was fifteen yards in front of me with less than a football field to run. I unleashed another shot of speed.

Then the scent of her happiness surrounded me, the pride of her accomplishment, the pulsing satisfaction. This girl had sacrificed countless hours to hone her body and refine her skill. She had earned her victory, yet here I was, about to use my demonic powers to snatch away her just reward.

Three murders to date and no end in sight, but I was still better than that. I slowed to a jog and strolled in at second place.

Matt enveloped me instantly. "That was so awesome! Second place! In your first meet!" Thank God for my super-human lungs, or he would have squeezed all the breath from my body.

The nuns quickly pried me from his arms. The joy that masked the sadness in their limpid eyes was the best gift I could have given and the best I could have received. However, I did not get to gaze upon it long as the entire Prompt Succor delegation swarmed in with shoulder slaps and high-fives. I had finished higher than any runner in school history, and the cheer went up again: "Jen-ni-fer! Jen-ni-fer!" Kyle hugged me, and Brandon kissed my cheek. Then I had to hug Matt again to make sure he did not punch anyone.

From the edge of the chaos, Jeremy caught my eye and gave a silent, congratulatory salute. It even looked like he meant it. What was his problem?

I turned away as the rest of our team began to spill from the course. Prompt Succor showed far better than Coach Taylor deserved, with Kelly coming in sixteenth and another girl twenty-third. April finished forty-first, a personal best, and we hugged each other and squealed as only teenage girls can.

"I think this deserves pizza," said Ms. Willette. "What say we all go out?"

I turned to Mother Lily. "Can I? Please?" A flash of uncertainty crossed her face, and I realized too late that I was still grounded. "Never mind. Let's just go."

She straightened her shoulders. "No, you've earned it. Go out with your friends and have fun."

"Are you sure?"

"Yes. I'm proud of you, Jen."

I hugged her again and wished I could do more.

The sisters decided not to stay. They had funeral arrangements to make and substitute teachers to call, so they handed me off to Mr. Derwin and Ms. Willette. All of the other girls agreed to join us, except Kelly, which was fine by me since it meant Jeremy would not be tagging along. Matt wrapped his arm around my shoulders and put the roses in my hands, and I was just about to cap the best morning of my life with a long draught of his fragrant love when a voice behind me froze the blood in my veins. It only spoke a single word: the word that spelled the end of everything I had ever known.

"Nicole?"

17

My foot froze mid-step, half-way to the ground, but I forced myself to push it down. *Don't turn around. He'll go away.* Matt peered curiously around me, trying to see who had spoken.

"Hey, Nicole?" Muffled footsteps approached on the grass. He was not going to go away. *Deep breaths, Jen.* I turned around. There, just feet away, stood a boy in a McKinley High School running uniform with brown eyes and floppy blonde hair, the same boy whose hand I had shaken last night, Martin's friend.

"My name's not Nicole."

"But I met you last night. At the theater?"

I could smell his confusion mounting. Maybe I could just smile, brush his arm, and convince this boy he was mistaken. The muscles of my mouth crept upward . . .

Matt put a protective arm around my shoulders, pinning me to his side. I had never charmed anyone without touching them before, and if I tried to touch this boy, Matt, with his skin against mine, would bear the brunt of my allure. I put the smile away and shook my head. "Sorry. Must've been someone else."

Martin's friend frowned, the line between his brows deepening in disbelief.

Matt clutched me tighter. "She's not Nicole, and she was with me last night."

"Do you have a twin?"

"No."

He squinted and finally shrugged. "Sorry. That girl looked exactly like you."

"No problem." I tried to smile, but it probably came off as a grimace.

The boy walked away, and I had no choice but to let him go. The Fates had caught up to me at last.

The boy — the witness — probably did not know that Martin had never gone home, but he would find out soon enough. Then he would tell the police that the last time Martin was seen alive, he had been arm in arm with me. I had always known this would happen, but I had figured I would be impossible to track based on nothing but a description and a false name. But now he had seen me in my Prompt Succor uniform. He knew I was lying about my name. Any day now, detectives would be knocking on my door.

Damn my mother for leaving me here to do this alone.

I climbed mechanically into the Suburban and belted myself in, the buzz of panic drowning all other noise. I had to find the witness before the police could, but I did not even know his name. I thought of searching all the social networking sites. If I could find Martin, maybe the witness would be linked to his page. Or if I could get a McKinley High yearbook, I could find his name by looking up his picture. Problem was, the police might be waiting at his doorstep right now, while I was heading off to spend a pointless hour watching my friends eat pizza. The outing that had been so promising, so beautiful only moments before, now seemed like just a collection of wasted seconds in my race toward The End. Was it worth it to fake being sick so I could go straight home?

"Jen? You okay?"

"What? Oh. Yeah, fine."

"You look worried."

"I was just thinking about Mother Celeste."

Matt wrapped his arms around me. "You loved her, didn't you?"

"I don't know. I hardly knew her."

"Does that mean you couldn't love her?" The weight in his voice was unmistakable; he was not talking about Mother Celeste. I bit my lip as a sudden wash of anger cut through the buzz. Did he really have to do this *now,* while the world was crumbling down around my ears?

As I searched for a way to shut him down with a modicum of tact, a smile crept along his face, showing off his dimples like two inverted chocolate chips. His glasses glinted in the sun, the eyes behind them sparkling with a light all their own. Yes, we did have to do this now. Now was the only moment we might ever have.

I touched his face and whispered, "Thanks for coming today."

"Wouldn't have missed it for the world." Those glorious, credulous eyes saw me as I had always wanted to be seen. "You're beautiful," he whispered, and I knew he was not talking about my lustrous hair and porcelain skin.

Tears pooled in my eyes as I tried to imagine looking at myself through his, and suddenly, *she* appeared, so vibrant, so clear, that other Jennifer, the one I had spent my whole life trying to ignore – that phantom Jennifer, the ugly, awkward, flawed girl I would have been if only Helen Carshaw had chosen someone else. *That* Jennifer still had acne and mousy, lackluster hair. No man had ever been seduced by the power of her smile. *That* Jennifer's real mother had waved from the front row at her second-grade school play. *That* Jennifer had prayed, and God had not turned away. Matt could see *that* Jennifer, feel her and know her as the strength of his conviction made her almost real. If this were truly going to be our last hour together, I could not waste it worrying about some witness whose name I might never know. This moment – this precious, ridiculous droplet of time – was one not even Helen Carshaw could steal. *That* Jennifer was finally going to live.

Matt brushed away my first tear before it could fall. "Hey, it's okay. Don't cry."

I leaned across the seat and pressed my lips to his. "I love you," I whispered so his dad would not hear.

He cradled me in his arms. I could not see his tears, but I could smell them blossom with his joy. "I love you, too."

I laid my head against his chest, needing nothing more than to be with him, to hear the beating of his heart, the rise and fall of his lungs. *Please, God,* I begged, *don't let this be goodbye.*

I had forgotten how much garlic people use in pizza.

The fumes racked me with nausea, a poisonous cloud so thick I could not even smell my friends. I spent the entire lunch attempting to smile instead of gag while spewing lies about food allergies to my teammates and slurping at a glass of water. It did not help my stomach, but at least I couldn't retch with a straw in my mouth.

Fortunately, Mr. Derwin hurried us out as soon as the pizza had disappeared. There was an LSU football game scheduled to kick off in an hour, so he did not allow Matt to dally over our goodbye. I got home just as the chapel bells tolled one o'clock. The sisters were all in the kitchen eating lunch, so I waved hello and slipped off to consult my PC.

I found three Martins from McKinley High on Facebook, but two were from schools in other states. The third was from the right school, but he was not the right boy. I tried some other sites with no better luck. McKinley did not have its yearbook available online, and the only place I knew to get a hard copy was the school library, which would not be open on Saturday. I still had my lock-picking kit, but what if it had an alarm? If cloak-and-dagger operations were supposed to be a part of vampirism, they were not a part my mother had taught me.

After two fruitless hours in front of the computer, I fell back in my chair, my eyes glassy from strain, my body limp with failure. I picked up the phone and called April.

"Hello?"

"April, it's Jen."

"Hey, what's up?"

"You know anybody who goes to McKinley?"

"I don't know. Maybe. Why?"

"There's this boy I met at the movies last night. We were talking while Matt was in the bathroom. I'd really like to find him, but I don't know his name."

I could sense April's eyes narrow with cunning despite the fact that we were on the phone. "What about Matt?"

The sound of his name was a thorn in my heart, but seeing me hauled off to jail was certain to make Matt break up with me. "I don't know. I might stay with Matt, but this guy and I sort of clicked, you know? But then Matt came over and we had to shut up before we could exchange names. I just want to get a McKinley yearbook, so maybe I can find out his name and look him up."

"There's a guy who takes piano with me that goes to McKinley. I can ask him on Tuesday at my lesson."

I had no idea April played the piano. I was such a lousy friend, but I pushed that aside, knowing any chance of our continued friendship depended upon my finding the witness. "Could you call him? Tuesday's kind of a long time to wait."

"I don't have his number."

I sighed. "Okay. Thanks."

"Hey, you know who else goes to McKinley? Jeremy's sister. I bet if you called him, he could bring a yearbook to school."

I stood breathing into the phone, numb with the horror of such a thought. I had already known about Jeremy's public-school sister, a random fact buried deep in the carpet of useless information on the floor of my brain. Still, calling Jeremy

Higginbotham ranked just below ordering pizza with embalming fluid sauce on the list of things I wanted to do.

April snickered at my lack of response. "Jen, he likes you. You should talk to him."

"To ask him to bring me a picture of another boy I like?"

"Good point. You'll have to make something up."

I sighed. "Okay, thanks. And . . . don't tell anybody, okay?"

"Okay. Good luck."

I hung up and immediately re-tread my steps on the Internet, refusing to think about calling Jeremy. I told myself it would be madness, anyway. When the cops showed up, they would want to talk to my classmates. April was my friend; I could sell them the same story I had sold her, but how could I justify calling a guy I hated to ask for a McKinley yearbook? That had "guilty" painted all over it.

I wasted another hour scouring every search engine ever invented, but without a name, it was like searching for a needle in the ocean. I did find a picture of Martin – the right Martin – but it did not give his last name, and there was no link to the witness.

As the clock crept toward the dinner hour and the end of my life, I pulled out the school directory and turned to H. I spent five minutes just staring at the page, pondering what I could possibly say to convince Jackass Jeremy to do me a favor, especially such a bizarre favor, but I had no choice. This humiliation did not even compare to what I would face when the police knocked on my door.

I dialed.

"Hello?"

"Hi, Jeremy. It's Jennifer Carshaw."

Silence. I drummed my fingers on the handset. More silence.

"Are you there?"

I heard him swallow, but he spoke with his usual bravado. "To what do I owe the pleasure?"

"I need to ask you a favor."

"Really? Well, I guess you can ask."

Why did we have to do this on the phone? I could not see or smell him to gauge what he was thinking. "I need to borrow your sister's yearbook from McKinley."

"Why?"

"Never mind why. Can I borrow it?"

"What do I get in return?"

I had been afraid of this — prepared, but afraid. "I'll do your homework for a week."

"Won't work. The nuns know your handwriting."

"Well, then, you know that . . . suggestion you made a while back?"

"You mean you'll go out with me if I bring you my sister's yearbook?"

"One date. And it can't be a real date because I'm grounded."

"Right. Angie." He laughed. Stupid, musical laugh. "So, what kind of date are we talking about?"

"I'll ditch cross-country after school one day. We can do whatever you want as long as I'm back by the end of practice."

"*Whatever* I want?"

This is why I love Matt, I reminded myself as my hand trembled around the phone. "Within reason."

Silence again. Probably trying to make me sweat, and succeeding. "Do we have a deal?" I asked when I couldn't take it anymore.

"Are you done with Matt?"

I knew I had to tell him yes, say anything to make him agree. I had already given Jeremy enough ammo to ruin me with Matt, but still the memory of "I love you" bound me to the truth.

"No."

"So this is just a bribe. You haven't actually changed your mind."

"Correct."

"Let me get this straight. You're giving me half an hour of your time, during which I can attempt to steal a geek's girlfriend, in exchange for my sister's yearbook?"

"Yes."

"You are one weird girl, Jen."

"I know. So will you do it?"

"Hell, no. I told you this morning, I'm with Kelly now."

I slammed down the phone as my body temperature spiked, my lungs flooded with lead as I lusted for his blood — not to drink it but to spill it, tear his heart out, gouge his eyes . . .

On second thought, it was probably a good thing we'd had that conversation on the phone.

I indulged in a few more half-hearted fantasies of dismembering Jeremy, but reality quickly overshadowed my rage, and I fell prostrate onto the bed. I had failed. All that remained was to wait for Judgment Day to arrive. Hot tears stung my cheeks as I imagined Matt's heartache, Mother Lily's outrage, the cold, profound disappointment of Sister Diane.

I threw myself upright and pulled out the note she had left the night I ran away. I held it to my heart, clutching vainly at the words that would never again be true. *God loves you. I love you. You will never be alone.*

Alone. Forever, irrevocably, eternally alone. The fate that had awaited me since the day my mother left, when I lost the only other soulless, God-forsaken hellion in a thriving, animate world. The curtain had finally closed on my farce. My illicit hourglass had run dry. Don McLean's voice echoed through my mind, singing pointlessly, *Bye bye, Miss American Pie, this'll be the day that I die.* Even now, the Grim Reaper stood knocking at the gate, ready to harvest my happiness into the darkness of oblivion.

As if on cue, the doorbell rang.

18

I waited until Sister Diane's feet had passed my bedroom door and then opened it to listen. *Let it be Mormons,* I prayed. I always got a kick out of watching laymen attempt to evangelize nuns, and I could use some comic relief right now. Unfortunately, the voice that greeted the open door was far too rigid for the Latter Day Saints.

"Good evening, Sister. Are you the principal of Prompt Succor school?"

"No, that would be Mother Lily. She's in New Orleans right now. Is there something I can help you with?"

Mother Lily was in New Orleans? I sneaked a peak out the window. The car was still here. How did she get there?

The rigid voice jolted me out of my questions. "I just need to borrow some yearbooks from the last couple of years. Can you get that for me, Sister?"

"Of course, Officer. Come right in."

Martin had been missing less than twenty-four hours. These guys didn't waste any time.

"Can you tell me why the police need our yearbooks?" Sister Diane asked.

"A boy went missing last night. His friend thinks he was with a girl from your school, but he doesn't know her name."

"Ah. Well, please make yourself comfortable. I'll be right back."

I could not hear her retreat because my heart was pounding like a jackhammer, filling my ears and threatening to shatter my sternum. If the police wanted yearbooks, I was at least on the right track with my own investigation, but I could not flash a badge at McKinley's principal to catch up to the game. There had to be another way.

There was. The school directory lay next to my pillow, still conveniently opened to H.

Facing a squad of detectives, even a full-blown murder trial, might be less painfull than that. I swallowed hard, remembering that mine was not the only peace of mind at stake. *Do it for Matt. Do it for Sister Diane.* I took a deep breath, then used the computer to map out the address. I was out of the window and running before Sister Diane could return with the books.

Jeremy only lived six blocks away. I did not even have time to sweat before I was on the front porch. My hand had acquired a life of its own, positively refusing to knock on the door, so I finally kicked it instead.

"Germy! Get the door!" That would be his sister shouting across the house.

"It's fourth and goal!"

Oh, crap. The game was still on. LSU football was the religion of Baton Rouge, and I was about to interrupt High Mass.

I heard a mangled scream, then footsteps pounded heavily toward the door. The snarl stretched grotesquely across Jeremy's chiseled features told me the outlook for the Tigers was grim, but when his livid eyes met mine, the snarl fell slack into an open-mouthed "O."

"So, I'm not asking anymore. I'm begging. What's it gonna take?"

I counted twelve Mississippis before he managed to close his jaw; twelve eternities during which the TV announcer declared, "Final score, South Carolina 21, LSU 17," and Jeremy's scent slowly resolved from the excitement and disgust of football back into his ordinary fear.

He cleared his throat and looked back toward the TV. "Fucking Tigers."

I nodded. "You going to get it, or do I have to ransack your house?"

"What the hell, Jen? It's a stupid yearbook."

"Okay, fine. There's this guy, sometimes I see him outside my window at night. Then today he calls and starts saying all this crap . . . Look, he wears a McKinley jacket. I just want to find out his name so I can call the police."

Jeremy studied my eyes, and for the first time in our eleven-year acquaintance, he gave me an honest gaze, person-to-person, eye-to-eye. His fear waned as he beheld the desperation I did not need to fake. He almost smiled as he stepped aside and motioned for me to come in.

"Germy, who is it?"

"Salesman." He added to me, "Stacy's getting ready for a date. She'll be in the bathroom for hours. Come on." I followed him up the stairs, nearly tripping on the odor of something that reminded me of friendship. "Did you see the game?"

"No."

"Damn offensive line is made of Swiss cheese."

No point telling him I had no idea what an offensive line was. He would just use it for ammunition later.

He turned right at the top of the stairs. "Should be in here."

Stacy's teal-and-purple comforter, the myriad of framed photos of happy young girls, the poster of an actor endowed with heart-throb status for playing a teenage vampire, seemed almost like they were trying too hard to be normal. I lingered in the doorway, staring at the vampire actor and wondering how he could close his mouth with such protuberant fangs while Jeremy rifled through the desk. "I don't know where she keeps it," he explained as he came away from the last drawer empty-handed. He went to the bookshelf and pushed aside a bunch of pictures that blocked the actual books. On the third shelf, he finally tugged out a thin blue volume and flashed the Hollywood smile. "Woila." He mispronounced the word like the illiterate moron he was, but I decided to let it slide.

"Thank you."

"So, when are we going out?"

"I thought you were with Kelly."

"You're with Matt. If it's just one date, who cares?"

"Are you seriously going to use this guy who's stalking me to coerce me into a date?"

"'Coerce?' Jesus, Jen, who talks like that?" He grinned and held out the book. "Here, but it's your loss."

I took it before he could change his mind, but I did not open it. I just stared at him, trying to work up the courage to ask, "Do you really like me, or is this just another one of your jokes?"

"Guess you'll never find out, will you?"

I shook my head. What else had I expected?

He walked me back downstairs. "I'll bring it back to you at school," I said.

"Whatever."

"Hey, don't tell your sister, okay? It's just, she might know the guy."

"Don't worry about it."

"Okay. Thanks again." I opened the door.

"Hey, Jen?"

"Yeah?"

"If the cops don't catch him, let me know. I'll kick his ass."

I actually smiled. Something *Jeremy Higginbotham* said made me smile.

Maybe I should start paying attention in "therapy." I was clearly losing my mind.

He closed the door behind me and I ran home at top speed, then climbed back through my window and tore open the book. Before I could even begin to look, Sister Diane opened the door and announced, "Dinner's ready."

Thoughts of the patrolman speeding toward the witness with my photo in hand burned like acid through my gut, but I put the yearbook on my desk and followed her to the kitchen. Painful as it was to set my quest aside, the point of all this chaos was to preserve my charade. That meant I had to eat dinner as if nothing were wrong. Sister Joan had over-seared my beef to almost medium-rare, but still I swallowed every bite.

"I see your appetite's back," said Sister Diane.

"Running makes me hungry." I chugged a glass of water, then darted off and locked myself in my room.

The thin blue volume smelled of dust and stale perfume. I wanted to dive in, flip the pages so fast they would tear from their seams, but I stopped myself. *Be logical, Jen. You know where to start.* I found it on page fifty-six: a group photo of the boys' cross-country team.

Martin's face erupted from the page, the smile that had tasted of such heavenly desire circled boldly in blue marker. Scrawled beneath the picture in identical ink were eleven words I would never forget as long as I lived.

Stacy —

Have a great summer. See you next year.

Martin Reed

Martin's handwriting. His very own illegible "s," his dot over the "i" that looked like a slash, and his name. Martin Reed. Not Martin the Student or Martin the One Who Taught Me How to Seduce. Not an alias, like Benji Gardener or Violet Barista. Not Martin whose identity belonged to the moment that had given me new life. Martin Reed had lived and laughed and run and held this very book in his hands, just like me.

He smiled at me, this creature whose life I had taken for my own, so guileless and carefree. He had draped his arms around his teammates, all of them grinning and dripping with sweat, so hot and friendly and tired. And alive. How could it be that this was the only way for me to live, by turning photos of happy memories into reminiscences of ghosts?

Stop it, Jen. You can't change the past.

Still my eyes remained riveted, my heart thumping cruelly as it fought to return to the ignorant bliss those inane blue words had forever stripped away. Would the boys in this photograph grieve for him, hold prayer vigils for his return? Would they wrap their arms around his mother and wish they could replace her vanished son? I wanted to reach out to them, to lay my hands against theirs and let them see the meaning of the life he had given. I wanted to erase my fatal forgery of love and let him rise to grace another yearbook with his smile. Yet even in my dream, Martin Reed had not come back. Martin Reed was gone.

Get on with it, Jen. Getting caught won't help him now.

What was I going to do, just have my moment of remorse, then go out and kill again? No. Dammit, *no.* I could not stave off the next murder forever, but it would not be tonight. I had weapons in my arsenal other than my teeth.

I was hyperventilating as I finally forced myself to turn the page. I stared at the Spanish club for a full five minutes — the banal grins of strangers — while I caught my breath. I had to keep searching. I had to survive.

I skipped the seniors. They had all graduated last year, and I knew my witness was still in school. I scanned the pages of the junior class, miniature faces crammed together like sardines in sterile shades of gray. I recognized a few: Stacy Higginbotham, a girl I had beaten in a speech contest two years ago, a boy who had transferred out of Prompt Succor in sixth grade. Martin again.

I swallowed my tears and moved on.

I found the witness on the last page of sophomores. That made him a junior now, like me. I almost did not recognize him. His acne had cleared up since last year, and the harsh lights of the camera had faded his golden hair to a colorless drab. I thought of my own transformation, last year's picture of the quintessential nerd who bore only superficial resemblance to the goddess I had become. Was it enough of a disguise? Could I trust him not to recognize me?

No. His own photograph proved that appearances might change, but the indefinable something that marks an individual never does. He would find me unless I found him first. I matched his photo to his name, Trey W. Varnado, then I opened the Baton Rouge white pages online and typed in his last name.

Eighty-eight entries found. Well, at least he wasn't called Smith.

I scrolled through, looking for kids. A few entries listed minors, and, for the first time in my entire life, luck was on my side. I found an entry for Varnado, Lyle C. and Deborah, Trey and Kate. The address was on the other side of town, near the Amite River, miles from McKinley High. It might be wrong, but it was the only chance I had.

I hid the yearbook and left a note: *I'm sorry. I will come home.* Then I climbed out the window and ran full-throttle toward the home of Varnado, Lyle C.

The pavement pulverized my heels, Reeboks disintegrating underfoot as friction became fire. Solid air cracked before my onslaught as I sawed through fiberglass smog. *I'm going to crash and kill myself,* I thought as I raced through the world at a speed my optic nerves could not comprehend. Even blind my feet flew on, aided by a perception I could not name or understand. Every car, every curve, every pothole yawning with destruction, I evaded them all. *How?* I wondered, as I dodged left, then felt the whoosh of air as a reckless driver just missed me on the right. I had no answer. I only knew that I could.

Before I had even gotten used to the sensation of sightless navigation, I arrived. I pulled up panting on the lawn of a run-down 1970's ranch-style suburban home and collapsed to the grass, tugging off the smoldering remnants of my shoes. My scorched socks fell away like brittle straw, but my feet were miraculously perfect. My mind flashed back to the day I knocked a bookshelf on top of Mrs. Jones. My head wound had healed before I even got out the door. I had never stopped, then, to appreciate the wonders of immortality.

You can marvel at how cool you are later, Jen. Get up and find the witness.

I raised my head to survey the scene, and my pounding heart stood still. The carport stood vacant, the lights dark, the curtains drawn. Nobody was home.

My breathing accelerated as I edged toward the windows, hoping to catch a peek inside. I tried the front door – locked – so I scaled the fence and quelled the barking German shepherd with a smile. He nuzzled my ankles as I crept along, and finally I found a window where someone had left open the Venetian blinds.

A bedroom stared back at me, rife with mounds of unwashed clothes beneath which protruded an electric guitar and its amp, a laptop, a backpack in desperate need of washing. Posters of rock bands adorned the walls, accented by a colorful picture of a nebula shot from space. A lamp shaped like an LSU Tiger sported a pair of real sunglasses while a model airplane, red paint faded to a dingy not-quite pink, hung forgotten from the air conditioning vent. *A Tale of Two Cities* lay abandoned on the desk, a ragged yellow post-it note marking the reader's place – and a McKinley High School Letterman's jacket lay draped across the foot of the bed.

I groaned and sank to the ground, my back pressed against the brick while the German shepherd licked my hands. I was too late. The police might already know my name. They might even bring Trey Varnado home, and if they found me here, that would be the end.

I got to my feet, scratched the German shepherd one last time behind the ears, gathered up the melted remnants of my shoes, and returned to the convent at a speed my tear-stained eyes could bear.

19

I tossed my shoes into the neighbor's garbage bin, then crawled along the side of the house below the windows to be sure the nuns would not see me. I peeked into my bedroom for signs of trouble before I climbed up, but no one should have noticed my absence. I had only been gone thirteen minutes. Sure enough, I found my room exactly the way I had left it. Just to be sure, I poked my head tentatively into the hall. No sounds of frantic searching, no voices on the phone, no worried musings or fervent prayers. In fact, the only sound was the television. Sister Joan was watching a cooking show on PBS.

Phew.

I picked up my farewell note to destroy the last damning evidence of my illicit foray, and tremors of terror rocked my hand. I blinked, then again, trying to convince myself it was an illusion that made my heart stand still, but, like everything else in my nightmarish life, the tidy slanted handwriting was real. Beneath my promise to return perched three new words I had not penned:

I can't wait.

The unmistakable scrawl, the unmistakable sarcasm, of the one and only Sister Diane.

❖

"Come in," she called to my tremulous knock, so calm, so eternally unperturbed. I entered her room to find her on her knees, rosary in hand, eyes fixed on the ceiling. She did not disturb her prayers, leaving me to wait in unholy silence while her fingers moved deftly over the beads. She did it on purpose, I knew, to put me in my place and make me sweat about what was to come. It worked.

She kissed the tiny crucifix at the end of the chain and finally turned to face me. "Well?"

I opened my mouth to speak, to lie, but nothing would come out.

She realized she had better prompt me or else we would be gawking at each other all night. "It wasn't Matt because he called while you were out. So where then?"

"I . . ."

"Spit it out, Jen. You're not leaving this room until you do."

"I was at Jeremy's." I realized the mistake the moment the words left my mouth. I said it because I could prove it, but using Jeremy as my alibi was probably more idiotic than telling the truth.

"Jeremy Higginbotham?"

"Yes."

"The one you so lovingly refer to as 'Jackass Jeremy'?"

"How'd you know . . . ?"

"I'm a teacher, Jen, I hear things." She folded her hands in her lap. "All right, I'm intrigued. What were you doing with Jeremy?"

Words tumbled forth without stopping to be processed by my brain. "He, uh, he's been hounding me to go out with him. I keep telling him no, but he won't go away. At cross-country this morning, it was really bad. He kept saying all this stuff . . . it was disgusting. I wanted to tell his mom, but when I called, Jeremy answered the phone. So I went over there, but she wasn't home."

Sister Diane stared at me, reeking of suspicion, then retrieved her school directory and dialed the phone. My knees knocked so loudly, I was surprised she could hear the person on the other end.

"Hello, Dr. Higginbotham? This is Sister Diane from the school. Is Jeremy in, please? I don't know if he's in trouble yet. I just need to ask him a few questions, if you don't mind. Yes, thank you." She held the line, her gaze never wavering from mine. "Yes, Jeremy, hello. This is Sister Diane. I'm calling because Jennifer claims she was at your house this evening while she was supposed to be here, in her room. Is that true? I see. If you don't mind my asking, precisely why did Jennifer pay you this little visit?"

Oh, crap. Why had I pinned my hopes on a jackass?

"Really? And what did you say? Okay, then. Thank you. Yes, that will be all for now. Good night." She hung up, her eyes attempting to eat me alive. "Jennifer?"

"Yes, ma'am?"

"Jeremy confirms you were there, but he has a rather different interpretation of what happened."

"What did he say?" How could I possibly explain the yearbook?

"According to Jeremy, you went to his house to beg him to go out with you. He says, quote, 'I felt so sorry for her, I finally said yes.'"

I stared, blinked, and tried to find something coherent to say, but it was a lost cause. Jeremy had lied for me without my even asking him to. He had done exactly what I hoped he would do, and I couldn't even use it. If I let Sister Diane believe Jeremy's version of the events, that would be the end of me and Matt.

Which was probably why he had said it. Jackass.

"Last chance, Jen. What really happened?"

"I told you what really happened. You can't believe I'd want Jeremy when I've got Matt?"

She studied me intently, noting the sweat on my brow, torn between the voice that told her I was lying and the one that knew Jeremy was one hundred percent capable of everything I had just described. "You're both lying. I don't know why, but I will find out."

God, this woman was good. Still, it was my job to protest. "I didn't . . ."

She held up her hand. "It's your turn to listen now. You're still coming to the funeral. The sisters deserve your condolences, and you're going to pay them. But when we get back, you will not leave this house again except for school. No more dates, no more cross-country, you won't even come along to the grocery store. You will not close the door to your room for any reason whatsoever. There's not going to be any more sneaking out through windows. You're going to be in plain sight, under our thumb, even when you're asleep. And you're going to start acting like you live in a convent: daily Mass, morning prayer, vespers, and I'll get Mrs. Hargrove to lead you in noon prayer."

"But . . ."

"No buts, Jen. Until you start telling the truth and obeying the rules, that's the way it's going to be."

"Mother Lily might not agree to this," I muttered feebly.

"Maybe it hasn't penetrated your little self-centered world, but the head of our Order just died. Mother Lily is down in New Orleans trying to figure out what will happen to the Sisters of Prompt Succor, and she may not be back full-time for several weeks. It's just you and me now."

I nodded, letting that soak in. "How long am I grounded?"

"Until you tell me the truth. About tonight, about the last time you ran away, about everything."

I bit my bottom lip, working through this newest dilemma, but there was no way out. I had nothing to barter with, and Sister Diane would only scoff if I begged. Nor did there appear to be any loopholes in her scheme. I doubted the nuns would actually post a guard over me while I slept, but I would not put it past them to install an alarm. I could never hunt under these rules unless I used force to escape, but I did not think I could bring myself to actually harm the sisters.

"If you're looking for a way out, there's only one," she said. "It runs through me."

The tragedy of it was, she was doing everything right, everything a rebellious teenager needed her parent to do. If I had been sneaking out to take drugs or have sex or do anything but commit murders I was biologically programmed to commit, I had no doubt her efforts would have reformed me in the end. What a shame to waste this good woman on such a daughter as me.

I squeezed her hand. "You're the best mother any girl could ever have."

"Flattery won't get you anywhere. Now go get ready for bed."

"I mean it. You're everything my mother could never be."

Her eyebrows drew together. I almost never spoke about my mother, and the fact that I mentioned her now seemed to trigger warning bells in Sister Diane's mind. "Jen, whatever this is, we can face it. Just tell me."

I kissed her cheek. "I would, if it could change anything."

She pushed me away so she could glare more effectively. "Jennifer Carshaw, you can tell me what's going on, and we can change things. The only thing stopping us is that you're a coward."

That hit me square between the eyes because it was true.

She rolled her eyes. "Go call Matt. And if I hear one word about you dating Jeremy behind his back, you're going to find out what punishment really means."

"I'll never hurt Matt. I promise."

"Really? Make sure you tell him all future dates are canceled, and that it's entirely your fault." She turned her back and picked up her Bible, signaling that my freedom had ended.

20

The nice thing about talking to Matt, apart from the fact that his smooth voice dripped with the healing balm of love, was that the police could not call with the phone line tied up. If they wanted me, they would have to knock on the door and look me in the eye. I would at least have the chance to smile and pray they could be seduced. But finally, Sister Diane ordered, "Hang up and go to bed," and I had enough sense to not be told twice. Then the waiting really began.

It was not quite the longest night of my life. That had been the night after my mother went away, when I lay terrified and alone, with no indication of how long she would be gone or what would happen next. That night had not really ended for three entire weeks, until I finally ran out of frozen steak and decided to risk calling the school. This night, at least, had a time limit. We would leave for New Orleans at 8 a.m. I only had nine hours to lie in a sleepless dread, waiting for the knock on the door. It felt like nine years.

What was taking them so long? Surely the police had not given up and gone home for the night. Was it possible Trey Varnado had not been able to identify me? Or was there a more sinister reason for the delay? Were they tracking down my past, digging up the cold case file of my mother's disappearance, or waking up Matt and April to ask about my recent behavior? Were they getting their ducks in a row so they could come at me with a warrant rather than just questions?

Paranoia has a way of seeming logical in the cold gray light of a restless dawn.

Somehow morning arrived, sunny and law enforcement free. Father Henry said a quick Mass for the four of us, and at eight o'clock sharp we piled into the Volvo and hit the road. Who would have guessed that driving to Mother Celeste's funeral could make me so ecstatically happy?

The atmosphere in the Volvo did nothing to echo my glee. Sisters Theresa and Joan took it as a personal affront that they had put their grief on hold to support me in cross-country, and this was how I repaid them. They spoke to me as little as being stuck in the same car would allow. Sister Diane spoke plenty, but only to reiterate the terms of my punishment, and I knew Mother Lily's tirade awaited me at journey's end.

We stopped for gas at a truck stop in LaPlace, just before I-10 dove out over Lake Ponchartrain. I asked, "Am I allowed to go inside?" Sister Diane gave the briefest of nods. I used the restroom and then purchased the only item that meant anything right now, ten dollars' worth of minutes for my phone. My cell phone was the no-contract, re-loadable kind, so I could use it whenever I wanted as long as I had cash to spend. My stash had never been replenished since I ran away, so I was still the proud owner of eleven dollars and sixty-six cents. I squandered it shamelessly now.

The police were going to call; it was only a matter of time. Fortunately, the nuns were not home. I would check the convent answering machine every hour and hopefully intercept any messages that spelled my doom. I typed the calling-card code into my phone and then tucked it into my pocket, praying that this paltry defense would be enough.

We arrived at the New Orleans home of the Sisters of Prompt Succor a little after ten a.m. Mother Celeste's casket, a plain box of varnished wood, lay almost hidden at the far end of the rotunda, the stained-glass hall overflowing with several florists' entire inventories of wreaths and bouquets. Yet the plain wood box cast a shadow over all that color, as macabre and yet as splendid as the crucifix that stood on its closed lid.

Mother Lily and the eight New Orleans sisters were kneeling in a circle by the coffin with Sister Louisa's clear soprano leading them through a sung Divine Mercy Chaplet. Sister Diane nudged me to follow as she, Sister Theresa, and Sister Joan fell to their knees and added their voices to the prayer. Sister Louisa intoned, "For the sake of His sorrowful passion," and the rest of us replied, "Have mercy on us and on the whole world." The prayer repeated these same words over and over, and after the first six or eight responses, I was shocked to find myself really praying. "Have mercy on us" – on *me,* I wanted to cry – "and on the whole world" – all the nameless victims I would send to an early grave over the course of my immortal existence. "Have mercy on us" – these poor, good women deceived into harboring a monster – "and on the whole world" – Martin Reed, Violet Barista, Benji Gardener, and Mother Celeste.

The Chaplet ended, but the response still rang unceasingly in my ears. The tune haunted me as I repeated in endless, useless silence to a God who refused to hear, *Have mercy on us and on the whole world.*

The New Orleans sisters bid us welcome with hugs and repressed tears, then showed us to the rooms they had prepared. I leaned to stash my suitcase under the cot in the room Mother Lily and I would share, and the door closed behind me with a thud. I looked up into Mother Lily's brimstone glare and tried to steel myself for the barrage.

"Jennifer, let me begin by saying that if you hoped I would soften Sister Diane's punishments, you were wrong."

I sat down. "I hadn't bothered to hope."

"Would you like to tell me what's going on?"

"I would, but I can't."

"Did I do something to make you believe you can't trust me?" She said it sternly, rhetorically, but I could smell her very genuine pain. I took her hand.

"No. I know I'm being impossible, and if I were in your shoes, I'd probably come up with a punishment twice as harsh. But I need you to believe that if you were in my shoes, you'd do exactly what I'm doing, too."

She tore her hand out of mine. "You're not getting any sympathy from me, Jennifer. The time for that is past." She turned so I would not see her wipe her eyes on her sleeve. "I'm going down to the sisters. You're going to stay here, in this room, until I call you for lunch. You'll come to the wake tomorrow and the Mass on Tuesday, but otherwise, you're going to stay in this room until we go home."

She left, and I heard the lock click after she closed the door, but I did not care. I had just realized that none of the sisters' punishments mattered at all. The dreaded four-letter word had reared its ugly head once again.

Mass.

The funeral was coming on Tuesday, and I was going to die.

❖

In all the confusion of the last thirty-six hours, it had not occurred to me that Mother Celeste's funeral would be a Mass. I had never actually been to a funeral before (my mother was only "presumed" dead), so I had imagined a Hollywood graveside scene with a priest droning the twenty-third psalm while actors in heavy black overcoats stood in the rain, shedding fake tears. I should have known better. Catholics rarely do anything without celebrating Mass. You *can* be baptized or get married without it, but that's not the norm. Catholics are trained to include Holy Communion in their lives at every possible opportunity — apparently, even after they have died.

This was not going to be some humdrum Mass where I could hold my breath ten seconds longer than usual and come out okay. This was a funeral for a Mother Superior to be held in historic St. Louis Cathedral. At lunch, I asked how many people were planning to attend, and the answer made me want to wet my pants. "As many as they'll let in," Sister Constance said, "but there will probably be a line around the block of the ones who can't fit." She went on to say that the archbishop would preside, and nearly every priest in New Orleans would be there. The governor, a congressman, four state legislators, and the mayor had all promised to come. The Catholic TV channel would carry the whole thing on tape-delay, and the police and the fire marshal would be on hand to control the crowds. I was supposed to sit there, right at the front, and watch patiently while everyone in that enormous New Orleans gumbo drank the Blood of Christ. Everyone but me.

Yeah, right.

As if doomsday's noose were not tightening quite fast enough around my neck, at four o'clock I called home and heard on the machine, "This is Detective Luis Noriega, Baton Rouge City Police. I need to get an address for one of your students, a Jennifer Carshaw. Please call me back as soon as possible." I copied down the number just in case and promptly hit delete.

The wake on Monday began at noon and did not end until the last mourner left, sometime after nine o'clock. Mother Celeste had touched a lot of lives. Any number of her former students came to pay respect, plus teachers who had served under her administration , and herds of clergy, including Protestants, Muslims, and Jews. Doctors and attorneys mingled with housewives and longshoremen, shopkeepers and janitors, blacks, whites, Hispanics, Asians, and everything in between. Moved as I was, contemplating the depth of the impact one small woman could have upon the world, I still felt like I was staring at a world-class buffet I must not dare to touch.

I lurked on the edges of the crowd, shaking hands whenever someone wondered who I was, trading condolences with anyone who came my way. Through it all, I knew I ought to leave. I had to run away, and this time I could not come back. I had reached the end of the nuns' forgiveness already, and this newest betrayal would crush them. If I never returned, they would come to understand what Sister Diane had known on that very first night: *If you're taking this drastic step, it is because there is truly nothing we can offer.* They would accept in time that cataclysm had come and left them forever changed, but that life does go on.

I imagined what life would be like, out there on my own. I would hide in the slums until I found some way to contact the world's omnipresent network of criminals. Any "dangers" I might encounter did not matter. Gang-bangers and rapists could not hurt me. I just had to stay hidden until I could find someone to forge my new identity. I would get a new birth certificate, social security card, driver's license, and whatever else I needed to prove I was really Some New Girl, age eighteen. Then I could disappear. I could get a job, rent an apartment, maybe even get a degree. I would live as my mother had taught me to live, hunting by night and moving to a new place before anyone could get too close. The time had come. All I had to do was walk out the door.

Still I stood, my feet rooted to the floor, watching as the sisters hugged necks and shook hands. I would never leave, not until the sisters kicked me out or else carried me to my grave. Sister Diane had hit the nail on the head. I was a coward, and eternal loneliness terrified me more than the police or funeral Masses. I chewed my lip and racked my brains, determined to be Jennifer Carshaw for just one more stolen, empyrean day.

❖

I had not thought to pack my lock-picking kit, which had lain unused under my bed since my return from the mausoleum. When I sneaked down to the chapel sacristy at midnight, I brought a hairpin and my library card and set to work.

My musings had yielded nothing, no way to get out of the funeral, no way to be present and survive. But a plan had slowly emerged, like a paper drawn from a file labeled "Inevitable," as if I had always known it would come to this. My stomach felt like an eager Boy Scout had used it to win his knotsmanship badge, but I pressed on.

The sacristy of any church is a holding place of sacred things: dishes from which Communion is served, clerical vestments, bread and wine that have not yet become Body and Blood. Consecrated bread does not return to the sacristy. It is kept in the tabernacle, there to be adored, or taken out and distributed among the faithful. However, consecrated wine is not kept at all. At each Mass, the ministers pour only enough to serve the congregation, and if there is any left over, the ministers drink it, and the cups are then washed clean. I was not here to find the Blood; I wanted the smell, the residue of the Presence that I was sure no soap could ever wash away. I would face the greatest temptation, learn the truth about that half-forgotten echo with all its possible meanings, and I would live to tell the tale.

But first I had to get inside, which did not look promising as the hairpin snapped off in the lock. I tried to jimmy it out with the remaining piece, but the broken part was in too far. The library card was no good, especially with a broken hairpin jamming the door. In the end, I either had to break down the door or give up.

I sat down and tried to catch my breath. I could go back to bed, and tomorrow someone would discover the jammed lock. The sisters would call a locksmith, and the locksmith would find the hairpin. I would not be any closer to living through the funeral, and Sister Diane might be sharp enough to suspect me of the vandalism. If I broke down the door, I would find out everything I longed to know, but the noise would bring the nuns, and I would be caught for sure.

Run away, Jen. Just get up, walk out, and vanish. Any kind of life is preferable to death. Plus, it's New Orleans. Who knows? There might be other vampires here.

The voice of reason was alive and well, yet ineffectual, as always. As I felt the hard press of the stalwart wood against my back, I knew I was not looking for a way to survive the funeral. If I walked through those cathedral doors tomorrow, I might as well bring a stake and mallet, too. I had come here because I needed to know.

This battle, this longing, cut to the heart of the question I had never dared to ask because the answer — the fact that there might *be* an answer — drove me toward the brittle, ancient apathy, the darkness I had always known but yet denied. It was the answer that gave birth to amorality so vile, it could rip an infant from her mother's womb and with the same breath drink her soul. It was the wisdom my mother had sought to teach above all else, the one part of her lessons I had refused to comprehend. I had convinced myself it did not matter because I, the lowly creature, did not deserve to understand the ways of the Creator. But His ways, His answer, lay behind this very door.

With one fluid motion, I sprang to my feet and ripped from its hinges the last barrier between the girl I had always wanted to be and the monster Helen Carshaw had ordained. The question burst from my lips, the sum of all the anguish the world had ever known.

"Why don't You love me, too?"

On the wall of the sacristy hung a mirror. I had barely glimpsed my wild, tear-stained face before one whiff of the mere remnant of the Presence filled me with its power, and through the looking-glass I fell.

21

I see a shepherd bathed in sunlight with his rod and staff upraised. Across a pasture green as envy roam His lambs toward deep blue springs. I watch them drink. My parched throat gasps to join them.

A drop of oil rains upon my brow, igniting in the Light. I swat it with my hands as I wipe away my tears. *Why,* I yearn to cry, but my empty words fall mute while the shepherd smiles. He strikes his staff against the ground, and from it rolls a path. Right at my feet, it stops, and there a banquet spreads – first a table, then a cup; in it, one red drop – one drop that overflows to spill the glory of the dawn. I know that I must drink to set my feet upon the path. I know that one drop must pass my lips, and I will drown into all time.

But behind me, a chasm yawns, lined with shards of mirrored glass. In broken panes I see myself flushed with violet pride. The shepherd moves his hand – to beckon or to cast me out, but which, I cannot tell. My tears fall; they touch the chasm, and the darkness grows. With every drop of me, the valley crumbles into dust. The cup pours forth its wine; though I'm parched, I shield my tongue. My swollen eyes I close. I leap into the chasm, desperate now to get away, for in that valley, I am shadow. In that valley, I am Death.

I never realized I had blacked out. It seemed I was conscious all the while, conscious beyond all ordinary definition of the word, witnessing what lay behind the earthly veil. But when I opened my eyes, pieces of the shattered mirror lay around me on the floor, and Sister Constance was standing over me with a kitchen knife. "Jennifer?" she squeaked. "I heard a noise."

Sensation flooded back, a torrent of horror poured into the cast of flesh and bone. My tongue cleaved to my palate; my throat felt packed with sand. My eyes blinked with agony, lids of steel wool tearing across parched scleras. My limbs lay palsied near to atrophy, torture even to move.

Sister Constance put down the knife and leaned her face close to mine. "Jennifer? Are you okay?"

With my only instinct, my only strength, I lunged and sank my teeth into the flesh that divided me from life. My body healed with every swallow, the wine of my Sister calling me back into the night. I could not stop any more than I could fly, yet with every mouthful, I cried. I knew who this was, what she meant. And I knew now the celestial heights to which her blood could never help me soar. I had glimpsed the true paradise I could never call home, and its echo gave lie to this earthly ecstasy. This was everything, this physical sensation for which rapture seemed too pale a word. Yet this was nothing, a glass of muddy water, sumptuous no more.

Filled, I gazed into her vacant eyes and wept. I did not care when footsteps filled the air, when sobs poured forth beyond my own and aged throats gasped to scream. I did not care when frantic cries demanded explanation only to be silenced by more resolute calm. I wept for life, for death, for pain. I wept because I would go on, forever wallowing in my own ignominy, but the woman who gave me reprieve from heaven's sorrow would never breathe again.

Soft hands finally pried me from my prey, soft steps steered me to my room. Soft arms held me close until the tears at last ran dry. A voice, monotonous even in the face of death, whispered, "It's okay. Whoever did this, he's gone."

Sister Diane's words bled through the fog of my despair. I had been caught red-handed with a body in my arms, and still she could not equate murder with her darling little girl.

I could stay.

The door opened, and the moment Mother Lily's scent touched my nostrils, I knew why this woman tempted me beyond all others. She smelled of Him, a love so pure that to taste it might almost lead me back to that green valley.

Mother Lily touched my shoulder. "The police are here. They need to talk to you, but it's okay. We'll be with you."

I dug my fingers into Sister Diane's back. I wanted to yell for Mother Lily to run, to save herself, but still the monstrous question gnawed, the presumptuous need for *why*. I knew the answers were not pulsing there, inside my guardian's veins, yet her scent so near perfection taunted me, promising a glimpse of the divine that it could never really give.

I let go of Sister Diane and stood. Mother Lily's tear-streaked eyes met mine. "I love you, Jen."

"I killed them," I heard myself say. "Sister Constance, Martin Reed, a barista with purple hair, and a gardener named Benji. That's the secret." I looked back at Sister Diane. "That's the truth."

Two hellish shadows passed across those two hallowed faces, and whatever still remained of my heart dissolved. "I love you. I swear." Before either of them could find the strength to move, I broke the lock on the window and vanished into the rising dawn.

Wind lashed the tears from my face faster than I could cry while rays of early morning light bored like needles through my skin. I wished I had put on sunblock before I confessed, yet the poetry of the moment was not lost to my pain. The blistering sun cried with the voice of Light, driving me back to the darkness. *Too late,* I wanted to scream. *Too late. I will never know light again.*

The sun had devoured the horizon by the time I arrived back in Baton Rouge. I fished the spare key to the convent from a flowerpot and flung myself into the cloister, the welcome shade of home, but the chill of exile seeped in with the morning breeze. Home was just a phantom now, a dream that had died with the dawn. A dream that had never been possible for Jennifer the Damned.

Flakes of blackened, brittle flesh clung to my legs and face and arms, the air pervaded by a sulfurous stink of doom. I lay down on the couch and watched as the pink glow of life knit the embers of my dying body into tissue, freckles, and hair. There, on a bed of faded green upholstery, eternal youth asserted its dominion while the weight of endless ages hung around me like a shroud. Regret washed over me in waves, but regret for what I could not say.

That I had killed a Sister? That I had dared to look upon the face of God? That I had forever abandoned the life I loved? Or was it only that I had not drunk Mother Lily's fragrant blood while I still had the chance?

I stared up at the crucifix, the single death that had healed the wounds of all mankind. I had seen the true victory that awaited those who passed beyond the grave, but the grave was a portal through which I could never pass. Perhaps my charred skin turned so quickly back to white because I was not worthy to move beyond this broken realm. I had glimpsed true immortality, that verdant realm where souls could rest refreshed. But without a soul, my immortality was lost. I was condemned to dwell forever in this shadowed pretense of a life.

"Take it," I whispered to the cross, suffocated by the knowledge that I would always continue to breathe. "Just take it. It doesn't mean anything now." As usual, He did not oblige.

Maybe I would do it myself. I could run until I reached the ocean, dive in and swim until I blacked out. I could not drown, but maybe I could starve to death before consciousness returned. Just sink into the blue beyond and end, never to know the pain of loneliness again. But dreams of death could not make me die, as my body proved with every square inch of restored skin. Within minutes I was healed, whole, perfect once again. Even suicide had no meaning in my world of eternal sin.

I got up and went to my room. I spritzed on a hefty coat of sunscreen, then found an old duffel bag and tossed in the can. I added clothes and toiletries, my lock-picking kit, flashlight, and batteries. I put on my school uniform and packed the McKinley yearbook, then opened my desk and tucked Sister Diane's note into my bra, to carry it next to my heart. *I love you,* it said. *God loves you. You will never be alone.* Lies, all lies, but I would hold them dear, to remind me never to step into that trap, to remind me never to love again.

I could not help but curl up on my own bed just one last time. My ancient quilt caressed me, whispering dead dreams. I dropped a few last salty stains onto its careworn threads. *Drink deep, old quilt,* I thought. *They're the last tears I ever plan to shed.* Then I hefted my bag to my shoulder and went into Mother Lily's room.

I stood in front of the safe for minutes on end, working up the courage to steal. There was not much inside, just a few hundred dollars for emergencies, but I needed it more than the nuns. I was literally penniless, my very last dollar left behind in New Orleans. Still, a voice whispered, *Jen, you're not a thief. You kill because you have to, but now you have a choice.*

I made my choice. I ripped the door from its hinges and stuffed the wad of cash into my bag. The paper sent spikes of reproach through my hand as it clawed to return home. *Home,* the walls still seemed to scream. *Home,* said the bolt as I slid it into place, locking myself out forevermore. I stood on the step, watching for the police, wondering what I would do if they came, but I could not leave without one last goodbye.

I waited for him outside homeroom. My classmates ignored me as they filtered in – I belonged here, in their eyes – but Jeremy stopped with surprise.

"Carshaw? What are you doing here?"

"It's my class, too, you know."

"I thought the funeral was today."

"It was yesterday. I'm back." I thrust the yearbook into his hands. "Here. Thanks."

He studied me, sensing the blackness of my mood. "Why were you in trouble for coming over? Seems like Sister Diane would want you to catch your stalker."

"It's complicated."

"Yeah, I bet." He gave me one last searching look, but finally went inside.

The object of my vigil arrived with less than a minute before the bell. Matt stopped in his tracks when he saw me there. "Jen?"

"Come with me. Please."

"Where?"

"Anywhere."

"Okay." He took my hand. Goodbye was all I had come for, but with his skin against mine, I knew goodbye would never be enough.

We did not go far, just crawled beneath the bleachers, where countless star-struck couples had gone before. We sat down, and he pulled me close. "What happened? Why are you back?"

"It's over."

"The funeral?"

"No. Everything."

He pulled away to look me in the eye. "Jen, what's going on?"

As I gazed into those goofy eyes, now grave, I saw the truth, the promises that lied. He would learn what I had done, and the love so brilliant, so cherished, would bleed. He would hate. He would mourn and grieve, but in the end, love would heal and flourish and grow. Someone else – someone *human* – would claim his precious heart for her own. Someone else would live the future that should have been mine.

"Do you love me?" I gasped, just to hear him say those words.

"Of course. I love you. Whatever it is, I'm here."

He let me take him in my arms. He let me press my lips against the soft flesh of his neck. He did not even seem to feel the first small scratch, the first trickle that spilled across my greedy tongue. Agonizing beauty burned my throat, succulent and dry. No fog appeared to drive me; no cement weighted my lungs; no atrophied limbs cried out to be restored. No desire but my own propelled my teeth, no justification but greed.

He gasped at last. "Jen, watch out, you bit me."

"I know." I pictured him wrapped in another girl's arms and drove my teeth further in. Fists pounded against my back as I drank and wished to die.

"Let go of me, you crazy bitch." The air rent with fury where kindness had been. He scratched and yelled and fought and bit until my blood flowed out with his. I soaked up the blows, the price of my crime, wishing they could kill me, too. We could go down together, united by blood.

The blows grew lighter, his protests more faint, his eyes waxing tired and confused. I remembered the words I had spoken just three days before. *I'll never hurt Matt. I promise.*

I pulled away, a dry sob breaking in my throat. He was still alive when I set him gently on the ground. "I'm sorry. I'm sorry. I'm sorry. Oh, God."

He looked into my eyes, white lips struggling for words . . .

"Jesus Christ, Jen, what did you do?"

I whipped around. Jeremy Higginbotham stood gaping at me with liquid eyes.

Rage bubbled in my throat, bitter as regurgitated blood, but I was too stunned to spring. Jeremy stepped forward, riveted by the sight of Matt's feebly struggling limbs. "Fuuuuck," he whispered as Matt gave one last shudder and fell still. Something drifted through the air, something decadent that called to me, crying for me to let go. With a jolt, I realized that I did not want to die.

Jeremy held my gaze without the slightest scent of fear. "You're a vampire."

"Yes." I ground my toe into the dirt. "I guess I'll have to kill you now."

"Jen, are you really that blind?"

I muttered, "Just go away."

"Seriously?"

"Do you *want* me to kill you?" I curled my lip into a snarl, but he came toward me, his russet eyes soldered to mine.

"Look at me, Jen. What do you see?"

"A jackass who won't go away."

"Okay, but what else?" He stopped, his face inches from mine, open, honest, and completely unafraid. "I know your secret," he whispered.

My body turned to water, but he caught me before I could fall. "No," I groaned. "Not you."

He laughed. He actually laughed, as if the world had not suddenly ceased to turn. He cradled my inert body in his arms. "You're not my first choice, either, but at least we're not alone."

22

"I know a place we could go," Jeremy said as he helped me stand. "An apartment complex, over by the golf course."

I forced myself to breathe. "Okay."

"We should hide the body first."

I dared not tear my eyes away from the future to look down at the past. "It won't matter. The police already know about me."

"The police already know?" He ran both hands through his golden hair while a vein in his neck began to throb. "Well, that's just great."

"I killed a nun in New Orleans last night. I had to tell the sisters the truth. I'm sorry." I told my fingers to take his hand, but they did not obey. "I'll have to carry you so no one sees us."

"Please don't tell me you can turn invisible."

"No. Just . . . you'll see."

He took three deep breaths, then stepped toward me. "What the hell, right? I'm just going to wake up before you can kill me, anyway."

I wanted to smile, but the glassy eyes still glared out judgment from the boy who had died of loving me. I did not turn to face them. I only hefted Jeremy over my shoulder and ran.

Seconds later, he was wheezing when I set him down in the parking lot outside our destination. "Damn," he muttered with what little breath he had.

"Is this the place?"

"Yeah. Number eight."

I left him there to catch his breath and set to work picking the lock. I had passed this apartment complex a thousand times and never gave it a second glance. It didn't deserve one: brown, boxy, utilitarian, a place where nothing and no one stood out from the backdrop of bland. My mother would have approved.

Jeremy sidled over to join me a few minutes later, still looking dizzy from the run. "I get the feeling you threw the cross-country meet."

"That obvious, huh? Is there an alarm?"

"I don't know. I've never been here."

"Well, one way to find out."

I opened the door and froze, poised to hoist him up and bolt, but no electronic beeping greeted us. After about ten seconds of silence, we went in. "What is this place?" I asked. A ratty old futon, a miniature TV, a card table, and two folding chairs wallowed in the septic fluorescent light.

"My mom's love shack," Jeremy mumbled.

"Wait, your mom keeps this place . . . ?"

"So she can fuck strangers, yeah." He stared at the walls as if staring could set them on fire. He finally cleared his throat and sat down on the futon. "So."

It seemed like the only right thing to say. I sat down next to him. "Yeah. So."

He twiddled his thumbs while I played with the edge of my skirt.

"So, how did it happen?" I finally asked. "I mean, you . . ."

He looked at me as if to pull the rationale for his existence from my eyes. "I was five. My mom used to work at Woman's Hospital. I met an angel at the company picnic."

Hate as strong as gasoline poured over my senses. "Helen?"

"Yeah. She climbed in through my bedroom window later that night."

A buzz of demons' laughter rang in my ears while he told his tale. An angel bright with promises, a pill to make him sleep, and a morning dawned to find his mother drunk and passed out from the horror. His world had collapsed "like a star imploding," a childhood forever orbiting the light that had shattered it, powerless to do anything but circle her from afar.

"She promised to make me immortal, but she never told me I was a vampire."

"You're taking it pretty calmly now."

He shrugged and flayed black flecks of paint from the futon's peeling arms. "I guess it's hard to freak out about being fictional." He peeled some more, until chunks of silver began to show through the black. "I did finally get to talk to her again. Right before she left, she came back and found me. She said that you would change before me, so I should go to you and you would teach me."

Every word was a needle tattooing questions on my mind. Had my mother never really intended to come back? And might that mean . . . she was still alive?

"So you knew. All those years you were sitting in those classes picking on me, you knew."

He dusted the paint flecks from under his fingernails. "Not when we were little. I always used to wonder about it back then. But, after she told me that . . . then yeah."

"Jackass."

"Yeah." He smiled and laid his hand on mine, but before I could pull away, his cell phone rang. "Hey, Mom," he said as I blinked away mirages of bliss that had blossomed under his touch. The fact that I had hated him all my life seemed less important, now, than the fact that he was here.

Jeremy's face drew taut as he listened to the person on the line. "Turn on the TV," he said to me, then, to the phone, "Yeah, I've got her. If you go to the police, I'll turn you in to the child protection people. By the way, I'm a vampire." He hung up and then, since I was sitting mesmerized by that scrap of conversation, he turned on the TV himself. "I guess we'll be seeing Mom in a while." He sat down next to me again. "After that little chat, she's bound to go get drunk and try to get laid."

I kept blinking, my jaw fallen slack. "But . . ."

"She's not going to turn you in. Mom is fifty shades of fucked up, but with stuff like this, you can trust her. Hey, look, there you are." He waved at the TV and, sure enough, there I was, last year's yearbook photo blown up to fill the entire screen. They had broken into the morning game shows to put the public on their guard. The agent who read the prepared statement was not police; he was FBI.

"Wow. You made the big time," Jeremy said as a red-eyed Mr. Derwin came on to offer a reward for my arrest.

I put my head in my hands. *I'm done with love. I have no need to cry.* Then Mother Lily's voice came through the speakers. "Jennifer, please. Turn yourself in. You do not have to face this by yourself. Please. I'm here."

I smashed the "off" button and collapsed in a blubbering heap into Jeremy's arms. Not for a single tear did my resolve falter, but wishful thinking could not kill love any more than it could kill me. I would have to suck its life out, just like any other living thing.

"Hey," Jeremy whispered as he stroked my heaving back. "Hey, come on, I'm here. We're together now." The heat of skin on pining skin, the waft of solidarity sang like sunshine into my pit of doom. But when I looked up into his warm, russet eyes, only Helen stared back.

"Jeremy." I lifted his hand away and did my best to swallow the tears. "Please don't take this the wrong way. I'm really glad you're here, but it's not going to be . . . like that."

"Why not?"

"Because the one thing Helen Carshaw could never do is give us love."

We held each other's eyes and watched our dreams spill into the silence.

"Was she really your mother?"

"She ripped me from my real mother's womb with her teeth."

He winced. I dried my eyes on my sleeve.

"I'm going to go get some steaks and stock the fridge." He stood and kissed me on the top of my head. "Don't worry," he added as I shrank from his lips. "No love. I get it. But you're still all I've got."

❖

The crushing fatigue of the last twelve hours caught up to me after Jeremy left. It turned out there was a bedroom behind one of the apartment's bland beige doors, so I went in to try to rest. Unfortunately, the bed smelled like lust and stale tobacco with a strong residue of sadness. I had never smelled emotions as a stain before, and it creeped me out so badly, I went back into the living room and opened up the futon. *That* smelled like a third-world sweatshop that made cheap beer, but at least modern chemistry could explain it. I lay there for a while, tossing to the erratic rhythms of my confusion, but eventually exhaustion won out, and I fell asleep.

I awoke a few hours later to the sound of drunken laughter and somebody fumbling at the door lock. "That'll be Mom," Jeremy said, smiling at me from the card table over a mostly-empty plate of steak. "You better hide 'til I can get rid of the guy."

I hopped up, still only half-awake, and headed for the bathroom. The sickly-sweet aroma of marijuana followed me as I closed the door and perched on the side of the tub. I heard a woman scream and then, "Hey, Mom," from Jeremy.

"Yo, bitch, what's the deal?" a man's voice said, the kind of voice that conjured images of gold teeth and prison tattoos.

"I'm her son," Jeremy answered. "If you know what's good for you, you'll walk out now."

"Man, I ain't lookin' for no trouble."

"Good. Then just walk out the door." I heard a few muttered curses, then footsteps and the sound of a slamming door. "Quite a place you've got here, Mom."

I sneaked a peak under the bathroom door and watched his mom sink into the open futon. I had seen Dr. Higginbotham plenty of times, at school events. Her rusty eyes were always rimmed with red, her hair a sickly chemical-brown, her wrinkles deeper every year. She always seemed mildly manic, too, like she thought she might have left the stove on. Now the brown had given way to Elvira-black, the wrinkles had been botoxed until she could barely move her face, and she looked like she *knew* she had left the stove on but was too tired to care.

"How long have you known about this place?" she asked her son.

"Four, five years. Since I found the rent bill in the mail."

"Fuck. Fuck fuck fuck fuck *fuck.*"

I had to hand it to her; she had a way with words.

Jeremy's mom reached into her purse and pulled out a cigarette. "She's here, isn't she?"

"Yeah. In the bathroom."

Dr. Higginbotham's hand shook so badly, she couldn't get the lighter to ignite. Jeremy lit it for her, and she took a drag. "You might as well come out," she called to me as she exhaled. "I've done everything you asked."

I opened the door and her wide brown eyes met mine. "I never asked you anything," I said.

Her head wilted into her lap. "Oh, shit."

"Did you think I was Helen?" The name thudded to the floor like an anvil from the sky.

"Wait," Jeremy stammered, "I thought Helen was dead."

His mother groaned. "That's what everyone thinks."

Fury coursed through me like a toxin, until my entire body shook with rage. "What do you know, Dr. Higginbotham? Any threat she made to you, I promise I can match."

Jeremy bounced to his feet crying, "Jen, what the fuck?" but his mother only glared.

"If you want to kill me, go ahead. I've been ready since the first time your mother drank my blood."

"*Helen Carshaw* drank your blood? And you're still alive?"

"Twice: once on the night she changed Jeremy, and again before she left." She pulled down the collar of her blouse to show a tiny pinprick scar. "If you think I still want to be here after that, then you've got a lot to learn about vampires."

"Wait." The color drained from Jeremy's cheeks. "Are you saying you knew?"

Dr. Higginbotham looked at him, the tenderness of a mother wrapped up inside the hatred of the living for the dead. "I couldn't tell you. She ordered me not to, and she swore . . ." She heaved a breath. "The point is, we're all here right now for the same reason — because this is where Helen wants us to be."

"Dr. Higginbotham, do you know where she is now?"

"Of course not. What I do know is, you can't hide out at this apartment with the FBI chasing you. Jeremy, go put some coffee on. We've got to figure out how to get Jennifer out of town."

Jeremy gawked while Dr. Higginbotham took another drag. My body trembled as if I could feel Helen tugging at it like a puppeteer, my feet forever doomed to dance upon her heinous stage. I knew now why I had not managed, despite my best efforts, to die. It was because, if I died now, I would die as Helen Carshaw's slave. From inside the black depths of oblivion, I could not sever the strings that bound us. If I were dead, I could not kill my mother.

23

Creating my new life proved to be a whole lot easier with help. We spent a couple of hours formulating plans and parceling out duties. Dr. Higginbotham would procure the essentials of disguise: hair dye — which I hoped would be more subtle than her own — contacts, makeup, a new wardrobe, plus a laptop and cell phone. Jeremy would get Carter Guidry, Prompt Succor's most notorious underworld liaison, to forge a new birth certificate, driver's license, and social security card. I got stuck with the part that required thought and imagination: figuring out who I should be and where in the world I could go.

"All right." Dr. Higginbotham stood up when we had done what we could do, dusting a few stray ashes from her slacks. "That's that. Jeremy, let's go."

He lingered in his chair. "You going to be okay here?" he asked me.

"As long as the cops don't come."

He nodded and started to reach across the table, but then wrung his hands instead. "All right. Good night."

"Good night."

Dr. Higginbotham said nothing, but ushered her son outside and firmly locked the door. I lay on the futon until morning, listening to the echo of the emptiness.

❖

"We have a problem."

Jeremy returned around eleven o'clock the next day, after I had numbed my brain with three morning talk shows and four consecutive episodes of *Family Feud*. He had evidently run, because his clothes and hair were dripping. The scent of his sweat sent an assortment of shivers down my spine.

"Okay," I said from the sunken place on the futon that had molded itself to my rear end.

He marched to the sink, wiped his brow on his shirttail, and stuck his head under the tap. Not until he had chugged about a half gallon did he right himself and say, "It's Stacy."

Stacy Higginbotham had featured rather prominently in my own musings this morning, but only as a solution. "What's wrong?"

"The nuns told the police about your habit of only eating raw meat and always wearing sunscreen. It's all over the news. Stacy knows I'm the same way, and she's enough of a bitch to call the cops."

"So, did she?"

"Not yet. She's too busy storming around the house in tears. Did you kill some guy named Martin who goes to her school?"

I swallowed. "Yes."

"Is that what the yearbook thing was really about?"

I turned down my eyes. "There was a witness. I was trying to find him."

Jeremy groaned. "Stacy's jumping off the deep end like she's his goddamn grieving widow. There's nothing that would make her feel better faster than to get me arrested."

I nodded with what I hope passed for understanding. "Is that why you ran here?"

He looked down at his drenched T-shirt. "No, that was just training. I've got a boxing match on Friday, junior welterweight semifinals. I mean, assuming I'm still here."

"Where else would you be?"

He cocked his head. "With you. That is the plan, isn't it?"

Deep breaths, Jen . . . but not too deep. I dared not fill my lungs with his heat and worry and craving. "I kind of need to talk to you about that. Your mom, too. I can't work out the details until I get the Internet, but the plan is that I'm going to go away to school. And, right now, it's probably better if you don't come."

Only his eyelids moved. It was a shame I could smell the truth of his pain, since he hid it so well.

"Why?"

"Because I'm a wanted mass-murderer and you're not. I've got to get the hang of this hiding-from-the-cops thing, and I'm probably going to screw it up a few times before I master it. Do you really want to be with me through all that?"

He gripped the edge of the card table. "You're the only person I can be with."

It felt like Eternity traced cold fingers down my spine. "I know. But Helen didn't change you until you were five, right? That means you've still got five more years before you mature. Just let me get settled someplace, let the trail get cold."

"So I'll come when it's safe."

"Yes." I did not tell him I would never be safe from him.

"And you'll keep in touch?"

"Yes. Somehow. I mean, it might be kind of complicated."

He nodded. "I'm supposed to meet Carter at IHOP for lunch. Did you figure out what name you want on your papers?"

"Yes, but you're not going to like it."

"Why?"

"Because I'm going to be Stacy Higginbotham."

This time, his eyelids flew back into his head. "Jesus, Jen, what for?"

"So it will look legal. Your mom can sign whatever I need — school forms, apartment lease, that kind of stuff. She can get me copies of Stacy's transcripts. As long as no one figures out there are two of us, it's all legal."

"And if *Stacy* finds out . . . ?"

Steel jaws of accusation clamped onto my courage, but there was no turning back. "Jeremy, I am supposed to teach you how to be a vampire. Vampires do not have families."

"So if one of the nuns came and stood in your way, you would kill them?"

"You're forgetting that I already did." I did not tell him that her blood still wept inside me. "But if you don't want Stacy to get hurt, it's very simple. Make sure she never finds out."

Black thunderheads gathered in his russet eyes. "I'm going to go meet Carter." He slammed the door on his way out.

I did not tell him that Carter would be his next lesson.

Carter Guidry was a senior at Prompt Succor, the kind of greasy fat guy nobody wanted to hang out with, except all the boys hung out with him because he sold porn under the bleachers during lunch. Being so far on the outskirts of Prompt Succor's criminal underground, I should not have known this. However, last year, on a particularly slow day for business, Carter had found me reading under a tree and informed me that he could get "stuff for girls, too," if I was interested. "I could just let you borrow it," he said. "I mean, I know you can't exactly take it home."

I shuddered. "No, thanks."

"That's cool. My brother's roommate grows some really awesome weed. I wouldn't charge you . . . you know, if you wanted to share."

I should have turned him in to Mother Lily. I would have turned him in to Mother Lily, except for the blush on his bulging cheeks that told me this was the only way he knew how to approach anyone. So I just said, "No, thank you," and went back to my book. He lingered and looked like he wanted to talk – like he wanted to sit down – and if either of us had had the social skills of a parrot, we might have become friends. Instead, we spent the next few weeks trading awkward looks in gym class, until we finally gave up and went back to ignoring each other as we always had.

The memory of the friendless longing in Carter's hard, gray eyes painted itself across every surface in the apartment that afternoon. For hours, I stared into the jaded depths of their atrophied potential, even when Dr. Higginbotham returned with the things on her shopping list. I learned how to put in contacts – green, just like my mother's eyes – dyed my hair a pretty, golden blonde, and got the computer set up to start my search for a school. I used a hefty dose of charm to convince Dr. Higginbotham that I should become her daughter, that she should pay for my schooling and housing, and that the plan in no way endangered the actual Stacy. Through it all, I saw nothing but Carter Guidry's eyes. Not because I was going to snuff them out; no, that I could have done. But I was not going to kill Carter Guidry.

Jeremy was.

❖

Every digital red minute of that night dripped a cell into my cancer. Carter's eyes retreated to make way for a different, russet pair. *Kill him,* conscience whispered, deadly echoes of compassion. *Helen made him. Kill him, and he cannot live her plan.* But it was the ageless music of her voice that brushed my ears. She tainted even conscience now; even compassion groaned with death.

I imagined that she smiled and kissed me and said, "You finally understand."

I could not meet Jeremy's eye when he returned the next morning. "I got 'em," he said, and handed me an envelope full of "Stacy's" papers. The birth certificate and social security card looked surprisingly real, but the driver's license had no photo, and the lamination was unsealed. "We'll have to do that part ourselves," he explained. "I couldn't tell him who it was for."

I swallowed. "Thank you. I wasn't sure you would go through with it."

He shrugged. "Stacy tried to kill me once. She got her friends to tie me to a flagpole in full sunlight and then tried to wash off my sunscreen. That's how she got kicked out of Prompt Succor."

"So this makes you even?"

He toyed with the unfinished lamination and did not answer. "Did you figure out where you're going to go?"

"Yes. Los Angeles."

He started. "Why?"

"Because by the time I got the Internet working last night, admissions offices were closed everywhere except the West Coast. I found a community college in L.A. that said they would let 'Stacy' come for her senior year." I did not mention that there was still the problem of convincing them I *was* Stacy. I figured Los Angeles had seen enough bad acting, my performance was sure to go unremarked. "Did you bring a camera? What color is the background on your license?"

He fished it out to check. "Blue, sort of a sky color."

"Like this?" I held up one of the shirts his mom had bought me.

"Yeah. Close enough."

I found a couple of pins in the stack of my new clothes. Jeremy held the shirt against the wall while I tacked it up. The heady, virile scent of him filled me with hope, purpose, and despair.

He took the picture, then used an iron to seal the photo into the lamination. "I guess you better start calling me Stacy," I said as I took the finished product.

"You have no idea how hard that's going to be."

I met his eye at last, just long enough to glimpse the fear that had already begun to assault my nose. "So," I said, twiddling my new license against my thumb, "did Carter do these himself?"

"No. He's just a broker for some paralegal up in Scotlandville."

I nodded. "So there are two."

"Two what?"

"Two loose ends we have to tie up before I leave."

Jeremy froze. "You just said 'we,' didn't you?"

I nodded.

He took a few loud deep breaths. "All right."

I packed my few possessions into my backpack and then climbed into the passenger seat of Jeremy's decade-old white Honda. He stared straight ahead at the windshield while the miles of I-110 slipped away, his knuckles white against the wheel.

"You're going to hate me after today," I said.

He rolled the car to a stop at a red light off the Scotlandville exit, just north of the city. "I can't say I'm happy about this, but I don't hate you. I already saw you kill Matt, remember?"

"You're going to hate me. Just remember, I didn't ask for this any more than you did. If I could choose to be human, I would."

He said nothing, only pulled the car up next to a house with peeling siding.

"You can stay in the car for this one if you want."

He nodded.

I did not charm the paralegal. I wanted the taste of his agony, the helplessness of his struggle. I wanted him to be my mirror, but it turned out the legends were right, after all. Emptiness casts no reflection.

Jeremy was still gripping the steering wheel when I returned. "Okay," I said, "let's go."

He drove us back into Baton Rouge, to the Garden District, to a little cottage-style house whose driveway had been broken to bits by the roots of a giant Live Oak. The car jolted like a carnival ride as he pulled in, but I did not think that was the reason for the violent pitching in my gut.

Jeremy cut the engine, but neither of us reached for the doors.

"You're probably thinking about bailing." My serrated voice cut the air. "You can, but it won't matter."

"Because you'll do it anyway?"

"Yes, but that's not why. It won't matter because nothing matters." I shut my ears against the screeching echoes of the paralegal's screams and got out. God help him, Jeremy followed me to the door. I did not even have to ask.

Carter's father answered my knock. "Hi. We're here to see Carter." Mr. Guidry's eyes unfocused as I shook his hand, but it was my sight that blurred. I had not known there would be two. I had come to draw a draught of evil Jeremy must drink, but now I could do more than pour it down his throat. Now, I could make him drown.

Jeremy closed the door behind us as Carter entered from the hall. "Hey, Jeremy. What's . . . oh, fuck." Recognition crashed into understanding the moment his eyes met mine.

"Hey, Carter. I came to say thank you for the papers."

He threw a glare at Jeremy and slurred, "You fucking piece of shit," then grabbed a baseball bat and came at me. I sidestepped his swing, but the blow felled Jeremy with a crack that sent him howling to the floor. Carter's dad came to his senses and tried some kind of karate kick, but I caught his foot and tossed him down. Carter tripped on his father and went sprawling to the floor. I knelt and touched their cheeks. "Shh . . ." Carter shivered and, for an instant, leaned his face into my hand. I cupped it to catch his tears. "I'm sorry. I can't help it. I'm a vampire."

"Jen . . . don't . . ." Jeremy wrenched the words from his lips, but I could not listen. If I let him see the wounds I was tearing in my heart, I could not save him from his own.

"Are you going to drink our blood?" Carter whimpered into the rug.

"No," I answered. "You are."

I kissed him with my mother's lips while mine were praying. *Stop me. Please, God, stop me.* Then I kissed his father, too. I used a single tooth to scratch a gateway to his vein, then turned to Carter and did the same. *This cannot work.* But it had to. Here and now, love had to die.

I guided their mouths against each other's necks and listened to them swallow.

Jeremy spewed his last meal across the Persian rug and gagged, "For God's sake, what's the point of *that?*"

"There is no point. There is no judgment for us, Jeremy. No heaven, no hell, no law, no morality. Nothing matters. We don't have souls."

Carter and his dad slumped together, too weak to finish the job. From the depths of his vomit-scented hatred, Jeremy cried, "Get out!"

I did not argue. "They're still alive, you know. You can leave them there to bleed to death, or you can put them out of their misery. Or you can call 911." I stepped outside. The door clicked shut. I lasted two whole heartbeats before I collapsed on the stoop and wept.

From behind the door came two sickening crunches of a baseball bat on skull.

I slung the backpack full of all my worldly possessions over my shoulder, and I ran: one hundred miles, two hundred, three, my shoes melting beneath me while my body caked with dead bugs. *Jeremy,* I longed to cry, to cradle him in my arms, to lull him and lie to him and tell him everything would be okay. But even as I spread a gulf of interstate between us, I knew the day would come. He would hate me, curse me, rejoice to be rid of me, but someday, he would come. He would come for the same reason *she* would come, though a thousand years might pass. They would come because nothing can escape a black hole — least of all the black hole itself.

II

THE RED SUN

FOUR YEARS LATER

1

"Ach, genius! That shadow on the jaw line . . . genius! I want to run screaming in terror!" Amos Maddigan's hairy Scottish arms enveloped me with a sensation akin to carpet burn. I had grown to enjoy that sensation because it meant success.

"All right, you're right. I do look pretty damn scary." Tommy Lee Jones swiveled in his chair to face me. The legend was doing a screen test today with some teenybopper James Dean wanna-be, and Amos had brought me along for my own screen test. Mr. Jones's suspected-ax-murderer-next-door makeup was my own design.

Mr. Jones stood up and extended his hand. "What's your name, kid?"

"Stacy Higginbotham."

"You look like an actress. You ever considered working on screen?"

I stifled a sigh. Being beautiful in Hollywood was supposed to be an asset — that is, if you were not wanted for murder. All I needed was for some FBI agent to see me prancing around on screen. Unfortunately, Tommy Lee Jones was the third person to ask me that question this week.

"Thank you, but I'm pretty camera shy."

"Well, you sure got a knack with a makeup brush."

I had not chosen my new career as much as it had chosen me. It turned out that, even in Los Angeles, being eternally young was a problem. I had not been at community college a week before people started saying, "You look too young to be in college." By the end of my first semester, I only had to look at the faces in my study group to realize I was screwed, so I invested in some Revlon and signed up for a stage makeup class. As they say, the rest is history.

Amos looped his fuzzy auburn arm around my waist and we watched together as Mr. Jones and the teenybopper held a stilted double-entendre conversation across a sound stage hedgerow. As usual, Amos held me tighter than necessary, and, as usual, I put up with it because he was Amos.

Amos Maddigan thought he was Sean Connery, but in truth he more closely resembled some small mythical creature: elf, leprechaun, Hobbit, take your pick. Pointy ears notwithstanding, he had a shelf in his office full of gold statuettes crammed together with studied disdain. My teacher at community college had invited him to do a master class with us. I suspect it was my vampiric good looks as much as my actual talent that caught his eye; no male makeup artist in Hollywood could get away with being straight, but Amos was renowned for his conquests on both sides of the aisle. Somehow, we kept my interview professional enough that I didn't kill him, and three years later, I was a full-time member of his staff. I figured that entitled him to an occasional hug.

Amos nuzzled my hair. "Stacy," he whispered while shooting was stopped, "Tommy is right. You should be on the screen. You're like Audrey Hepburn, Greta Garbo . . . stunning. These little starlets nowadays, they've got nothing on you."

"Except for one minor detail. They can act."

"Ach, anybody can act. It's *magnetism* that can't be taught."

"Then maybe the calendar on my fridge would look good on screen, too."

He grinned his crooked grin that meant I had won another skirmish. "Just remember, now's the time. You won't be young forever."

"I'll try to keep that in mind."

The director called, "Action," and I watched the scene unfold. A grip I knew waved hello across the set, and as I waved back, I could hardly believe I had become what Helen intended me to be: a functioning member of human society who secretly drank blood by night. Hollywood made it easy.

When I first started working for Amos, the after-hours social life of "the industry" had driven me into an introverted cocoon. Nearly every day, someone invited me to a house party or to grab an after-work cocktail. Every day, I blushed and stammered excuses, determined not to fall into the trap of friendship. Finally, Amos overheard me turning down drinks with a lighting designer and cornered me in his office. "Stacy," he said, "you're talented. I'm doing my best to open doors for you, but if you don't get out there and network, you'll never amount to anything in this town."

"Network? I thought he was asking me out."

"I'm sure Gary will gladly take you home if you're in the mood, but that was not his only motive. You've got to get to know people in this business if you want to move up. That's just the way it is out here, my love."

After that, I had quickly mastered the game. I went out when I wanted, begged off when I was hungry, laughed at shallow wit, and made the kinds of "connections" that could cement a successful, lifelong career. After every hollow hug, every kiss I blew goodnight, I knew if morning came without me, not a tear would dampen the dawn.

I was packing up my makeup bag after the shoot when the teenybopper sauntered toward me wearing the now-familiar lecherous grin of the ego-inflated elite. "Hey. What's your name?" he asked.

"Stacy Higginbotham. What's yours?"

His grin wavered a split second before it returned with a bravado so reminiscent of Jeremy, I dropped my tube of eyeliner. "It's Conner Brazel, but you already knew that, didn't you?" He swept up the eyeliner and returned it to my hand, his fingers lingering in mine. "So, Stacy, are you hungry? I've got a table waiting at Spago."

He smiled — *leered* — at me with such practiced nonchalance, it made me want to slug him, kiss him, and kill him all at once: exactly the way Jeremy had made me feel for my entire grade school career.

I whispered feebly, "Sure, why not?"

We rode in his Ferrari with the top down, plunging around corners at a speed that would have made me wet my pants if I had not been immortal. Thankfully, the wind drowned any possibility of conversation. It left me free to pretend the impudent hand on my knee belonged to a different blonde jackass.

Four years without a word. Four years without a glimpse of the damage I had done. Four years without a chance to say I'm sorry.

We squealed up to the valet stand and the teenybopper shocked me by opening my door and offering his arm. "Treat her good," he told the valet with a wink as he handed over the keys and a hundred dollar bill. I wondered if he put on this show for all the girls or if he had learned of my reputation from Amos. I had rejected so many romantic advances, people at the office called me Celibate Stacy.

We breezed past the maître d' with another lavish tip and settled into a corner table. "So, where are you from?" Conner asked as he perused the wine list.

"Louisiana."

"Really? What happened to your accent?"

I ground my teeth and forced myself to forgive him. Every person in Los Angeles had asked me that question since the day I first arrived: "What happened to your accent?" as if I had fallen off a Cracker truck and immediately gone into speech therapy.

"Nothing happened. I've always talked like this."

"Seriously?"

"Seriously."

"Lucky you. I'm from Birmingham, and I can't tell you how long I spent with the voice coach to get rid of the twang." He laughed. Stupid, musical, Jeremy-sounding laugh. "So, what do you like? Red or white?"

"Are you even old enough to drink?"

"I guess you don't read much. My twenty-first birthday party was on the cover of *Us Weekly*."

"Actually, I read quite a lot. They're called books."

"I remember those. I think they keep them in museums." He grinned, letting me revel in the depths of his sapphire eyes. "So, red or white?"

"I'll just have water."

"They're not going to card you."

"I'm legal. I just don't drink." Stacy Higginbotham was almost twenty-two, even if Jennifer Carshaw was not.

Conner gave me an appraising look and I let him appraise. I regretted coming already, and soon I would have to go through my charade about eating human food.

"You're not going to come back to my apartment after dinner, are you?"

His frankness caught me off-guard. I stammered, "No."

"You just came for the food?"

"Actually, I'm not hungry."

"So why are you here?"

Good question. I had to think about it before I said, "I guess because I didn't have anything else to do."

He stared at me a moment and then burst out laughing so loud that half the restaurant turned to watch. "Oh, God," he gasped when he could speak again. "Wow. I get a hundred fan letters every day from girls who would kill to be sitting in that chair, and you didn't have anything else to do!"

I didn't know how to respond to that, so I just fidgeted with my shirttail until he stopped laughing. When he recovered, he stood and took my hand. "Come on."

"Where are we going?"

"I'll drive you home."

We waited in silence as the stunned valet retrieved the freshly-parked car. I did not know what to make of the fact that Conner never let go of my hand. When the car arrived, he ushered me into the passenger seat, then climbed behind the wheel, put up the top, and asked, "Where to?"

"Venice."

"Nice." But he didn't drive. He just kept staring at me like he had never seen a woman properly before.

"Are we going?"

He took a breath, started to say something, then stopped. He stared at me a moment more, then tried again. "Can we start over?"

"What do you mean?"

"I mean, can I come pick you up, like this weekend maybe, and try this again?"

"Without all the bravado, you mean?"

"You're obviously still new. Around here, we call it charm." He grinned the devilish grin I remembered so well, and I could not tear my eyes away. *Tell him no, Jennifer. You can't be the girlfriend of Mr. GQ cover boy. It can't possibly work, your picture will end up in the tabloids, and you'll be dead. For God's sake, tell him no!*

"Sure," I said and smiled.

Not much had changed in four years. My reasoning skills were still in perfect working order, and I was still an idiot.

From Beverly Hills to Venice Beach we did not talk at all except that I gave him directions. On the drive to Spago, even his scent had broadcast "arrogant playboy," but now the air smelled of openness. What could possibly have happened to make him change?

He pulled to the curb in front of the orange stucco duplex where I rented the first floor, and his hand tightened around my knee. "Stacy, look, I just want you to know . . ."

"Stop. You're the one who needs to know . . ."

"No, I get it. You're the girl you bring home to Mom."

"I promise you, your mother does not want you to be with me."

"Why not?"

"Because I have the kind of problems you only act out on screen. The kind you don't want to be a part of in real life."

Conner tucked a strand of hair behind my ear, the touch of his skin sending shivers down my spine. "Come on, Stace, if problems stopped people from trying to be together, we'd all die alone." Compassion burst like fireworks from his luminous eyes, and the magnets of our mouths connected. Even as I felt myself falling in a way I had never fallen before, I knew this was the end, that Stacy had to go, that it was time . . .

He pulled away.

"What's wrong?"

He nodded toward the window behind me. I turned around — and there he was, glaring at me through the glass.

"Boyfriend?"

"No." I hit the button and the window slid down. "Conner Brazel, meet Jeremy Higginbotham. My brother."

Jeremy didn't say a word. He just threw a punch straight through the window.

2

I caught his fist and twisted until Jeremy groaned and fell to the sidewalk. Conner jumped out of the car and positioned himself between me and Jeremy. "Back down, man," he ordered, then wrapped his arm around me as I got out.

Jeremy looked up with disgust no actor could ever have matched. "Whatever you say."

"Conner," I whispered, "Jeremy and I need to talk."

"I can't leave if he's going to hurt you." Conner's arms around me were refuge, but Jeremy was the vault where I had locked away my heart.

"I'll be fine, I promise. I can take him."

Jeremy rolled his eyes.

Conner tucked my hair behind my ear. "I'm going to call you in an hour. If you don't answer, I'm calling the police."

"You do that," Jeremy mumbled. "That'll really make her happy."

I glared at Jeremy and handed Conner my business card. "Don't worry. I'll answer."

Conner held me captive with his azure eyes. "One hour." He kissed me, then got behind the wheel of the Ferrari and blazed away.

I sank down onto the sidewalk next to Jeremy. "Hey."

"Hey." He shook his head. "When did you become the type who falls for movie stars?"

"Today."

"That little knight-in-shining-armor act was pretty cute. Especially since he didn't have your number."

I allowed myself half a smile. "I was starting to think you hated me."

"What makes you think I don't?"

"That punch wasn't aimed at me."

He tugged at a blade of grass growing through a crack in the cement.

I sucked in a breath, working up the courage to ask the most important question. "So . . . have you heard from Helen?"

"No. You?"

"No." I sighed, not knowing if it was with relief or frustration.

We both watched an ant work its way along the sidewalk, carrying a crumb.

"Four long fucking years, huh?" he said.

"Yeah. Four very long fucking years."

We went inside, and he told me about the cloud of police suspicion he had lived under since the day I left. It had started with routine questions about my visit to his house, the yearbook I had borrowed, but the sergeant had seen a plate full of raw steak sitting on his kitchen table, and it had all been downhill from there. A failed polygraph convinced the FBI that he was helping me hide, and he had only avoided prison because the lie detector evidence was inadmissible. "They even looked at me for Carter and his dad's murders, but I poured about ten gallons of bleach on the rug to get rid of my DNA, and I guess it must have worked."

I squeezed his hand and felt every word stitching us together. "I didn't want to do it."

"I know. You had to show me what it feels like to kill, and it totally sucks." He grimaced at his own pun. "Not . . . like that, but . . . I'm just trying to say, it's hell, carrying that around. You don't have to carry it by yourself anymore."

I almost kissed him. I almost threw myself into his arms and let caution be damned. The only thing that stopped me was the scent of my own fear.

I settled for leaning my head against his shoulder. "Thank you for coming."

His fingers stroked the back of my hand. "Well, I kind of had to. I've been sort of . . . changing."

"It's less than a year now, isn't it?" I had to suppress a shiver.

"Maybe not that long. I haven't needed a haircut in about a year."

I sat up and stroked the golden strands as if I could will them to grow. "Are you sure?"

"I think I'd notice getting a haircut. Plus, I've been healing faster after my boxing matches."

I peered into his eyes, and now I saw the tiny, subtle flecks of green. He gazed right back at me, one abyss into another, as if the sum of nothingness might become more than its parts.

I looked down, and all I wanted was a lead-foot boy in a Ferrari to take me any place but here. "So, where are we going to go? I guess I'll need a new identity again. I mean, if the cops are on your tail, it will look pretty suspicious to be living with your sister who's supposed to be in Baton Rouge."

"Stacy's here. She goes to UCLA. I made sure of it, just so it would look normal to have you with me."

I blinked repeatedly. That seemed to happen to me a lot around Jeremy. "Really?"

"Yes, really. You're moving to Pasadena, but that's as far as you have to go."

"Why Pasadena?"

"Because I'm going to study astrophysics at Caltech." He grinned from ear to ear while my jaw fell open.

"Astrophysics? *You?*"

"Yeah. When Helen told me I was immortal, the only thing I could think about was how I might live long enough for space travel to really start picking up. I've been at LSU the last two years, trying to get good enough transcripts to convince Caltech to take me. Otherwise, I would have been here sooner." He looked like a kid in a candy store, not a soon-to-be-vampire who had come in search of his hellish mentor. "You can close your mouth now. Just because I'm a vampire doesn't mean I have to give up all my dreams."

I closed my eyes and saw myself inside a coffin with Jeremy standing over me, whispering, "Wake up." Then my cell phone rang.

"You better take that. Your little boy-toy looked like he meant it about calling the police."

The hairs inside my ears stood at attention as I slipped outside to answer.

"Hey. Are you still in one piece?" Conner's lilting baritone made my stomach turn cartwheels.

"Yes. You do realize he was aiming at you, not me?" The sudden shimmer in my own voice nearly blinded me.

"Oh. Well, then, he's lucky he missed. My face is expensive, and my lawyer's very good."

"I'll try to remember that next time you make me mad."

"Next time? We've known each other five hours. When did I make you mad before?"

"When you asked what happened to my accent."

He roared with laughter. "You don't mind being treated like a groupie, but you can't stand an attack on your Southern pride?"

"Something like that." I blushed, glad that he could not see.

"Ah tell you what," he drawled, "you come on over heeyer with me, an' Ah'll teach you a little sumthin' about Suthern charm."

"Is it a lesson your mother would approve?"

"Just because I would bring you home to *her* doesn't mean I don't want you home with *me.*"

The word "home" hit me in the gut, and the light in my mood faded. "Listen, Conner, thanks for checking up on me. But I really mean it; you don't want to be with me. People who get close to me get hurt."

He sighed. "Look, Stacy, I like you. If you don't want to go out with me again, just say so. Otherwise, I'm not going away."

I opened my mouth, but no words came out.

"Thought so," he said. "Okay, I've got to go, but I'll call you tomorrow?"

"Okay."

"Goodnight, Stacy."

"Goodnight."

I went in and sat next to Jeremy, his presence soaking into me like cyanide and balm. He had been through hell the last four years, the kind of hell I had managed to avoid precisely because of him. He had been more faithful to me than I could ever have dreamed, but that could not change the fact that he was as soulless as I. Together, we formed a vacuum where no spark could ever shine. But Conner glowed so brightly, the entire world called him "star."

He's not real, Jen. I had pretended not to know him because I hated the condescension of swollen Hollywood egos, but Conner was one of the fastest rising stars around. He had broken out with a supporting role in last year's Best Picture, and now he had something like four movies set to release this year. Movie stars did not date orphans who had been raised in convents, much less vampires who were wanted by the FBI. He would disappear as quickly as he had entered, like headlights passing through the night, but I could not un-see the girl those lights had shined upon. That girl was no less riddled with torment and sin than I, but at least she still knew how to laugh.

"Hey, Jen," Jeremy murmured into my hair.

The name caressed my homesick ears. "It's Stacy," I said.

"Right. *Stacy* . . . I missed you."

How could I tell him the ways I had longed for him, that every breath I took without him crushed me with deprivation? How could I tell him that, here with him, I would suffocate and decay?

"I missed you, too."

We fell asleep together on my couch, one big, messy tangle of futility.

3

I woke up before Jeremy the next morning and did something I had forbidden myself to do for the last four years. I got on the Internet and searched for the Sisters of Prompt Succor.

They were all over the Louisiana newspapers, mostly in articles about my killing spree and its aftermath. *Funeral for Mother Superior Put On Hold, Nuns Reveal Startling Details of Killer's Childhood, Sisters of Prompt Succor to Hold Memorial Mass for Victims.* I read no more than the headlines, damming my carefully desiccated life against an old, familiar flood. But even the headlines shot bullets through my barricades.

Our Lady of Prompt Succor Academy

Will Not Reopen For Fall Term

Sisters of Prompt Succor to Close Convent in June

The article was dated from April of the year after I left. I couldn't help myself; I skimmed the text. Enrollment had dropped off so steeply after Matt's murder, the sisters had put both the Baton Rouge school and convent up for sale and moved to New Orleans. Remorse, that old antagonist, bubbled up from the depths, but I slammed the screen shut on my laptop and held it down.

The noise woke Jeremy. "Hey," he said. "You okay?"

"Yeah, of course." I glanced at the clock, realizing that today was Friday and I was actually supposed to be at work. "I have to go call in sick for the day. I guess we need to go apartment hunting."

"I already have one. We just have to get you packed up to move." His smile wrapped me in possibility. "Just for the record, are you still stuck on that 'vampires-can't-love-anybody' stuff?"

I thought about a shepherd and a boy with cow-licked hair. "Yes," I mumbled to the wall.

Jeremy sighed. "All right, whatever. Go call your boss."

The phone call took longer than it should have. Amos had seen me leave the screen test with Conner, and no amount of protestation could convince him my "sick day" was not the result of luxurious debauchery. "Stacy, a dish like that is too big for one little girl like you. Just think of all us other poor souls starving for a taste."

"I'm telling you, he drove me home before we even had dinner. Nothing happened."

"Fine. Have it your way. But I've got my eye on you, Miss Celibate Stacy."

I had barely finished hitting "end" when my phone rang again. "Hello?"

"What's your dress size? I'm sending Willa to Dior."

The gears of my brain squeaked and smoked, trying to decode that transmission.

"Stacy? Are you there?"

"Yes."

"I've got a premiere tonight at Mann's. Not mine, actually, but the agency wants me to go. We need to get you something to wear."

"I . . . Wow." I think I turned a somersault in mid-air. Or maybe it just felt that way.

"So what are you, about a four?"

"Look, Conner, thank you, but I can't. I have to move this weekend."

"Where to?"

"Pasadena. Jeremy's going to Caltech. We're going to share an apartment."

"No problem. We'll just get you some movers, and your brother can be there to supervise."

"It's not that I don't want to, but I can't. I really, really can't." The little girl who had spent her childhood yearning for pretty things could not believe I was turning down a walk on the Red Carpet in a Dior gown, but for once I let reason prevail. There would be cameras at a premiere.

"All right. How about if I come tomorrow and help you move?"

"Are you serious?"

"Why, you think movie stars don't do manual labor?"

"Well . . . yes."

"I do a lot of things movie stars aren't supposed to do. Hey, there's Willa beeping in. I'll be at your house tomorrow at nine." Before I could formulate a thought, the line clicked dead.

I wandered back into the living room and found Jeremy watching TV, one of those celebrity gossip shows that glorified every mortal sin except the one that sustained my life. I cringed at the very timbre of the brash blonde anchorwoman's voice. "You don't have to buy into that crap just because you moved to L.A."

"Neither do you." Jeremy let the barb linger long enough for me to squirm, then scooched over to make room for me on the couch.

I sat down. "So, you're going to have to explain this whole astrophysics thing. You barely scratched out C's in school."

"That's because I was always over at the Highland Road Observatory learning about stars instead of doing my homework."

"Since when?"

"Since I was six. They had a summer day camp. I actually went to the real Space Camp when I was thirteen. I just didn't tell anybody."

"Why not?"

"Because . . . well, because I figure I'm going to be about three hundred years old when the stuff I really want to do starts happening, and that sounds pretty stupid to brag about at school." He suddenly looked back toward the TV and turned up the sound. "Hey look, there's your Boy-Toy."

Sure enough, Conner was smiling out from the screen, as phony and plastic as any movie star could ever be. "It's just such an honor to play this amazing person. The best part was working with him one-on-one, getting to hear him tell his story. He's really become one of my personal heroes . . ."

I groaned.

"Aren't you glad you got rid of that loser?"

"Actually, he's coming over tomorrow to help me move."

It was Jeremy's turn to blink in disbelief. "So vampires can't love, but they can fuck over everyone around them by dating a guy who lives his entire life in front of cameras?"

"It's not a date. He's just helping me move."

Jeremy rolled his eyes. "I know you're not aging, but I still thought you would have grown up." He turned up the sound on the TV again, making sure I heard every chortle of Conner's counterfeit, pretty-boy laughter.

❖

A haze of silence hung over my house that day. I felt as if I were twelve years old again, caged inside my own home with a monstrous creature I dared not question or defy, except that I was the monster now. Mine was the life I dared not examine or explain, Jeremy's the not-quite-innocent eyes that probed my silence. I wondered if this was the reason Helen had left me — if the strain of my scrutiny had stirred in her some distant echo of shame. But as quickly as the thought appeared, I dismissed it. To credit Helen with a conscience meant that killing her would not assuage mine.

I had not been prepared for the aura of Helen that accompanied Jeremy's arrival. It was as if the sight of him pierced an abscess in my mind, releasing all the poison that four years of careful forgetfulness had collected. Since the moment it first occurred to me that Helen might be alive, I had never thought of her without succumbing to murderous rage. Every day, I read the *LA Times*, keeping tabs on my own crimes, and I never scanned the stories of murder without wondering if one of them had been hers. Yet I couldn't allow myself do to more than wonder. As dearly as I longed to plunge a stake through her haughty, copper-skinned breast, I had not tried to find her. Cowardice abetted by inertia always prevented me, both of them comfortably rooted in the soil of insecurity. Who was I to condemn a monster? What right did I have to act as an agent of Right? Now with Jeremy packing knick-knacks into boxes beside me, his presence demanding that I impart to him the evil Helen had imparted to me, I feared more than ever that when I saw her again, I would only see myself.

When Jeremy left to go pick up the U-Haul truck, I hated that I felt relieved. I called my landlord to break my lease, then retreated to my bedroom to fold away my linens because I could not fold away my disgust.

4

"I'm hungry," Jeremy announced around two o'clock that afternoon. The arms bent across his chest ended in balled fists.

"Okay." I tried to extend an olive branch. "There's a market down on the boardwalk. We could go to the beach, if you want."

"Why? Are you hungry, too?"

I swallowed. "I was just thinking we could take a swim. I can get something . . . later." I *was* hungry, though. It was time.

"How much later?" Jeremy demanded.

"Look, it doesn't matter. We'll go spend the afternoon at the beach, and I'll do what I have to do tonight. You can stay here and watch a movie or something."

"Right, because a movie is going to do me a lot of good when my turn comes."

Now I understood the clenched fists. They were holding tight to the part of himself that would die tonight just as surely as the person who would fall victim to my teeth.

"Jeremy, watching me won't help you. When the hunger first hits, you still won't be able to control it."

"At least I'll know how to try." He set his lips in a hard, thin line. "We're still cleaning up the mess you made figuring this out on your own. I'm not saying you should have known better, just that I'm not going to repeat your mistakes."

I held my breath as if to stop myself from inhaling the truth, but he was right. "After dark," I whispered. "It's always easier after dark."

❖

Dusk found me in the passenger seat of Jeremy's same old beat-up white Honda, winding our way up toward the San Fernando Valley. Ordinarily, I would have run, but Jeremy could not keep up with me yet, and the long ride gave me a chance to deliver the lecture I had been unwittingly composing all afternoon.

The Logistics of Vampirism by Jennifer Carshaw:

"You have to hunt more often right at first. After your body adapts, it's only about once a month."

"When you're hungry, is it . . . normal? I mean, like, does your stomach growl or . . . ?"

"Not really." Blinding fog, cement in my lungs, the urge to dive into abandon — they were with me, forever with me. Only rhythm and regularity kept them down. "It's more urgent than that," I said, then changed the subject. "I try never to go to the same place twice. Definitely not within the same year."

"What kind of places?"

"Any kind. Bars are the easiest because people are looking to hook up, but it can be anywhere. Once I just walked up and knocked on someone's door."

"Someone you knew?"

"No. Never someone you know. Your name might come up in the investigation."

He nodded toward the GPS. "Where are we going?"

"A gay bar I found on Google. Otherwise, everyone will assume we're a couple and not approach. When you get there, you just sniff out the crowd until somebody catches your attention."

"You mean that literally, don't you?"

"Yes. You can salve your conscience and look for the scum of the earth, or you can find the most mouth-watering person in the room, or you can take the first one who smiles at you."

"What do you do?"

"I've tried them all."

"And?"

"It doesn't matter. They're all the same." I could not tell him what I really meant: that every one was so exquisitely different, so beautifully unique, no choice could ever be wrong. That every one brought me closer to the heaven I had glimpsed in that sacristy so long ago, and that every one fell short. Every taste of humanity reminded me how desperately I longed to be one of them; every life I took fueled my vengeance against the demon that had stolen mine.

"What do you do once you've picked someone?"

"You just smile and touch them and turn on the charm. They'll do whatever you want."

Jeremy swallowed, and I knew he was picturing the same proof of this that I was: a father and son sprawled helplessly across each other on a Persian rug.

"Where do you go once you have them?" He pulled into the parking lot outside our destination, and I opened the door.

I shrugged. "There's only one way to find out."

❖

Bars have a talent for making even light look dingy. Convenient as they might be, I hated hunting in places where otherwise sane people came to put their dignity on sale for the price of a martini. The smell of self-abasement always dampened my appetite.

As Jeremy and I searched for an empty table, I took in the crowd. The place had a definite Rainbow Coalition vibe, but this was the Valley, not West Hollywood. A handful of flamers were offset by businessmen fidgeting with their wedding rings while they flirted awkwardly over tequila. My nose drew me toward an exception, a woman whose gardenia perfume complemented perfectly her fragrance of high standards, but I set the thought of her aside as Jeremy spotted a table near the dance floor. The pulsing bass beat ensured we could shout at each other about murder and no one would notice.

I ordered two cosmopolitans from a waiter with a spandex shirt. Jeremy raised an eyebrow but waited until the waiter was gone to ask, "What'd you do that for?"

"You're more approachable with a drink in your hand. And this is a gay bar, so you need a cosmo. At a regular place, you would get a beer."

"And do what with it?"

"Pretend, or drink it, if you have to. It won't hurt you." I settled back as much as the chrome barstool would allow me to "settle" and once again surveyed the room. "So, what do you think?"

"I'm not the one who's hungry." He took a sip of his drink, then winced and wiped his tongue on his sleeve.

"Jeremy. Look at me."

He did, his gaze both fearful and defiant.

"You killed Carter and his dad, but you didn't choose them. I did. Every time I need to eat, I choose someone else's death above my own. That's what being a vampire is."

Jeremy shook his head, looking even greener than his sip of cosmopolitan could account for. "It's no good. I can't smell like you."

"I told you. It doesn't matter. They're all the same." I tried to smile, but I could not find the will. I knew what I was creating, the lesson I was failing to teach. A part of me wanted desperately to leave this hopeless place, to break down another sacristy door and allow Jeremy to experience the love that surpassed all loves.

But the love that flowed into the souls of men from whips, thorns, and nails was a libation we could never drink. To even know that it existed chewed at my mind like the jaws of Dante's Satan, a cold, mechanical torment from which I could never escape. If I never let Jeremy learn the truth, I could spare him from my affliction. If he never glimpsed true paradise, he could believe the lie of satisfaction told by the carnal rapture of the kill. I was unleashing a ruthless monster upon the world, a creature that would never share my longing for the life I had lost on the day I was born.

It was the only gift I knew how to give.

Jeremy looked at me, still refusing to take in the crowd. "Do you have to kill them?" he asked.

"A living victim can call the police."

"You're a sick bitch. You know that?"

"Yes, and you're the sick bastard who wanted to come along. Now, who in this room is going to die?"

He closed his eyes. When he looked at me again, the flint in his glare told me I had won. Victory should not smell so much like despair.

Jeremy scanned the room at last, his eyes flitting madly from one person to the next, never wanting to settle, but finally they stopped. He nodded toward the bar. "That guy with the rainbow tattoo."

I looked up at a shirtless man in his late thirties sporting a dyed-black pompadour and white hot pants with rhinestone-studded go-go boots. The tattoo ran vertically across his abdomen, pointing toward the pot of gold. He held a martini glass with his little finger outstretched, giving off an aroma of insecurity that did not surprise me; I had smelled it often among the brazen, gay and straight alike. What I did not expect were the analytical overtones, the keen, orderly mind I most often noted in accountants and engineers. Try as I might, I could not picture that pompadour sitting inside a cubicle at H&R Block.

Jeremy swirled his cosmo around the glass. "I know. You want me to go get him. But I don't have the charm."

"You don't need it. Talk to him about astrophysics."

"*That* guy?"

"Trust me. All you have to do is get him to this table. I promise I'll take over from there."

He stared at me with those russet eyes that knew the profound perversity of my being yet somehow still wanted to be with me, then he leaned in close to my ear. He could not whisper – the music would never allow it – but I could feel his warm, moist breath against my skin. "I'll get him for you. But someday, I'm going to want *you* in return."

A chill ran down my spine. What would happen when someday came and he realized there was nothing left of me to give?

He did exactly what I would have done. He leaned on the bar as if waiting to catch the bartender's eye, then waited for his victim to approach. I could see the subtle lines that creased Jeremy's forehead as he fought to control his revulsion, but Mr. Rainbow either did not notice or did not care. Soon he was circling Jeremy like a vulture in drag, and the businessmen put down their glasses to watch. I could not hear a single word, but

Rainbow's eyes got big and he actually licked his lips. A vein in Jeremy's neck began to throb, and I prayed he would not knock the guy out cold.

Then something changed. Rainbow's devil-may-care mask cracked, revealing the scholarly eyes that matched his scent. He said something, and Jeremy's revulsion melted into surprise. Suddenly he was racing back to me without the prey.

"I changed my mind."

"He's a scientist, isn't he?"

"He's the head of physics at UCSB."

I nodded. "But I don't think he's going to let you change your mind."

Mr. Rainbow was walking toward our table. Jeremy closed his eyes as I stood to shake Rainbow's hand. "Hi. I'm his sister."

"Luke Paulson. Nice to meet you." I cringed. Even after four years, I still never wanted to know their names.

Mr. Rainbow sat down. He looked even more ridiculous, wearing the demeanor of a professor with his hot pants. "I think I scared your brother. I just wanted to apologize."

"It's all right. He's kind of new at this."

He leaned toward Jeremy. "Listen, I came on too strong. I should have realized you'd just come out. I know how hard that is. If you're still interested, it's cool. If not, I understand."

Jeremy didn't look at him; he looked at me, his eyes swimming in the sea of moral tumult I knew all too well. "Well?" I asked. "Are you still in?"

He darted his eyes toward the professor, then nodded once at me. Mr. Rainbow smiled sweetly and put his hand on Jeremy's. Jeremy flinched away, but I touched our victim's arm and smiled. "It's all right. Everything is going to be okay."

Jeremy buried his head in his arms. I reached to comfort him, forgetting that I was super-charged with charm. I felt him relax beneath my touch, and something noxious filled the air.

Acceptance.

Jeremy took Mr. Rainbow's hand and led him toward the door.

5

I did not sleep that night, but Jeremy did. The taste that fell just short of ecstasy lingered on my tongue, warring against the labyrinthine guilt from which I would never escape. It loomed even darker and more twisted now, Helen's reflection mocking me from mirrored fun-house walls as I led a new monster down her path. Yet my protégé lay snoring softly on the sofa. He did not toss or turn the whole night long.

I did what I always did on nights when my conscience hung heavier than my eyelids; I thought about the future instead of the past. I sketched designs for the creature feature Amos had just signed, human-lizard hybrids that were *not* supposed to look like Godzilla. I updated my bank accounts to the Pasadena address. I shopped for curtains for a bedroom I had never even seen. And I thought about Conner.

I slumped in my chair beneath the weight of my hypocrisy. The more Jeremy followed exactly where I led, the more I wanted to run from him into Conner's open arms. The more I saw the truth in Jeremy, the more I ached for the illusion Conner could provide. I did not care that Conner was a pretentious Don Juan, that surely I had imagined the gorgeous flavor of his friendship. He still wanted more for me than *this*.

Jeremy finally roused around eight-thirty. He yawned and stretched and gave me a friendly little smile. "Hey. You're up."

"Yeah." I decided not to tell him I had not gone to sleep.

"So, how does this work? I mean . . . Do we talk about it?"

"Not unless you've got something you feel like you need to say."

He thought for a second, then replied, "Looks like good weather for the move."

"This is L.A. It's the only kind of weather we have." I went to the fridge and got out a steak. "You better go ahead and eat. Our help will be here soon."

That wiped the smile off his face. "Right." He stormed over and tore into the meat with his teeth, the knife and fork forgotten.

I sat by the window watching for a yellow Ferrari, half hoping it would not come. At 9:05 a.m., a black Lexus sedan drew to the curb. I thought my neighbors were having company until the door opened and out popped the face with the million-dollar smile. He was wearing beat up cargo shorts with a University of Alabama T-shirt that had been washed at least a hundred times. If it had not been for the Louis Vuitton sunglasses that cost about as much as I made in a month, he would have looked like someone I might reasonably expect to know.

Jeremy groaned. "He's an *Alabama* fan? Really?"

I shrugged. Maybe they would have something to talk about, after all.

I opened the door before Conner could knock. He rewarded me with the kind of hug I had dreamed about all my life, warm and friendly and without agenda. He was a good six inches taller than I was, so he kissed my hair instead of my face. "Good morning," he said, as if he had said it to me every morning of our lives.

My knees melted. It was a miracle I did not fall down.

He let me go and strode toward Jeremy with his hand outstretched. "Hey, look, I know we got off on the wrong foot the other day."

Jeremy's temples throbbed. "Yeah."

"Just to clear the air, did I do something to make you want to hit me? 'Cause I don't want to repeat it."

Jeremy wrinkled his nose as he took Conner's hand. "It's complicated, but we're cool."

"Good." Conner smiled, and my heart skipped a beat. He was real. He was beautiful and perfect and loving and *real.*

What was I going to do?

❖

"No way they're going to win the division this year. They lost four defensive starters."

"They drafted Allen at defensive end and that safety out of Nebraska."

"Yeah, but they're rookies. They'll get run over."

I rearranged boxes at the back of the U-Haul, listening with half an ear as my "brother" and the man who might be my boyfriend dissected the minutia of off-season football. I had already suffered through a full morning's debate about the fairness of the college playoff system. Now, they had mercifully moved on to the NFL. I was almost jealous, but every once in a while, Conner flashed the smile that made my skin tingle, and I knew he was doing what he needed to do, courting the person who still needed to be won. Jeremy never noticed they had slipped into a friendly beer-buddy chat, but I did, and the occasional wink from Conner informed me it had happened by design.

"Have you seen the reports from training camp? Allen's bulked up twenty pounds. No one's going to get past him."

"That still leaves three holes they gotta fill."

I finally butted in. "Excuse me, but could one of you leave the gridiron long enough to help me get the dresser?"

Jeremy glared — he knew I could lift it by myself — but Conner wiped his brow on his sleeve and said, "Sure." He turned back to Jeremy. "Thirteen and three, and they'll take the division. Mark my words."

Conner followed me down the loading ramp and back into the house. Somewhere along the way, his hand found its way into mine. I couldn't help myself. The second we made it through the door, I slammed it shut and pressed my lips against his. "Thank you," I breathed when we finally came up for air.

"Hey, I'll do this every day for a kiss like that."

I stared into his glowing azure eyes and wished with all my heart I would never have to see them cry. "You're amazing."

"Yes, I've heard that once or twice."

I wriggled out of his embrace. "You're also a jerk. Come on."

We got the dresser from my bedroom and loaded it onto the U-Haul. With a few last adjustments to the jigsaw puzzle of my possessions, we were ready to hit the road. An arm around my shoulders led me wordlessly toward the Lexus, and I realized Jeremy was already pulling away with the truck. It was forty minutes to Pasadena, and we were finally alone.

"So," said Conner as he opened a bottle of Mountain Dew, "I have to admit, I'm pretty mad at you for moving."

"Why?"

"Because I live ten minutes from here, and now I'm going to have to drive to Timbuktu all the time."

"Where do you live?" Only now did I realize I didn't know.

"Santa Monica, up near the pier. I was pretty psyched when you had me drive you home to Venice. And now here you go, traipsing off to Pasadena."

"A single guy with two cars? Doesn't seem like you would mind the drive."

"Four, actually. I've got a pickup for my fishing boat, and the Aston Martin just came in. I promised my friend George I'd let him take it for a spin tonight, but I can come pick you up afterward."

"An Aston Martin. Yeah, I don't want to hear another word about the drive."

He put his hand on my knee. "By the way, that test for *Blades of Sand* I did the other day? I got the part. So I guess we're going to be working together, too."

I sucked in a breath.

"What? That's a good thing, right?"

"Of course." *No.* Working together meant people would find out. Everyone from Amos to Tommy Lee Jones to the P.R. staff would know about us, and that meant the press might get word, too.

"You don't sound like you mean that."

"I do. It's just . . . I had been hoping this conversation could wait."

"We're back to this 'no one should get close to me' stuff, aren't we?"

"Yes."

"Okay." He cut across four lanes of traffic to make the next exit. Before I knew what was happening, we were parked at an In-N-Out Burger. "Talk to me. Whatever it is, I can help."

I had heard that invitation before. I pictured Mother Celeste lying lifeless in her casket, Mother Lily sobbing on TV, Sister Diane's face stone-pale with pain at the moment I confessed. "You can't. No one can."

"Bullshit. Now tell me what's wrong."

There was something magically un-nun-ish about that command. A whiff of arrogance filled the air, its very flagrance tantalizing. "There are people after me," I heard myself say.

"What kind of people?"

"The kind that if they find me, that's it. I'm done."

He knit his brow, studying me in the waning light of a smoggy afternoon.

"So you can see . . . I mean, you're *you,* and if I end up on the cover of a magazine or something . . ."

"You're dead serious, aren't you?"

"Yes."

"What happened? Is it like the mob, are you in witness protection?"

I didn't say anything. There was nothing I could possibly say.

He ran his fingers through his hair. "Wow. I gotta say, I was thinking more like you had an abusive dad you were afraid for me to meet. You really can't tell me, can you?"

"No. I'm sorry."

"What about Jeremy?"

"He's in almost as deep as I am."

"Stacy, Jesus, what are you doing, working on movies?"

"Think about it. What do I do?"

"Makeup." The lightbulb flashed on above his head. "Wait . . . you're not even *you,* are you?"

"I guess that depends on how you look at it. But you can go watch the behind-the-scenes stuff for the movies I've done. I'm never in the shot. I won't let Amos put my picture on his website. Everybody from the people I work with to Tommy Lee Jones has told me I should be acting, and I won't even go for a test. This is serious, Conner. You don't want me. I don't exist."

He cringed and put his head in his hands. "Wow. I . . . wow."

"If you could just drop me off at my new place." My throat started to swell with tears, but I held them in. *This is the right thing. I'm doing the right thing.*

"No. Stacy, I'm not leaving." He grabbed my hand, his eyes probing me as if they could unearth the rest of the tale. "Whoever these people are, they can't win. We're going to figure it out."

I could not stop the tears from falling anymore. "You're insane. You don't even know me."

"Maybe not, but I will." He pulled me tight against himself, and the weight of his kiss almost made me believe. I almost lost the vampire inside the humanity of his arms. I almost saw a future that held more than misery and fear.

Almost.

6

"We're on a mission from God."

Dan Aykroyd's deadpan delivery wrung a smile from my lips every time. Even if they hadn't been a couple of criminals raised by a nun, I still would have fallen in love with *The Blues Brothers*.

"Your laugh sounds rusty," Conner teased. "We might have to watch this a few more times."

"Jesus, could you keep it down?" Jeremy shouted from the other room. But he didn't close his door.

"Is it wrong that I think this is better than *Citizen Kane*?" I asked.

Conner had discovered that, despite my years in Hollywood, my cinematic education still contained some rather gaping holes. We could not go out without risking paparazzi cameras, so we had spent two weeks' worth of evenings watching Netflix together on the sofa at my new apartment, with Jeremy studying and griping in the other room.

Conner darted his eyes toward Jeremy's open bedroom, then stole a kiss from me. "Nobody really likes *Citizen Kane*. It's just uncouth to admit it."

"But not uncouth to admit loving a movie where a woman takes a machine gun to her ex-fiancé?"

"Right. You're learning."

"Would you two shut up? I've got a test in two days."

I resisted the urge to remind Jeremy that Caltech had plenty of libraries. I knew good and well why he was here instead of there; Conner was not likely to push the bounds of propriety very far with my "brother" in the next room. Part of me wanted to kick Jeremy for hanging around, but another part was grateful. It was easier to laugh at John Belushi when I did not have to ponder where that laughter might lead.

"So, tomorrow's the big day," Conner said as he slipped his arm around my shoulders.

"Yeah. It's going to be hard, pretending not to know you." We would begin principal photography for *Blades of Sand* tomorrow, in close proximity to each other and to plenty of prying eyes.

"I'm not going to ignore you. People would know something was wrong if I didn't flirt with a girl as pretty as you." I glared at him, but he was serious. "I get it about the secrecy, Stacy, but the most important part of acting is that it shouldn't look like acting."

I sighed. "So what am I supposed to do?"

"Whatever you would really do when some stuck-up, over-privileged little rich boy hits on you."

"You better be glad Jeremy never taught me how to box."

"I can hear you, you know."

Conner walked over and, very deliberately, closed Jeremy's door. He sank back onto the couch and whispered, "There's one more thing."

"What?"

"My place is a whole lot closer to the set than yours."

My spine tingled with a dizzying combination of excitement and fear. "Don't the paparazzi stake out your place?"

"I'm not new to this game, Stacy. I know how to make it safe."

His fingertips traced a tremor across my thigh. "It's not a game," I said, though all I wanted to say was, "Yes."

He took my hands. "Not *this*. This is . . . I don't have words for this. But that — out there, with the press — that will always be a game. I know how to play it. I need you to trust me."

I nodded while the heat of his ice-blue eyes melted the last semblance of my will.

"Tomorrow, after we're done shooting." He squeezed my hand. "Come over."

I swallowed. "Okay."

Jeremy threw open the door to his room. "Y'all done whispering sweet nothings yet? It's ten o'clock. You've both got work tomorrow."

❖

The next day was torture. We were on location in Redondo Beach, and the sun kept beating down so hard, I had to use three more coats of sunblock than usual, and still I could feel my skin just on the verge of charring. Tommy Lee Jones kept sweating through everything I put on his face, so I was constantly out on the set touching him up while Conner sat right next to me, waiting for the scene to resume. True to his word, Conner flashed his million-dollar smile full of cheap insinuations, but the best I could do was stammer and blush. It was awkward and stupid and Mr. Jones raised a curious eyebrow a couple of times, but thank God, at least *he* could act like a professional.

By the end of the shoot, I was starting to shiver as my temperature spiked. I had not eaten since my hunt with Jeremy, and after that much sun, I could not afford to put it off any longer. Yet the promise of tonight's rendezvous tempted me more than blood. For twenty hours now, I had thought of nothing else. A freight train of objections had barreled through my mind, only to crash and burn against the steel wall of a single truth.

I wanted him. I wanted everything Conner was that I could never be, the forthright, carefree demigod soaring happily toward the sun. I wanted to soak him up like a sponge, to forget where Jennifer ended because I knew where Conner began.

If only *Jennifer* could have loved him, no amount of good judgment would have stood in my way.

I let Amos walk me to my car with his arm around my waist, lilting congratulations in that musical Scottish brogue. "Stacy, you were fabulous! Using his sweat to make the lines on his forehead stand out — ach! You're going to put me out of business if you keep it up like that!"

"Thank you," I murmured toward the pavement.

He stopped and held me at arm's length. "You're mumbling. You just nailed your first day as a primary artist for a major star, and you're mumbling. Methinks I detect sour romance, Miss Celibate Stacy."

As always, I could smell the genuine concern that might have gone unnoticed if I could only see and hear the brash, red-headed troll. "It's not sour. Only complicated."

"Ach, so there is a lucky young man at last! And now, I know it's all hush-hush, but it wouldn't happen to be that you're still with Conner Brazel?"

I let my blush be my answer. "You can't tell anyone. Please, Amos. *No one.*"

"Never fear, your secret is safe with me. Although, I must say, if it was me, I'd be broadcasting that good luck to the world. I've never seen an ass quite as firm as his." He made a gesture that made me feel slightly ill, then without transition put his arm right back around my waist. "Now, what's the complication? We can't go having you ruin this before I get my vicarious thrills."

"I'm supposed to go to his place tonight."

His eyes twinkled. "Ah. I thought Mr. Brazel would have crossed that bridge before now. You must have him enchanted, to make him wait so long."

The same thought had occurred to me. "I know. I think it must mean that he's expecting long-term results."

"And is there a reason you don't want to commit to him?" Amos flicked off the bravado like a switch, putting on the persona of able mentor I loved in him so well.

"Yes."

"Which is?"

"I can't tell you. What's worse, I can't tell him."

"Then tell him that, and then see where it goes." He kissed my hair. "Great work today, my love. Don't forget, whatever happens, I need you here at six a.m." He opened the door and ushered me into my car, then walked away whistling a tune I did not know. That was probably for the best; I was sure it was Scottish and very lewd.

I backed out slowly, my lungs growing heavier with every breath. I had never been less in the mood for taking human life, but the sad fact was that if I did not eat, I could not go. The danger would be too great.

I was supposed to give Conner a half hour's head start so we would not be seen arriving together. I took the 405 freeway north, then veered off to my old stomping grounds in Venice Beach. I parked and set off toward the boardwalk, which had not been made of boards for many decades but nevertheless still bore the name. I sat down on one of the few swathes of grass and tried to let the beloved nonsense of the place soothe me. Storefronts filled with psychedelic bongs flanked beachfront stands full of tube socks; children slurped on snow cones while barbells clanged at Muscle Beach; Rastafarians peddled incense, and Skaters turned three-sixties in midair. Such a place belonged in a storybook, not on a prime stretch of California sand.

The shops were closing as the sun went down; the man with the unicycle who made a living charming rubber snakes was stashing them in their case. I watched as the last few sun-seekers packed up for the day. Three women in bikinis and flip-flops strolled by and I sniffed without enthusiasm. One smelled faintly of passion, the kind I knew I could charm and enflame until it made my mouth water with desire, but I let her pass. Hers was not the passion I wanted to know tonight.

I spent ten minutes just sitting, sniffing and trying to decide. With the minutes to my assignation ticking swiftly by, I finally closed my eyes, resolved that the next person I smelled would be my meal.

Out on the sand, a dog began to howl.

A thought occurred to me then as it never had before: animals had warm blood, too. Helen had taught me that no blood but a human's would suffice, and the scent of an animal had never tempted me to drink. But why should I take her word?

Like a bolt, I darted toward the sound, snatching the dog from its master's feet with the speed of a rapturing angel. It panted against me, slick with sweat, as I raced toward the alley beside my old duplex. I paused only to note that it was a black Lab, beautifully groomed and probably expensive. It whimpered once before I drank.

It had no soul.

Warmth and life coursed over my tongue, the taste of iron I knew so well, all the trappings of a meal, but these were merely the china on which my food was served. Nothing here could mimic the fulfillment of a single, irreplaceable human life. I pulled away from the poor beast and realized suddenly that my mouth was full of fur. I spat, then stroked his coat, cradling this victim as I had so many before. "I'm sorry, doggie. I had to try."

I ran the half-block to the ocean and tossed him into the tide. Then I shuffled back to the boardwalk — back to the hunt — swatting vainly at my tears.

7

I did not go to Conner's place that night. I could not face my demigod with the stench of murder heavy on my breath. I called with the excuse of a flat tire and promised I would make it up to him tomorrow, but the next day we shot scenes of Conner running on the beach. At three o'clock, he texted to postpone because he was dead tired. On the third day, we moved production to the Warner Brothers lot in Burbank, barely ten miles from Pasadena. We fell back into spending evenings at my apartment, with Jeremy our reluctant chaperone studying in the next room. By the time the weekend finally came and Conner insisted I must come visit him at last, his golden smile had banished all but the tiniest flicker of my conscience.

I could not talk him out of preparing dinner. I tried everything in my repertoire: food allergies, finicky eating habits, specialized doctor-ordered diet. He just said, "Come on, Stacy, you're from the South. You know you have to eat to call it a date. Now, what can I fix that you will actually deign to try?"

Supposedly, we would be having steak tartare, but I suspected there would be side dishes even more expensive and less palatable. He had at least promised not to use garlic. The most awkward part of our relationship thus far had been trying to kiss him after he had eaten pesto.

My hands were trembling that afternoon as I packed a change of clothes. Jeremy came and stood in my room to watch.

"You're really going through with it." His jealousy sprayed like mildew through the air.

I added my toothbrush to the bag and did not look at him.

"You do remember what happened the last time you tried to date a human, right?"

"I killed the boy I loved and vowed never to love again." Looking back, I could not decide which had been the greater crime.

"So you're clear about where this is going."

"It is going to end. But maybe . . ." I shook my head. "When I said I would never love again, I had never really tried. I had been *in* love, but I had never done anything to really show it." I sighed. "Just let me try. I have to prove to myself that it's worth it to try."

A hot cloud of confusion rippled from his body, making him shimmer like the mirage he would always be. He took a step toward me. "If it's worth it to try, then what?"

The heat of him made me dizzy, but I dared not let myself be drawn into that all-consuming flame. "If it's worth it to try, then I'll try. Past that, I don't really have a plan."

He sniffed. "Whatever. I've got a school thing to go to, anyway."

"On a Saturday night?"

"Yeah, well, vampires might not be nocturnal anymore, but astronomers always will be." He stuffed his hands into his pockets and scuffed away.

❖

Sunset tinged the clouds with caramel as I drove to Santa Monica, wrapped firmly in my naiveté as if it were a suit of mail. Conner's high-rise featured a real live guard who checked my ID and issued a parking tag. I took the stairs to the lobby, half-expecting to end up in a room that looked like something from Versailles. It turned out to be much more modern, but likely still required the wealth of the Bourbon dynasty to decorate. The Italian furniture looked custom-made, and the Jackson Pollack painting did not look like a reproduction.

No white-gloved operator greeted me inside the marble-tiled elevator to the stars, and I was glad. No one could hear my knees knock as I watched the little red numbers ascend. I tripped on my own feet as I stepped out at floor nineteen.

Conner caught me. With the grace of Fred Astaire, he swept me downward in a kiss, then grinned from ear to ear. "Hey," he said.

I stood and straightened my hair. "Hey."

He glimpsed the overnight bag on my shoulder, and a different kind of happiness lit his eyes, so full of sweetness, of simple school-boyish relief, I almost threw myself into his arms again right then and there. Instead, he took my hand and led me through the door. "So, this is it. What do you think?"

I took in the open floor plan of coordinated neutrals, the sculptured bronze fixtures, the color-block wool rug that just captured the gold undertones of the silk houndstooth curtains, and I smiled. I had seen Conner wear three hundred dollar jeans with a T-shirt from his high school drama club. No way had he put this together.

"I think it looks like you called a decorator, said 'elegant bachelor pad,' and wrote her a blank check."

He grinned. "It was a he. And the word was 'chic.'"

"Right. Why settle for elegant when you can afford chic?"

"Exactly."

I picked up a script from the coffee table. *"Pulse and Prejudice?* Are you going to play the vampire Mr. Darcy?"

"Maybe. But I heard Ben Barnes is up for it, too, so maybe not."

"That's good. Vampire or not, Mr. Darcy really shouldn't be from Alabama."

He punched me playfully. "Come on. Dinner's ready."

He pulled out a chair for me, and I watched as he spooned "dinner" onto our plates. The steak tartare was as promised, but my worst fears had come true. "The vegetables have a truffle sauce, and this is just caviar and crostini. You're not allergic to fish, are you?"

I wanted to say yes, but he had obviously worked hard, and I could not bear to quash his sunny pride. "It's fine. I've never had caviar before. Or truffles, either." Or anything else on that plate that was not steak, but honesty was best served in small portions.

He set the plates on the table. "You're going to love it."

I forced the corners of my lips upward and dug in. Even the steak had onions and capers and spices I did not trouble myself to identify, but I basked in the glow of Conner's joyful eyes and managed to choke it down. "It's glorious," I lied. "Who taught you how to cook?"

"Food Network. And, uh, this girl I dated. She was a chef." His blush was so cute, I forced myself to take another bite.

"Looks like she knew her stuff."

He studied me until I wondered if my face had betrayed my roiling taste buds. I worked harder at pretending to smile until he said, "Stacy, I just want you to know, that asshole who took you to Spago, he's gone now."

"I know." I put down my fork. "But God help me if I know why."

"You're why."

"But . . ."

He held up a hand. "I know we can't hide forever. If this is going to happen, then I'll probably have to quit acting, maybe work for my dad or something. The thing is, you're worth it."

I put down my fork. "Conner, I'm just some random girl you picked up on a movie set. That's all I can really ever be."

He brushed the tears from the corners of my eyes, and skimmed away the truth I spoke to see the truth that screamed inside me, ravening for so much more. He took a breath that seemed to fill his every pore. "Two years ago, I went home to

Birmingham for Christmas. That was right after *Shelly's Cradle* came out, when it was getting all the Oscar buzz and people first started calling me a 'star.' There was this video of me on the Internet that went viral. I guess you didn't see it?"

"No."

He sighed. "Fine. There was a whole row of naked girls, and I was doing shots off their boobs." He closed his eyes. "Anyway, my grandmother, who's on the board at church, reads the Bible every night, she saw it, and after Christmas dinner she pulled me out into Grandpa's tool shed and went off. I mostly tuned her out because I was a cocky little prick, but right at the end, she said, 'The worst part is, someday the right girl is going to come along, and she's going to look you in the eye and tell you to go to hell. And then it's going to be too late.'" He swallowed as he twined his fingers through mine. "Every day, I thank God that she was only almost right."

A flood of passion swept me past the shores of my excuses, my arms a riptide pulling him into my heart. His buoyant hands lapped against the currents of my body, and waves of surrender washed us toward the island of his bed. He met my gaze and drowned me in the ocean of his eyes. "Stacy, I love you."

"I . . ."

I love you, too. Words of sand collapsed inside my mouth, though never had they been more true. I loved him more than I wanted to draw my next breath, but this girl in his arms pulsing with desire, this girl for whom he would sacrifice his whole career – she was not *Stacy*. This magic consummation was a fraud.

I had finally found a lie I could not tell.

"Conner, I love you. I want this. But I can't."

His brow creased, and I loved him more with every breath because it was not disappointment that filled the air. It was concern. "What's wrong?"

I fished for a lie, but I could only find the truth. "I spent four years in a convent. I think some of it must have rubbed off."

"A *convent?* Jesus, Stace, don't you have any normal stories?"

"No. I can pretty much guarantee you that."

He exhaled, then put a warm hand on my knee. "Okay, have at it. Tell me all about what it's like to be a nun."

We talked the rest of the night away. I told him about the sisters and the mother who had abandoned me, about going to school with Jeremy only to learn we were "related" at age sixteen. He told me about his father's Toyota dealership, how he had been bitten by the acting bug shooting a commercial for the annual summer sale, how his mother had moved heaven and earth to get him his first paying gig. We reviewed my one-week cross-country career and the myriad ways his sixth grade soccer team had lost. He played jazz for me on a stunning cherry wood baby grand; I made him listen to Shostakovich on my phone. When at last our eyelids began to flutter and no amount of magic could stave off the call of fatigue, I put on my pajamas, and he tucked me into his eight hundred thread count Egyptian sateen sheets.

"Stacy, thank you."

"Conner, my name isn't Stacy."

"That's okay. Mine's not Conner, either."

I started. "It's a stage name?"

"Yep. Clarence Brazelman, at your service. But I think I like Conner and Stacy."

Those blue eyes took me in, and this time it was really me, every single part of me except that one fateful word. That word seemed misty and distant now, a nightmare from which I might finally awake. "I think I like Conner and Stacy, too."

He wrapped me close in the warm blanket of his arms and held me safe until the dawn.

❖

I woke up the next morning with a pimple on my chin.

I thought at first it must be something on the bathroom mirror, a red smudge of fierce illusion, but I scrubbed the glass and it did not go away. It was real, a white-capped symbol of puberty, fresh and bright on my skin.

I had changed.

I sank down onto the side of the tub and laid my spinning head in my hands. This was not possible. Helen Carshaw had decreed it. Immortal vampires did not age; we did not grow; we did not have periods or catch colds or do anything to acknowledge that life was in any way fluid. Helen had sworn it could not happen.

Helen Carshaw had been wrong.

I wandered back to the bedroom in a daze, barely able to absorb Conner's loving smile as he gazed at me from the pillows. "Hey," he said, "is something wrong?"

How could I explain the cosmic significance of a single tiny blemish? How could I name the hope it stood for, unless I crushed it with the same breath?

"Stacy, are you sick?"

"I have to talk to Jeremy." Mechanically, I put on my jeans.

"Stace, you're scaring me. What's wrong?"

"I can't tell you." His blue eyes narrowed. I kissed him with all the words I could not say. "I hope you understand how much I wish I could."

He squeezed my hand. "Call me. Soon."

"I will."

All the way to Pasadena, my mind raced even faster than my car. What could have caused this? I had drunk animal blood and eaten human food. Could it be food poisoning? Both of those meals had made my stomach churn, but I did not feel sick now. *I had changed.* If I could do it once, I could do it every day, from now until at last I *died.*

"Jeremy!" I burst through the door. "Jeremy, I need to talk to you!"

His scent reached me before I saw him, drenching me with its power. He wore a smile almost as grand, adorning a face chiseled to new heights of perfection. Green fire flecked his russet eyes with an ecstasy I remembered all too well. "Oh, God." The heat rippling from his body had been no mirage.

I was not the only one who had changed.

He touched my hair and my whole body thrilled, some metaphysical electricity flowing between our skins. "You should have told me." His ruby lips brushed my ear as his seraphic voice coursed through my bones. "You never told me how perfect it would be."

"Jeremy . . ."

"Shh. I've waited for this long enough." He laid his lips on mine, and his gravity engulfed me, the inescapable belonging I could swim against no more.

"You should've had ten more months," I whispered, mere words into a solar wind.

"Time doesn't matter. It never did." The primal sameness of him branded me, a spell that burned us as it bound. "I don't care what you did last night. You know as well as I do, eternity has no future unless we share it. And I will love you *because* you are a vampire, not in spite of it."

Conviction rippled from his body, the glamour of the dream, the intoxicating scent of fate, of everlasting bliss – but it was not love. It was close, so close, tinged with such rosy sweetness that it taunted my nose as I searched beneath it, aching to uncover what I knew he really meant to give. *It can grow, Jennifer. You can build it, the two of you together. It will be real someday.* His iron lips sought my neck, my chest, roving with the fury of vindication until they found my chin.

I pulled away. "Jeremy, stop. Look at this."

He squinted. "Is that a pimple?"

"Yes. I changed."

He staggered back. "What happened?"

"I don't know. But everything you're saying, everything you're feeling, it's only because Helen told us there was no other way. She was wrong."

"You think we're free and clear because of a zit?"

"No, but if we can figure out why it happened, maybe we can age, go longer between kills, I don't know. We can do *something*."

The green-gold brilliance in his eyes grew black. "You still don't get it, do you?"

"Don't you want a normal life?"

"What life, Jen? Why would you want to be mortal if you don't have a soul?"

My mouth fell open and my thoughts flew backward into a world that only my mind's eye had ever seen.

Mother Celeste brushed the wrinkles from my soul and hung it just above me, dangling it like laundry from Gabriel's bright horn. It hung there, taunting, just above my reach . . .

Jeremy stood above me, brandishing a grin. "Jen, it's time to wake up now," he said.

I gaped at him in the flesh as a tear ran unchecked down his chiseled cheek. I had thought I was meant to be Jeremy's guide on this journey toward devastation. In truth, he was mine. Helen had left him with me as a part of herself, a guarantee that I would not turn from her ways. "*Jen, it's time to wake up now.*" Even before I had known what he was, my subconscious had followed. But was he waking me from the hopeless phantom of a dream, or was he standing between me and my soul?

He held my gaze, and pain surrounded us, the suffocating agony that no amount of blood would ever cure. This was the true future we held for each other: nothing but the empty ache of wondering what might have been.

I wiped his only tear as it dripped. "If Helen was right, then so are you. Nothing matters, and the best we can hope for is each other." I put his finger on my chin. "But Helen was wrong."

I turned my back and left him there, alone with the world turned upside down. He could not help me now. "*Wake up, Jen,*" but now I knew my future lay inside the dream. I did not know where I would go, what barriers of time or space I would need to bend, but I knew at last what I had to do. I would climb up out of that coffin and take back my soul.

8

Bless me, Father, for I have sinned. To date, I have killed sixty-three people because I am a vampire.

Oh, to see the look on the priest's face – any priest – as he listened to that confession! Like every good Catholic school student, I knew where lost souls were supposed to go. The first step toward recovery was to admit weakness, the second to invite a Higher Power to help; Alcoholics Anonymous had stolen its formula for healing from the Catholic Church. But confession was rather problematic in my case. For one, it would be hard to find a priest willing to give me absolution instead of a prescription for psychotherapy. For another, confessing would require setting foot inside a church, where the scent of the Blood of Christ would force me to extend my death toll. Irony mocked me until I had to laugh.

I had been driving aimlessly for an hour, pondering how to begin my pilgrimage. Should I try a church that was not Catholic? Journey to some far-off holy shrine? Look for other vampires who had been down this path before? None of those ideas seemed quite right, but then again, who knew? I had no map for this quest, not even a compass to point the way. Only a zit and a dream.

You're insane, Jennifer. It's just a stupid pimple. Turn around and go home to Jeremy. I might have done it if my phone had not rung.

"Hello?"

"So, Celibate Stacy! Do we need to change your nickname yet?"

"Hello, Amos. This isn't really a good time."

"It's a simple yes or no question."

"Short answer, no. Now, if that's the only reason you called . . ."

"All right, if you're in so much of a hurry, we changed the call time for tomorrow. I need you there at seven."

"Okay."

"Stacy, I expect some *progress* between now and then. For God's sake, what are you waiting for, an engraved invitation?"

"Goodbye, Amos. I'll see you in the morning."

I hung up and sighed. How was it possible the universe had been upended, yet my everyday life remained intact? Here I had embarked upon one of the greatest crusades ever undertaken, and I was still supposed to show up tomorrow and put paint on a grown man's face for money. The Fates must be falling over in hysterics.

As I traveled east, the urban sprawl of Greater Los Angeles slowly gave way to a drier landscape. *The desert* . . . that quintessential symbol of spiritual transition lay just miles ahead. Maybe I needed to take a walk. I drove as far as Palm Springs, then left my car at a gas station and ran east across the unknown until civilization disappeared. I sat down, alone with the horizon and the big, blue, open sky.

The expanse of nothingness taunted my senses, a vision of forever as false as the one Helen Carshaw had foretold. She had buried me inside an illusion of barrenness and brown, but now, at last, I saw beyond the limits of my beguiled eyes. A continent lay past that far-off dip of sand, an ocean beyond that, a world of mountains and rainforests and glaciers. The vastness of this sterile hell existed only in my mind.

Get up. Go find the end. My legs uncurled beneath me, leading me toward whatever lay beyond earth's curve. I absorbed every lizard, every cactus, every rock, wondering what temptation the devil had prepared. The Joshua trees flared like crooked crosses, talismans of God's country sent to ward away the damned. I turned toward a hawk's discordant cry, half expecting to behold winged Lucifer smiling down. The hawk merely circled and flew on.

I slogged forward despite the charring ache in every pore as the desert sun devoured the film of lotion that alone preserved me from daylight's scarring rays. The warmth, the sun, the Light of Life still sought to bar the darkness from their realm. *Get out of here, Jen. If you burn, you'll have to kill someone to heal.* Yet why had I come, if not to suffer and be tried?

The trial I had already endured wafted around me at every step, Jeremy's inebriating odor still clinging to my clothes. The power of his eyes, the savage ecstasy of his lips — how had I found the strength to leave? How could I turn my back on the man who had stood by me when even the nuns could not bear my sins? *Do this for him. Go find his salvation, too.*

The desert sizzled with audacity. I reached to touch my chin, the sacred blemish that gave lie to everything I had ever known. *Be methodical, Jen. What could have happened last night to make you change?* I had eaten dinner with Conner; a possible culprit. I had turned down the chance to sleep with him; hardly the first time I had told a man no, so file that under "unlikely." Then we had talked and shared and loved.

My head swam as the air shimmered and a word flashed through my mind, a word I had rejected as the dream of fools. A word that stung like needles of fire.

Soulmate.

But that gorgeous, taunting word — what did it mean? My soul had existed once, in that one brief moment of my infant life before Helen stole it away. Where was it now? Could Conner's soul draw mine back from the abyss because the two were halves of the same whole? Had we been born for each other, drawn together by some star-crossed cosmic gravity physics could not explain? Or was it choice that bound us, action that notched and grooved our lives into keys that unlocked each other? I did not know, but I also did not care. I could not fight the cosmos, and I was finally ready to take action.

I raced like lightning back to my car, lamenting the need for this slothful machine as my RPM needle jolted into the red. *This really won't help Jeremy,* I told myself. But it would if he could find his soulmate, too. *Don't get your hopes up. It's only a hypothesis.* No matter how loudly logic screamed, it could not drown the peal of wedding bells, the happy wail of newborn Brazels. *Stop. You know what happened the last time you let yourself dream those kinds of dreams.* But that love had never had what this one did: a prayer.

The miles to Santa Monica slipped away, my body wrenched with longing so profound, I could barely drive. At last I dipped my headlights into the garage and lowered my window to address the guard. "Stacy Higginbotham. I'm here to see Conner Brazel."

Recognition flickered and he set his jaw. "He's not expecting you right now."

Damn Conner for his philandering. This guy probably had standing instructions never to admit the same woman twice. I put on my most brilliant vampire smile and brushed my fingers against his hand. "It's okay. I'll be a welcome surprise."

With glassy eyes, he issued a pass. I parked and scaled nineteen flights of stairs without even pausing to breathe. "Conner! I'm sorry for barging in, I just . . ."

The flash of a camera bulb stopped me dead.

Conner sat posed on the sofa, arms open in a gesture that invited the world to take a load off, have a drink. Hoards of people packed the room: hair stylist, makeup artist, wardrobe assistant, photographer, and a reporter with the eyes of a lion on the prowl.

"Stacy!" Conner stood, his gentlemanly smile drooping into fear. "Marissa, this is Stacy, my . . . cousin. Stace, is everything okay?"

"It's . . . I . . . yeah, I'll just come back when you're done."

"No, no, please, stay, come in! We're doing a get-to-know-you piece. Who better to help us than his cousin?" The lioness padded toward me, claws outstretched. "Marissa Pritchard, *Entertainment Weekly*. So, Stacy, which side of the family are you from?"

I locked eyes with Conner, panic abruptly freezing my faculties of speech. He pasted his smile back in place and saved me from an answer. "My father's, but Stacy is a very private person. If you'll excuse us just a moment." He steered me outside and closed the door.

"Why didn't you tell me you had this scheduled?"

"You left before I had the chance. How the hell did you get up here? I specifically told the guard not to let you in!"

"He tried. I just thought . . ."

"Never mind, it's too late now." He ran his hands through his carefully sculpted photo shoot hair, then took a measured breath and met my eye. "Is everything okay?"

"I can't be in that article, Conner, if anyone saw . . ."

He held me to his chest. "Hey. It's okay. They're not paparazzi. If I tell them you don't exist, you don't exist." He lifted my chin. "Do you believe me?"

He wrapped me in the safety of his poignant eyes — so deep, so wide, so much more infinite than any stretch of desert sand. I swallowed and whispered, "Yes."

"Good. Now, is everything else all right?"

"I had a falling out with Jeremy. I can't go home."

He squeezed me tighter. "We'll figure it out. I'll do the interview, and then we'll figure it out. It's going to be fine."

I filled myself with the glory of his embrace, and with every breath my pounding heart slowed down. He was right. He was my soulmate. Everything was going to be fine.

9

He filled the world with so much magic, I wanted to start wearing glass slippers.

Conner's realtor found me a new apartment within a day, a cute little place overlooking a garden of bougainvillea less than ten minutes from Conner's high-rise. It was an amazing find, especially on my makeup artist's budget. An open-concept living room flowed seamlessly around a stainless steel island into the kitchen. Both were freshly remodeled, finished in an old-Hollywood art deco style that included a black-and-white checkered tile floor and a refurbished period gas stove.

I did not even have to face Jeremy to go back and get my things. Unbeknownst to me, Conner sent movers while I was at work. I showed up at my new home the day after I signed the papers to find all my worldly possessions not only delivered, but unpacked.

Conner gave up flirting with me on the set, so I was able to spend my days placidly absorbing his genius at his craft and my evenings basking in his golden smile. We pushed all his furniture against the walls so he could teach me how to tango; I took him to the cleaners in *Monopoly*, but the next day he kicked my butt in *Risk;* he screamed himself hoarse at a football game on TV while I plugged my ears and polished my nails. I even let him introduce me to something called "churrasco," which turned out to be nothing but over-cooked meat.

Three weeks had passed since the morning I woke up with a pimple – it had been a week longer since my last meal – but despite my magical life, my skin had smoothed itself back into hellish perfection. Once again, the familiar cement of my doom had crept back into my lungs. I sat on Conner's sofa and dipped my churrasco into the foul sludge of sauce, then chased the putrid Brazilian spices with a glass of water. *This is food. I am changing.* But my stomach clenched around the meat as it would around a vacuum, longing to be filled. What greater weapon did our fairy tale require to slay the vicious dragon at last?

"So," said my soulmate as he sipped a glass of wine, "George called today. He and Karina are borrowing a house in Malibu to go surfing this weekend. He wanted to know if you and I would join them."

"Conner, you know we can't . . ."

A burst of anger slathered its aroma across the stench of charred beef. "I'm not talking about some big industry party. It's my best friend and his girlfriend."

"I know, and I know you trust them. But . . ."

"This is not about trusting *them*, Stacy. It's about trusting me." He reached under a stack of mail and tossed me a brand new issue of *Entertainment Weekly*. "Read it."

With trembling palms, I flipped to the centerfold, where Conner smiled with put-on pretty-boy charm. My throbbing eyes skimmed the article, but nowhere did any mention of an intruding cousin appear. "I know how to play the game, Stacy. But that celebrity shit is not the only thing I have in my life besides you. If you can't trust me enough to be part of it, then . . ."

My heart fluttered against my solidifying lungs. "Okay." I still did not know what it meant to be a soulmate, what action of the cosmos or mine – or Conner's – could save me. But he was the only hope I had.

Conner took my hands. "Stacy, you're trembling." He screwed his eyes shut. "I didn't mean that to be an ultimatum. I love you . . ."

They were the only words that could have silenced my screaming paranoia. *Let him in, Jennifer. He cannot change you if you do not want to change.* I took a deep breath and said, "No. You're right. I'll do whatever it takes to make this work."

He kissed my cheek, and the subtle pulse under the flesh of his lips cried out to me, the flavor of my dark hunger. "Don't worry," he whispered. "So will I."

❖

By Saturday morning, I could barely take a breath without wanting to plunge my teeth into the nearest human throat. *Let him in,* became my mantra as I slouched into the Aston Martin's black leather seat and Conner turned up Duke Ellington. We pulled onto the Pacific Coast Highway, and I watched the blue waves dying and rising under the swell of Duke's piano, fleeting happiness dancing to the drone of eternity. Which tune was it that I sought out in the rays of beachy sun? I looked up at Conner's profile, and my famished heart longed, as always, to swallow him whole. He had to be the answer. What power but love could ever silence the screeching demons of my sin?

I took slow breaths in time with the waves until Conner pulled into the driveway of a beach-front home far smaller than I had expected. Karina stepped outside, a stunning, six-foot-tall woman from Barbados who worked as a personal assistant to a studio executive. The beach house belonged to her boss.

"Conner Brazel, did you get *another* car? Didn't anyone ever teach you the word 'invest'?"

He stroked the Aston Martin's hood as he got out. "It is an investment. In my ego."

"Stacy, I don't know how you can possibly put up with this guy, but I'm glad to meet you." She wrapped me in a hug. "Come on in. George is making Bloody Marys in the kitchen." I followed her inside, this smiling, laissez-faire Island girl who smelled of contentment. I hoped she was an omen.

George greeted us with a drink in each hand, a swarthy little imp with tousled black ringlets and wire-rimmed glasses. "Stacy! The woman who tamed the lion. It's an honor." He thrust a glass into my hand.

"What exactly has Conner been telling you?"

"Not enough, that's for sure. I've been begging this guy for years to date someone for more than two seconds so we could have a proper double, and here I had to borrow a beach house just to meet you. Cheers, man." He raised his remaining glass toward Conner. "Welcome to the joy of the ball and chain."

Conner laced his arm around my waist, neatly extracting the drink from my hand. "You were right, what can I say? I just had to wait for the right one." He sniffed the air while I tingled at his words. "Latkes! Man, you should have said you were cooking. I would have driven faster."

"That's why I didn't tell you. I've seen you drive."

We ate breakfast on the back porch, surrounded by fresh sea air and the fragrance of friends. I nibbled a few bites and managed not to grimace. Conner scarfed down stacks of potato pancakes while George, who had made quite a mark directing films for the festival circuit, regaled us with tales from his latest picture.

"So we go out to this stage that's got a giant tank for underwater scenes, and I've asked the animal guy to bring an octopus, like, two or three feet long, and we're going to put it next to models, use a long lens, all that, to make it look like a monster. So I get there, and the animal guy has this huge octopus taller than I am, and the actor has to actually go in the tank with this thing. The guy swears up and down that it's fine, it's a trained octopus and all he has to do is whistle, and I don't have the budget to rent this place for a second day, so we go ahead and shoot."

Karina gave him a dubious squint. "A trained octopus?"

"Yeah. I should've known. Anyway, long story short, I ended up diving in and prying tentacles off my star."

I motioned toward the surfboards on the deck. "Well, at least if we run into any octopuses out there, we know we're in good hands."

"Damn straight. You're eating breakfast with a regular superhero."

"Only if you got the shot," Conner said.

George grinned. "I'll win an Oscar for it if they don't throw me out of the guild."

❖

We waited until afternoon on this crisp October Saturday to give surfing a try. As I sat on the deck using SPF 50 to coat every inch of exposed skin before sliding in to my wetsuit, Conner came and sat beside me. "So," he said, "I need you to promise me something."

"What's wrong?"

"I just want to make sure you're still going to love me after you find out I'm a spaz." His sapphire eyes twinkled, but hints of real fear laced the air.

"Are you telling me you don't know how to surf?"

"I'm telling you, it's pointless even to try. I *will* try, but it's pointless."

I kissed him, though I had to pull away to keep from lapping up the fear. "Don't worry. I'm sure I'll be terrible, too."

As I should have expected, my prophecy proved false and Conner's true. We paddled out and watched Karina, who had practically been born with a board attached to her feet, and soon I was putting super-human reflexes to good use, taming the ocean. But poor Conner was hopeless. I had never dreamed that a man with so much grace, with a body honed to god-like perfection, could be so impossibly clumsy. Thank God he was a strong swimmer, as wave after wave toppled him into the depths. He kept getting up, letting George and Karina coach him, trying and trying, again and again, until I wanted to drag him back to the beach, set him right way up, and kiss him until the ocean ceased to roar. He stuck it out for more than an hour, until the rest of us were ready to go in.

Back on dry land, he gave me a good-hearted sneer. "Liar."

"Sorry. I didn't mean to be." I kissed his salty hair. "Go take the first shower. You earned it."

Conner wandered inside, stretching sore muscles as he walked. I got out of my wetsuit, then settled back down on the deck with his friends. George handed me a bottle of water as we watched the sun go down.

"So, Stacy, I was serious when I said Conner hadn't told us enough. I think you guys had been together a month before he told me about you. Which is strange, 'cause let me tell you, I've never seen that guy so smitten."

I blushed. "It's my fault. I'm not really into the whole celebrity thing. I asked him to keep me under the radar."

"I get that," Karina agreed. "George is lucky if I even go to his premieres."

"Yeah. It's actually kind of important in my case. I'd appreciate if y'all wouldn't mention me to anybody."

"Y'all?" George cocked one eyebrow so high it got hidden in his curls.

"Yes. I'm a Southerner. I'm entitled to say 'y'all.'"

George laughed and kissed my cheek. "Conner's lucky I've got Karina." He put his arms around her, and she snuggled her face into his chest. "You're doing good things for him, Stacy. Keep it up."

"Believe me, I intend to try." Try. And eat latkes. And deny. Yet the scent of sweat and serenity still made my body yearn. "If *y'all* don't mind, I think I'd like to take a walk on the beach."

"It's getting dark."

"It's fine. I'll take my phone, just in case."

I pondered the silent squish of the sand between my toes, hating myself more with every step. Like every other happy day I had ever known, this one was just one more lie. But why? I was becoming part of my soulmate's life, surrendering to his influence, trying to open myself to let him light the way back to the soul I'd lost. Yet here I was, still soulless, in the dark, tormented by a corrupt thirst that would sustain me, incorruptible. What was I missing?

My thoughts wandered back to my dream, to a soul that dangled out of reach, a soul that I could see but never lift my hands to touch. A soul I could not claim because death had first claimed me. The casket lay open, but inside it, my eyes were always closed. *Open them, Jennifer. You're missing something.* The line of victims brought color, renewal, the promise of life, but only Mother Celeste brought my soul. Mother Celeste, who poured out herself because she loved me, not because I had pierced her veins and sucked her dry. Maybe that was the kind of love I truly needed. Maybe someone had to *let* me drink her soul.

That's just great, Jen. Good luck finding a martyr in Malibu.

Still, what choice did I have? I searched the Internet from my phone, and soon my feet knew the way to the next great Faustian battle.

10

The stucco facade of Ocean View Hospice Care glowered over its yellow awning, condemning me for the mere thought of what I was about to do. I told myself this was an improvement over my usual hunting grounds. I could bring mercy to these suffering spirits instead of mowing them down in the flower of their youth. My hale and healthy victims did not stand a fighting chance no matter how physically able. Here, at least I might only rob someone of days, not decades.

All true. But still my heart recoiled as I found an open window and climbed through.

"Gavin? Is that you?" An ancient voice creaked from the bed, eyelids fluttering blindly in the darkness. I sniffed, but this one still had the will to live.

I brushed her hand. "It's only a dream. Sleep well." She sighed softly and began to snore.

I crept down the hall, following my nose through Demerol and disinfectant, searching for hopelessness and pain. I smelled them in abundance, but many of their owners were not conscious. I needed someone still capable of free will.

The sound drifted to me, so soft and familiar, I thought at first it was only a memory. I closed my eyes and let it flow through

313

me, the simple, subtle repetition I had heard every night whispered through convent walls. "Hail Mary, full of grace, the Lord is with thee. Blessed art thou amongst women, and blessed is the fruit of thy womb, Jesus." The tranquil clicking of the beads. The floral perfume of hope.

I found the woman lying in her bed, the crucifix of her rosary tapping the metal bedframe to the rhythm of her trembling hands. "Holy Mary, Mother of God . . ."

"Pray for us sinners, now and at the hour of our death. Amen."

My voice froze her in place. I knelt beside her to spare her the effort of looking up. "You're not the usual girl," she said.

"No. Do you mind if I pray with you?"

"Please." With aching slowness, she shifted the rosary into my hands. "You lead."

The woman placed my fingers on the bead where she had left off, only the eighth of fifty. I thought about Conner and George and Karina waiting for me at the beach. I did not have time to dawdle over dozens of prayers that would only fall on deaf ears.

"Nice and loud," the woman said.

"Hail Mary, full of grace," I began.

Together, we recited the jargon of faith, and with every halting breath, I tried to get up and go. I had come here to find a vanquished spirit aching for reprieve, but this woman trusted in her future, already brimming with the joy it would bring. As I watched her tired lips march resolutely through her prayers, I longed to trade the font of my eternal, rancid youth for the last fragile misery of her peace.

When at last in unison we made the sign of the cross, the woman looked at me and, with a word, opened the door. "Young lady, that was exactly what I needed tonight. Now, what can I do for you?"

"I'm sorry. I came here because I need your blood."

She narrowed the wrinkles around her eyes. "What is it, some kind of transfusion?"

"In a way. It will save . . . It will keep me alive. But if you do it, you will die."

"And I'm the right type, or whatever they call it?"

I bit my lip. "You're perfect."

"All right." No hesitation. Not even a tear. "I don't have much time left, anyway. Are there papers I need to sign?"

"No. You just gave me everything I need." I charmed her until I was sure she would feel no pain. Then she filled me and went home.

❖

I walked the last hundred yards back to the beach house. The woman's gift had left me drunk with beauty, but the blood! The taint of narcotics consumed me with the sour stench of death. I did not know whether it was the grandeur or the poison that made me stumble weakly on the sand.

I could just make out Conner walking toward me in the light of the rising moon. "There you are! I was about to call you. Come on in, dinner's ready."

I stirred the food politely on my plate and laughed at the right junctures of conversation, but George's superbly crafted pasta seemed a pale substitute for a martyr's soul, and I seemed a pale substitute for a friend. I took my leave as early as propriety would allow, wanting nothing but the healing balm of sleep and the solitude of my own mind.

Unfortunately, solitude was not on the agenda for tonight. The beach house only had two beds.

"Oh, God, I'm never doing that again. I didn't even think I *had* muscles in my toes." Conner groaned as he eased himself into his pajamas. "Ow, ow, ow, ow, ow. You're in love with a crybaby, Stace. Please tell me you're as sore as I am."

I flexed my calves with a grimace. For the first time since my sixteenth birthday, a tug of pain pulled back. "Ouch! I am."

He pulled me down and flopped his head onto my shoulder. "Thank God. I was starting to think you were too perfect to be real."

I stroked his golden hair, pondering my tender muscles. Had the woman's gift changed me, after all? I had never dreamed salvation would leave an aftertaste of morphine.

"Stacy?" Conner's husky voice drew me back from reverie. "I don't mean to pressure you, but I was wondering if that convent training might have an expiration date."

I stretched my back, the unfamiliar ache permeating my cells until I almost wanted to find out what aspirin would do, but beneath the soreness coursed a tentative elation. My body had changed again. "Maybe. If things keep going the way I hope they're going, then maybe."

"Where do you hope things are going?" His warm breath caressed my ear.

"I've been working on a resolution to my . . . problems."

"Oh." He sat up.

I gave him as much of a smile as I could manage through the pain in my bones. "Did you think I was waiting for a ring?"

"I should have known you wouldn't be that predictable."

"You weren't . . . Conner, you didn't bring me here to . . . ?"

"Of course not. It's been, what, two months? How would I explain that to my parents?" His eyes looked more nervous than they should, but I could not smell any lies. I could not smell anything but his aftershave.

He lifted his legs gingerly onto the bed. "Ow. Stacy, I just want you to know, your problems are my problems, too. Whenever you're ready to let me, I can help."

"You're already helping. More than you know." I reached to take his hand, but a wave of nausea wracked me. I staggered off the bed.

"Stace? Are you okay?"

"I think I'm going to be sick." I barely made it to the toilet before my mouth opened and the contents of my stomach poured forth into the bowl. Conner wrapped his arms around me as I slipped on the tile, saving my head from a collision with the floor.

"Holy shit, that's blood! Hang on, I'm going to get help. George!"

He set me gently on the floor. As the world went black, I thought that death had come to claim its faithful slave.

❀

"Watch this one carefully now, Jennifer. You don't want to make this mistake." My seven-year-old mind could barely absorb my mother's scornful tone, already too embroiled in the nightmare of her words. *Vampire*, she had called me, equating me with the fanged menagerie of revenants now parading across our TV. "Pay attention," she repeated, and I tore my too-wide eyes away from the majestic face where solace could never abide.

A woman in a torn Victorian bodice threw herself into the arms of a sultry, black-caped man. They kissed as if their lives depended on each other's lips, and then his sharp teeth pierced her throat. She gasped and let her eyes roll back, moaning softly with every swallow. The seven-year-old on the sofa could only imagine her pain.

"That is what Western culture has made of us," my mother scoffed. "Romantic demons, sexual gods. Don't be fooled by it, Jennifer. Don't ever drink the blood of any idiot who volunteers."

Death did not last very long. I awoke still lying on the bathroom floor, my head cradled in Conner's lap while Karina sponged my forehead. "Stacy, can you hear me?" Conner asked. "Nod if you're with us, Stace."

I nodded, the subtle movement sending knives through my brain.

"It's okay. George is getting an ambulance."

"No. I just need rest."

"Stacy, you're vomiting blood. You need a hospital. It's okay, I'll be with you."

"I can't . . . " I gasped for breath, still suffocating inside the memory I had not thought about in thirteen years. Helen had taught me so many terrible secrets that day, I had forgotten that one axiom until it was too late. From the heroine with her shredded bodice to Kamikaze warriors to Jesus Christ, Helen Carshaw would have scoffed at anyone who volunteered to die, but still truth reverberated through her words. My martyr had not made me more human. She had only made a vampire deathly ill.

I touched Conner with one hand, Karina with the other, channeling my last drops of energy into the power of my charms. "It's not blood. It's Bloody Mary. I don't need a hospital." Two pairs of eyes turned glassy, and I swiftly flushed away the evidence of my lie. "Please, just help me to the bed."

Karina left us and, like a robot, Conner carried me the short distance while a tear of guilt dripped down my face. I had never charmed him before, and above anyone else on earth, I had wanted to leave him free of my spell. "I love you," I whispered as he set me down. "I'm sorry."

"For what? I'm just glad it's not really blood." He pushed my sweaty hair away from my eyes. "I thought you didn't drink?"

"I don't, usually. I guess this is why."

Karina popped her head back in. "George canceled the ambulance. Can I get you something? I'll run out to the drugstore if you want."

"Thank you. Just water, please." She left to get it. Conner sat beside me, gently caressing my hand.

"How are you feeling?"

"Tired." And hungry. With the traitorous gift expelled from my body, my sense of smell had returned, and every particle of his humanity made me ache to be healed. "Conner, please don't take this the wrong way, but could you please leave me alone?" The hurt I had known he would feel filled the air, enticing me to rise. I gripped the sheets to hold myself in place. "I really just want to sleep."

"Then sleep. I'll be right here."

"I appreciate it, but you're kind of distracting."

He sighed. "All right, but promise you won't try to get up by yourself."

"I promise."

His kissed my forehead. I bit my lip as his closeness made my mouth water. "Call me if you need anything."

I waited for Karina to return with the water, then waited again, pretending to sleep, sweating and shivering as my temperature rose and the air hardened inside my lungs. I waited, cursing the folly that had forgotten Helen's teachings, cursing the devil that had taught me. Famine and pain, guilt and desolation danced a savage jig, pounding me against the newest dead end in my tangled crusade. Through it all, the resonance of Helen rang like cymbals in the gloom. Helen, who had formed me; Helen, who had trained me; Helen, who had sent me forth to perpetuate her bloody reign. I had been foolish to try to be human, believing she would someday return. The battle I had lusted for but never dared to fight would find me. How could I drive a stake through the heart of an immortal with the strength of a scrawny little girl? Lying on that beach house bed, I did not care whether my motive was justice or revenge. I did not care if my evil equaled hers, or even surpassed it. I only knew that the world needed Evil Vampire Jen to rid it of Helen's plague. Perhaps my soul was dust, swept and scattered beyond the reach of love, but I could still destroy the creature who had wasted it.

That thought alone gave me hope.

I lay trembling with hunger and hate until Conner came in to make sure I was asleep. One-two-three in, one-two-three out, I breathed while he kissed my hair and tucked the blankets around me. *You're asleep, Jennifer. Don't clench your teeth. Don't scrunch your eyes. Don't drink his blood.*

I battled every instinct I possessed until I nearly swooned, but he made it out alive. The moment he closed the door, I darted out the window into the night. This time, I left my pretenses behind.

11

The problem with becoming immortal in the twenty-first century was that it didn't have enough dramatic props. I spent three afternoons at the library, scouring the archives of every English-language newspaper in print, and when it all failed, there were no dusty pages I could tear or burn, no microfilm I could unspool: just a bunch of stupid windows on a computer screen to click very firmly closed. Technology was robbing me of catharsis.

"Can I help you find something?" the sleek-and-slender librarian asked as she glided through her rounds.

"No, thanks," I said, and opened up *The Assam Tribune*.

As a child, I could never figure out how Helen hoped to discover vampiric activity hidden amongst the myriad newspaper stories of murder. I still thought it would be difficult to identify vampires in general without a string of bloodless bodies, but it might be possible to find the hallmarks of a specific vampire's kills if one happened to know that vampire very, very well. I doubted that anything Helen had ever told me about herself was true, but I still trusted the things I had observed. The meticulous attention to detail. The insufferable confidence. The fact that she would never, ever leave a trace. It was tempting, after so many dead ends, to believe that somehow she had died, but Helen had vowed three times she would return: to me, to Jeremy, and to his mother. Far be it from such a creature to let her prophecy go unfulfilled. She was out there somewhere, biding her time, but nothing I found could tell me where.

For the third night in a row, I left the library when it closed, then drove home to choke down "dinner" with Conner before spending the night wide awake in my bed, remembering my mother's laugh. Such a joyless laugh it was, reserved for scorn and mockery, but it captivated me even in its deprecation. I lay and listened, watched and seethed, until vengeance infected my saliva and every swallow made me burn to see that villain die. If I could not go to her, I had to find a way to make her come to me.

I sleep-walked my way through the last day of photography for *Blades of Sand,* until I tripped and fell right into Tommy Lee Jones's lap. Conner leaped like a gazelle to rescue me, then ordered one of the accountants to drive me home. He followed after the filming was done.

"Are you sure you're well?" he asked as my feverish lips left his.

"Yeah. Just tired. Don't you have a flight you have to catch?" He was taking a red-eye to New York to promote another film.

"I had to make sure you weren't passed out here all by yourself. Promise you'll call someone if you start throwing up again. Amos or George . . . or Jeremy. He's still your brother, whatever else happened."

I shivered, wondering if he was right.

"Promise?"

"Yes."

"Okay." He tucked my hair behind my ear. "Call if you need me."

I watched the black Lexus pull away from my apartment, then sat down once more in front of the screen. From my laptop, I scoured the vast canon of vampire myth, hoping that someone, somewhere, had imagined a stunt with enough pizazz to provoke a response from Helen. Throughout the night, a parade of motley bloodsuckers cavorted, the fearless and the tormented, the glittery and the grotesque. They died, they rose, they laughed, they slayed, until my eyelids drooped with the weight of their profusion. However, if my confession back in Baton Rouge, the two bloodless bodies and the media blitz, had not managed to grab Helen's attention, then no bloodcurdling fictional exploit seemed likely to do the trick. Still, I read on.

```
Justine   slammed   the   door  and   flew  to   the
refrigerator,   sifting   wildly   through   the
vegetables.

"What are you doing?" Frederick cried.

"We need garlic! She's coming!"

"Who?"

"Rebecca!"

Frederick   gently   touched   her   arm.   "You're
dreaming, Justine. Rebecca's dead."

"That's what everyone thinks," she hissed as she
ripped herself from his grasp.
```

My eyes blurred across the mundane dialogue of another cliché scene, but something about it struck a familiar chord. I stopped, blinked, and read again.

```
"You're dreaming, Justine. Rebecca's dead."
"That's what everyone thinks."
```

I had heard those words before, not in some dime-store vampire romance, but in the heat of the strangest, most terrifying day of my life. I had ignored those words because the woman who spoke them threw up her hackles and explained them away.

"I thought Helen was dead."

"That's what everyone thinks."

Dr. Higginbotham. The woman who had raised a vampire. The woman whose veins Helen Carshaw had drained twice, yet who was still alive. The woman who had risked prison for me and financed my new life because she feared a demon whose death certificate had been properly filed. There had to be more to that story.

I found her number, but just as I reached to dial, I realized the FBI might still be surveilling her phones. Jeremy would know, and he would also know how to get through to her without arousing suspicion.

I leaned back, the draft from the air conditioner chilling me to the bone. Jeremy had been with me every moment since I left him. His redemption was every bit as dear to me as my own, and I had always intended to return to him when I had a choice to offer. Right now, I had nothing but my own failures, my own need. How could I face the monster I had created still steeped in my own sin?

I threw caution to the wind and grabbed the phone. Right now, federal agents scared me less than Jeremy.

No one answered at his mother's home, and a swift mental calculation told me offices in Baton Rouge might already be open. I searched the directory, then dialed anew.

"Women's Health, how may I direct your call?"

"Dr. Higginbotham, please."

"She's with a patient, can I give you her voicemail?"

"I'll hold. Tell her its Stacy."

The tinny hum of violins filled my ears while every few minutes a recorded voice advised me to call my pharmacy if I needed a refill. Did I really hope to track down a four-thousand-year-old immortal by listening to muzak on hold? Sometimes I wished I could sleep in a coffin or shape-shift into a bat just so my life would be a little less absurd.

The elevator music finally clicked off, and a voice I had not heard in four years said, "Stacy, what? This had better be good."

"It is. I promise."

Her stunned silence told me she recognized my voice. She finally said, "I see."

"The first thing is, I thought you should know, Jeremy's changed."

This time it sounded like the air traveled through her teeth. "I suppose that was to be expected."

"Yes. The main reason I called is, I just needed to talk to *my mother*."

The silence stretched until I finally said, "Hello?"

"I think your mother may not be quite ready to talk to you."

A plume of red anger blazed behind my eyes. Dr. Higginbotham had played me. "Any idea when you'll be ready, *Mom*?"

"These things take time, *Stacy*. Sometimes we just have to wait."

"I'm done waiting. You either find a way to make that conversation happen, or *your daughter* is going to stop talking to you for good."

I slammed down the phone, already regretting that rash threat. If Dr. Higginbotham was really still in contact with Helen, then I had probably just alerted my enemy to the fact that I was searching for her, but I had not even begun to prepare for the battle. Worse, I had antagonized Jeremy's family, and now I realized I needed him. In four thousand years, Helen had probably fended off greater foes than some pipsqueak, acne-prone vampire. I might not survive even with Jeremy for an ally, but without him, I was toast.

I grabbed my keys and headed to Pasadena.

❦

The sun rose slowly over Los Angeles, seeping hesitantly through the orange shroud of smog. The blanket of man-made toxins seemed a strange backdrop on which to paint my errand of supernatural war. I toyed with my phone, wondering whether I ought to tell him I was coming. How exactly did one approach a spurned, beloved vampire?

Beloved. My stomach fell to my heels as I realized how true it was. Jeremy had walked with me through the darkest hours of my life, following me to the brink of hell. He had offered me every part of himself, and I had left him cold. How must he see me now, this creature who had once presumed to teach him?

I swallowed my tears as I found a place to park and walked to the apartment that only weeks ago we had shared. He opened the door before I could knock. "I would know that scent of guilt a mile away," he said.

"I spoke to your mother this morning."

"I know. She called." He darted his eyes along the hallway, then finally opened the door wide enough for me to come in. He slammed it shut behind me. "Do you remember when you told me that if I didn't want Stacy to get hurt, I had to make sure she never found out about you using her name? Well, I've done it. I even moved her to the same city as you, and she still has no clue. You hurt her, and you're going to find out you're not the only one with super powers."

"I know. I came to say I'm sorry. I got caught up in the moment and said some stupid things, but I'm not going to hurt your family."

"You call my mom on a phone that might be tapped so you can threaten to kill my sister, and you call that not hurting my family?"

"It was stupid, all right? But I had to call your mom because I have to find Helen, and I was right. Your mother knows where she is."

He blanched. "So that's why you're really here."

"Yes. I need you." My voice leaked out as a whisper.

"Fuck that. I don't care what game you're playing. I'm out. You had your chance." Rage flared from his smoldering eyes, hatred so bitter and deep I nearly choked on the odor, but even his acrid wrath could not mask the core of his emptiness. His every molecule sang to me, drawing me into his desire.

"Please. I can't do it without you."

"You want to kill her, don't you?"

"I know you've thought about it, too."

"Yeah, and I've also thought about killing you."

I shook in the stark ferocity of his power. "Do it, then. Just help me get rid of her first."

He came towards me until his hand reached out, fondling a lock of my hair. I leaned my cheek against his palm. The jagged edge of his brokenness nestled perfectly against mine.

"Where's your Boy-Toy?"

"In New York."

"For good?"

"Until Saturday."

He pushed me away. "Jesus, you're an idiot. You want to go chasing after Helen, that's your funeral. Leave me — and my family — out of it."

"Jeremy, Helen is going to come. She made us both for a reason, and sooner or later, she's going to show up and expect us to fall into step with whatever she had planned."

"Yeah? And how much you want to bet her plan involves actually being around each other, acting like what we are, instead of leaving me hung out to dry so she can date a human?"

"I can still be here for you. I can still be with you, just like before. I just can't be . . . more."

"Why not, if nothing matters?"

I shivered. "I was wrong. Maybe there's nothing we can do to save ourselves, but at the very least, we can make sure Helen never makes another one of *us.*"

His scent engulfed me, so rich and conflicted, so ripe with decadence, I could not name his feelings. I reached to touch his hand, and sorrow leaped out from our fingers like sparks, scalding both our skins. He pulled away as if he had been bitten.

"Just go home, Jen. Forget about Helen, and in a decade or two, when you come to your senses, we'll figure it all out. Okay?"

The dry air cracked against my vocal cords as I edged toward the door. "I love you, Jeremy."

He shook his head. "No. You love the person you think I should be."

We stared at each other across the threshold, our hearts as deadlocked as our eyes. He broke the spell and closed the door.

12

Summer had ended, but autumn never really came. The bougainvillea in my garden bloomed year-round, a static fever pitch of life without season. Every day dawned exactly like the last, an enervating quicksand of time. I heard no word from Dr. Higginbotham, no whisper of my mother, and I dared not anger Jeremy by calling again. Conner returned briefly from New York, but left all too soon for Thailand, where his next picture was shooting. We talked on videophones every day, but any groupie with a dollar bill could see Conner on a screen. My soulmate slipped into illusion while I muddled through the monotony of makeup, just me and Amos and the crew with our latex lizard masks.

About a month into our separation, the tabloids published a picture of Conner walking arm-in-arm with a woman reputed to be a notorious Bangkok madam. Amos felt "duty bound" to bring it to my attention.

"Amos, do you honestly believe Conner Brazel needs to pay for sex?"

"You've never been to Thailand, have you?"

"No, but I'm pretty sure he's famous over there, too."

"Yes, but the groupies haven't been trained like the professionals."

Conner laughed about it and told me the woman was a crew member who had shown him where to get the best curry, but that night, the clean cotton of my sheets still felt too cold against my skin.

The insipid winter and I trudged on: soulless, friendless, vendetta-less, waiting mindlessly for any kind of spring.

Conner was due back in L.A. two days before Christmas, but with the long-anticipated day finally approaching, his face appeared on my phone wearing a sullen frown. "Hey, Stace, I've got bad news."

"You're not coming home for Christmas, are you?"

"Sort of. I'm still flying in at the same time. I'm just flying out again the next day."

"Seriously? You're working on Christmas?"

"No. I'm going to Alabama."

"Oh." A cold fist of fear gripped my heart as he slipped through my fingers.

"There's good news, too, though."

"What?"

"You're coming with me."

If he had not been on the other side of the Pacific, I would have wrung his pretty little neck. "You're really an ass, you know that?"

"Of course. I'll get Willa to send you the flight information."

"For future reference, Amos does pay me. I can buy my own plane tickets."

"Yeah, but then I wouldn't get to see that look on your face. Hey, I gotta go, but I'll see you in a few days."

Christmas Eve found me sitting in the VIP lounge at LAX, my palms sweating as I held hands with Passenger Clarence Brazelman. Not only had I never flown before, I had never actually been inside an airport, and having the TSA treat me like a wanted felon hit just a little too close to home. I watched a couple of teenage girls with Versace luggage elbow each other and laugh in our direction, and I shifted my newspaper to hide us both.

"You know, sitting next to a superstar in one of the busiest airports in the world on one of the busiest travel days of the year is not really my idea of keeping a low profile."

An ugly roll of his sapphire eyes darkened every golden feature. "Do you really still not trust me, or do you just not want to go?"

"I just thought . . ."

"No, *I* just thought, maybe it would be nice to actually hold your hand after spending six weeks busting my ass in some shithole backwater where nobody speaks English, where the one time I find someone fluent enough to have a decent conversation with over lunch, my girlfriend and my mom both accuse me of hiring a prostitute. I just thought, I promised Grandma I would come home for Christmas, but I'm fucking exhausted and I've lost ten pounds and I never want to see rice noodles again, and all I really want to do is go home and be with Stacy. Maybe I just thought some kind of idiotic shit like that."

I blinked a lot, trying to see past my own self-absorption. "I'm sorry. I'm really glad you're home."

"Whatever. Wake me up when they call for boarding." He pulled his baseball cap down over his eyes and soon began to snore.

Conner slept the entire way to Atlanta, the city where even movie stars had to go to change planes. This airport made me every bit as nervous as the last, especially when Conner bought a pretzel and the lady at the stand winked and said, "Thank you, Mr. Brazel," as she handed him his change. The second plane was too small for a first-class cabin, so we had to sit like sardines among the rank-and-file. I trembled the whole way, both because I thought someone might post our picture on Facebook and because the scent of glad anticipation made me ache with thirst. But somehow, we made it to Birmingham without incident.

"See, you survived," Conner said as he kissed my hand in the backseat of our chauffeured car.

"Uh-huh. When you land some big franchise role like Spider-Man or something and then you ask me what I want for my birthday, the answer is a private plane."

"So much for humble convent values." Sleep had done him good, and his smile now returned. "By the way, don't let Grandma hear you say that."

"Why, she has something against planes?"

"She has something against gold-diggers. And sarcasm."

With that happy pronouncement ringing in my ears, we arrived.

The car pulled into the horseshoe driveway of a white colonial structure I could only call a mansion. Three stories tall, bedecked with columns and balconies, it overlooked a manicured courtyard arrayed with fountains and statues.

"Is this where you grew up?" I gasped.

"Yeah. Why?"

"I just didn't realize . . ."

"That I was always this spoiled? Sorry, it's ingrained." He clambered out the opposite side as the chauffeur opened my door.

A woman stepped onto the porch, thin and blonde and every bit as stunning as one would expect a superstar's mother to be. Conner wrapped her in his arms. "Merry Christmas, Mom."

"Merry Christmas. Your father's unpacking Grandma's bag. They'll be down in a minute." She gave him another squeeze, then turned to me. "Stacy, I'm so glad to finally meet you."

"Thank you so much for having me."

"Of course, it's our pleasure. Clarence, grab the bags and let's get in, it's getting cold."

I followed Molly Brazelman inside as I tried to come to grips with the fact that Conner was not "Conner" here. He had warned me about the name change, but still it sounded strange.

Someone had gone to great effort to make sure the mansion was also a home. Rustic wood furnishings abounded, giving off the comfy scent of a log cabin. Fires blazed on numerous hearths while children whose origins I had yet to learn chased each other from room to room. Adults laughed gaily in knots of three and four as they lounged on sofas and settees, munching on truffles and macaroons. They descended upon Conner, getting up to trade handshakes and hugs, bombarding me with their names.

"It's okay," Conner whispered. "No one expects you to remember them all."

"Where did they all come from? I thought you were an only child."

"I am, but Dad's one of six and Mom's one of five, and all of *them* had three or four each."

The vastness of such a family made my head spin. I had never met anyone to whom I was actually related.

He showed me down a hallway lined with family photos, where I got my first glimpse of Conner the Child. He stuck out his tongue as he rode a bike with no hands, held up a rod and reel with a catfish on the end, smiled for the camera in a Halloween cowboy costume, complete with a saddle bag for his candy. If not for the piercing blue eyes no woman could resist, he might have been any ordinary boy.

"I like this one." I pointed to him, about six years old, dressed as Joseph in a Christmas pageant. He stood like a holy sentinel above the five-year-old Mary and her baby doll.

"Ah, yes, my first big role. The birth of a legend."

"You, or Jesus?"

"Take your pick." He grinned and led me on.

We walked to a room with two twin beds, one with a suitcase on it already open and unpacked. Conner set my bag on the other bed. "You're sharing with my cousin Stacy, so that won't be confusing at all."

"Wait, you actually have a cousin Stacy?"

"Yes, and she knows about the *Entertainment Weekly* thing. I told her just in case they called." He slid an arm around my waist. "Sorry we couldn't be together, but Grandma would have a stroke if Mom put us in the same room."

"That's fine. I can think of a few nuns who would agree."

He nuzzled my hair, then let me go. "Go ahead and unpack. My room's down the hall, third door on the left." He left, and I sat down on the quilted blue comforter, lost in the wilderness of this thing so commonplace, so utterly bizarre: a family.

Into my silence intruded the step of a firm, sensible loafer. "Well," its owner muttered, "you certainly look like his type."

I jumped up to greet the gray-haired matriarch, a woman nearly as tall as most men, but her stiff spine made her seem taller. She appraised me over the bridge of her nose with all the cordiality a Montague might show a Capulet.

"I'm Stacy," I mumbled, extending my hand, but ready to snatch it back in case she snapped at it like a turtle. "You must be Grandma, er, Mrs. Brazelman."

"I can't believe that boy finally had the gall to bring one of you here." I gaped at her dumbly while my self-esteem swirled toward the sewer that Grandma Brazelman's wrinkled nose seemed to smell with every breath in my presence. "How dare you flaunt your lust under my son's roof?"

"Grandma!"

We both wheeled to face Conner, standing framed in the doorway like a portrait of fury. He strode forward and put an arm around my shoulders, shielding me as once he had shielded little Mary. "I think the proper greeting for a guest here is, 'Hello.'"

She shook her head, adding the aroma of dashed hopes to her hostility. "Clarence. I should never have let your father encourage this acting nonsense. I knew this would be the result."

"It's not what you think," I said. "I'm not . . . we're not . . . I'm not what you think I am."

"Really? Well, by all means, please enlighten me. What are you?"

I looked to Conner, searching for the right words, but he found them first. "She's the girl who looked me in the eye and told me to go to hell. I listened, Grandma. I did it right this time."

Grandma's sharp eyes flitted quickly over my face, then settled on his. "Are you toying with me, Clarence?"

"No, Grandma. I love her." He kissed my hand, and my heart swelled with happiness.

"I guess it's easy to fall in love when the girl looks like *that*." She pointed sternly at Conner. "You had still best watch your manners under this roof, young man."

"I will if you will." He raised a jaunty eyebrow, and she returned it with a smile. Perhaps there was hope for her sense of humor, after all.

"Fair enough. Now come on down, dinner's getting cold."

I spent the evening with a whirlwind of relatives, and although Conner's mother squinted dubiously in my direction, the rest of the Brazelman clan proved quite keen to get to know the girl whom their infamous rake of a relation had decided to bring home. I chatted with sundry aunts and uncles and cousins, some of whom worked for Conner's father at his car dealership here in town, but also a doctor from Jackson and a teacher from Charlotte, a chemical engineer from Tulsa and a photographer from Seattle. Hidden tensions and phony smiles occasionally jarred my senses, but these people had come from far and wide to share hugs and trade stories and give each other the very best of themselves. They had left their headaches and their heartaches and their petty sins behind and wrapped themselves in Christmas cheer as bright as the star atop the tree.

As the fires simmered to embers and children began to yawn, everyone poured one last cup of eggnog or hot cocoa and gathered to hear Uncle Somebody read *The Night Before Christmas* aloud. Then Grandma went to the piano and led us in a chorus of "Silent Night," and afterward packed us straight off to bed. Conner kissed me goodnight under the mistletoe (making sure Grandma did not see), and I headed upstairs full of smiles.

"Is this what your family Christmases are like?" Cousin Stacy asked as we both got into our pajamas.

"Not exactly. My mother died when I was twelve, and I've got a brother I didn't know about until I was sixteen. That's all the family I have."

"Wow. This must be weird."

"A little, but I like it."

"Yeah. Hallmark Channel ought to make a holiday special about us."

"I'll give Conner's agent a call when we get back," I replied as I snuggled under the covers.

I awoke in the pre-dawn gray to the sound of children scampering downstairs, crying, "Santa Claus came! Wake up! He came!" Conner held me close as we watched the glee of torn bows and giant boxes, bicycles and dollhouses and video games.

"Was Santa Claus good to you when you were a kid?" he asked.

"Santa Claus never brought me anything I asked for in my letters. I grew up believing elves must be illiterate." In retrospect, it was a miracle Helen Carshaw had bothered with Santa Claus at all. She later explained that it was "important to understand the cultural rituals of your society."

"Well, I don't know what you asked him for this year, but I hope this comes close." Conner took a tiny foil-wrapped package from his pocket. My heart raced as I uncovered a velvet box, the kind that only jewelry came in. *Please, don't be a ring. I can't say yes right now. Don't make me explain in front of his family.*

I popped open the hinge, and a tiny crucifix stared back. Threads of gold as fine as silk crossed and wove and intertwined, dazzling in their perfect, random loveliness. "It's beautiful, but I don't understand . . . ?"

"I know you're not really Catholic, and I know that whatever bad stuff happened made you lose touch with the nuns. But when I was in Thailand, and of course almost everyone is Buddhist over there, one Sunday I went walking, and I saw this little church with a couple of nuns going in. It made me think of you, so I followed them. The Mass was just about to start, so I stayed, and it was . . . I don't know. It was like you were almost with me. So, afterward, I saw they had a little shop, and it turned out one of their church members was a jeweler who made this stuff by hand, and I got this for you." He took the crucifix from the box and clasped the chain around my neck. "I missed you so much."

Tears of gladness fought against the bitter irony that he should feel me with him in a Mass, the one place where I could never go. "Thank you. It's a whole lot more beautiful than what I got you." I handed him my gift – an old playbill signed by his idol, Gregory Peck – to hide the war of emotions raging in my breast.

"This is awesome. Perfect." He took my hand. "Stacy, I love you. Thank you for coming here with me."

"I wouldn't have missed it for the world."

When the last box had been pried open, the last toy endowed with batteries, breakfast appeared magically from the kitchen. Then people started changing out of their pajamas, returning in dresses, suits and ties, and I realized the Christmas tradition here included church. Thankfully, church for the Brazelman family did not mean Holy Eucharist, so I was only mildly terrified as we drove toward Olive Street United Methodist.

The reader of *The Night Before Christmas* stepped into the sanctuary. "Isn't that your uncle?" I whispered.

"Yes, Uncle Thomas. He's the pastor."

"Merry Christmas, everyone," Pastor Thomas announced. "Rejoice. The Lord is come."

We sang carols, and my squeaky alto blended into the lush harmony of the congregation's single voice. We read scripture, and the old familiar stories of the Nativity fell new and welcome on my ears. Pastor Thomas preached of birth and redemption, and my heart listened with joy. My hand clasped Conner's while my lungs filled with the truth no one else here could know: the Lord *had* come, his presence filling every heart gathered to worship. But I did not rush like a crazed monster through the Body of Christ, quaffing the summit of my desire from their veins. I did not cry out, demanding knowledge of mysteries that were not mine to know. I simply sat — and *was*.

We shook hands all around, offering peace, and peace they truly gave me. Every face that smiled with welcome, every hand that reached for mine poured peace like a wellspring into my shriveled life. I did not deserve their goodwill any more than I had deserved the nuns' patient care, but no one here deserved to be a vessel for the Love they served. All around me, cracked and bruised and unworthy, they became part of a mystery that soothed and bound and healed me. Conner's eyes were lit with the joy of home, and I dared to hope that this oasis of heaven might someday be my home too. My cracks were deep, my bruises black, but if God's children could welcome me . . . could He?

I touched the crucifix around my neck, the body willingly broken, and I understood what a soulmate really was.

13

"It all depends whether they can move the ball on the ground. From what I've seen, they don't have the legs, but supposedly this Granger guy's an all-American track star, so we'll see."

I listened languidly that afternoon as Conner and his father analyzed Alabama's chances in the upcoming Sugar Bowl. "I don't think it matters. Granger can run like Usain Bolt, but he'll still be too small to get past our line." I thought vaguely how disconcerting it was to hear a conversation in my native language where I only understood about one word in three, but mostly I swirled the water in my glass and thought about Helen.

God had let me sit with Him today. He had allowed me to enter His presence, to mingle among His children in His own house, and no one had died; not even me. Despite all my failures, my faulty hypotheses, I found myself right back on the road that might lead to my soul. I thought I knew how to follow it this time. I thought I knew what to do. But Helen was still alive; Dr. Higginbotham had confirmed it. I could not let myself be weak.

You can't wait forever, Jen. Your body is still sixteen, and Conner is already twenty-two. The makeup will only take you so far. Not to mention that the longer I waited, the more people must inevitably die.

I had no better idea how to find Helen now than I had months ago when I devoured vampire fiction in search of an answer. I still believed she would come back for me someday, but how long was I willing to wait? Helen Carshaw had stolen my every hope of happiness. How long would I allow her to keep me hostage? Yet was it not my duty to vanquish her, to garner my strength and free the world from her evil? How would I ever live with myself if the moment came and I was too weak to face her?

You won't have to live with yourself. She'll kill you, and Conner, too.

"Stacy?" Conner's mother jolted me out of reverie. "Would you mind helping me in the kitchen?"

"What? Oh, of course." I followed her, half-dazed, and began clearing away stray dishes.

"I see you haven't developed a taste for football yet. I guess Clarence has been in Thailand most of the season."

"Yes. He'll have to indoctrinate me next year."

"Don't worry, he will. If you're still with him."

I bit my tongue against a sharp reply. She was right to doubt me, even if she did not know why. "I, uh, don't know where you want these."

She took my stack of dirty plates and put them by the sink. "About the sleeping arrangements. If you're uncomfortable, Grandma will be leaving tonight after dinner."

"I appreciate the thought, but I'm fine where I am."

"Stacy, I know my son. I'm not saying I approve, but he's an adult now, and so are you."

"Thank you, but I'll tell you the same thing I told him. I grew up in a convent, and some of it stuck."

She cocked her head, the piercing blue eyes she had passed on to her son studying me in the light of the chandelier. "You don't have to pretend. He gets his straightforwardness from me."

"I'm not pretending. I don't know why your son is willing to put up with my 'convent training,' as he calls it, or any of my other quirks that would have chased off any other man, but he is, and there's not a minute that goes by when I'm not grateful."

She looked me up and down, just like her mother-in-law. I was beginning to wonder if my clothes had been woven from the Emperor's invisible cloth. "Yes, I imagine men flee from you wherever you go." She started piling spoons onto the plates. "I can tell you why he 'puts up with' you. Clarence sees people in a way most of us never will. Their masks never fool him. It's why he's so amazing on screen." She let the dishes clatter into the basin and met my eyes. "Whatever he sees in you, he's never seen it before, and he figures he'll never see it again. He's too young to realize none of us are really that unique." She rinsed her hands and looked me in the eye. "Stacy, do you love him?"

"With all my heart."

"And if he suddenly lost his fortune and fame?"

"In a way, I would be glad, because life would be much simpler."

"Hmm. The girl with all the right answers. I wish I could believe you."

"What can I do to convince you?"

"Truthfully? Nothing. He's too great of a temptation — and so are you." She turned on the tap and poured dish soap into the sink. "Don't get me wrong. I'm glad you're here. At the very least, you're a step in the right direction."

"Please let me finish those dishes for you," I said because I did not know what else to say.

"That's okay. You'd better go back and start learning about football. Just make sure you can say, 'Roll Tide.'"

Jeremy will never forgive me, I thought as I echoed, "Roll Tide."

❖

Molly Brazelman's words haunted me all that night as I lay listening to Cousin Stacy's breathing. *"People's masks never fool him. Whatever he sees in you, he's never seen it before."* From the very first day we met, Conner had seen something in me I had not known existed. That girl was better than any version of myself I had ever known, but who was he that he wanted to be with her? How often did I stop to think about what Conner might need from me?

He needs you to leave. Get out of here before you hurt him anymore. I had often given myself that advice and then ignored it to dire consequences, but this time, the voice of reason was wrong. I belonged with Conner. Maybe I would never find a way to stay, to create the life I dreamed of as his normal, human wife, but even so, I had to give him what I could. I knew now that love was only love when it was given as a gift, and the only gift I had to give him was the truth.

I poked my head out to check that the hall was clear, then made my way softly toward the third door on the left. I found him snoring, draped in a ratty crimson bedspread that had probably been his since childhood. I could just make out the swoosh of the Alabama "A" in its folds. *He never went to college*, I realized. *I wonder if he regrets it. I wonder if he ever plans to go back.* What did he want the future to hold? What had he dreamed about before I came along to change it?

I took in what I could see of the room: old black-and-white movie posters, a set of weights, a few stray photos. They did not tell me much, but Conner spoke to me through the gentle buzzing of his snores. When had he first looked at me as more than just another one-night stand? When I told him I had gone out with him "because I didn't have anything else to do." When had he first intoxicated me with his acceptance? When I told him I had problems greater than he could handle. When had he awakened me to change, to grow that tiny, treasured pimple on my chin? When I gave him every part of my true self but one. Was it possible the trait Conner cherished in me was *honesty?*

My throat had swelled with its share of lumps in my day, but never one quite like this. "Oh, Conner. If you only knew."

But he did know. Not the full extent of it, not the thirst for human blood, but he knew I had secrets. My truthful moments might have drawn him in, but he knew honesty did not define me. What was it, then?

I watched him snooze in the comfort of this sweet, old-fashioned home, surrounded by a family who had gathered from far and wide to celebrate Christmas together, a family who said grace before meals and sang carols around the tree and piled into their cars to bring a caravan to church. I thought about his life of glossy close-ups and plastic interviews, public relations handlers and industry parties, beach houses and Aston Martins and location shoots in Thailand, and it clicked. I understood what it meant to lead a double life, and I could share both of his. I could bridge the divide between Clarence Brazelman and Conner Brazel. A Steel Magnolia with a Hollywood job and a secret identity; his mother was wrong. He was not likely to find anyone like me again.

But even this could not account for why he would sacrifice his multi-million-dollar career, his chosen way of life, to be with me. Logic alone could never explain such a choice. Conner was willing to let my secret identity dissolve his public one for no other reason than because he loved me.

Was I willing, in return, to let his love dissolve my secret?

As I sat and watched my soulmate breathe, I knew the choice he presented me, the same choice Mother Celeste had offered me when I was twelve. *"You can come to me, and I will help."* I had chosen, then, to lie and hide. I had chosen to trust Helen, who despised love, more than the people who embraced it. Here I stood again, at the same fork in the same road, still paralyzed by the same fear. What if Conner cursed me, threw me out, or called the police? What would I do if the glass slippers shattered, if anger like a flaming sword slashed away the bud of hope? The only way to love him was to lose him to the truth. But maybe — just maybe — in the light of truth, I might find myself.

I spent the plane ride home rehearsing my confession. If Conner noticed my ceaseless fidgeting, the blush of panic on my cheeks, he never said so. He only sat beside me, holding my hand and poring over his next script. I had just about written my own script when the captain turned on the "fasten seatbelt" sign for our descent, and Conner turned to whisper in my ear. "We shouldn't stand at baggage claim together. People tend to take pictures."

He saw my eyes fly wide, and I wondered if he could hear the blood pounding in my ears.

"It's fine, I promise. I'll just get off first, and you wait a while to follow. We stand on opposite sides of the carousel. It's no big deal."

I squelched my fear and took his hand. "Conner, when we get back to my apartment, I want to tell you . . . what happened."

The peace that flowed out from his azure eyes washed me with courage. "Good. And I'm still going to love you, no matter what you say."

"I won't make you promise that." But the hand that clung to mine was a vow. All the muscles in my body uncoiled, as if they knew it was time to move over and make room.

The wheels touched down, and he left me with a smile. I waited ten minutes on tenterhooks, then followed. Conner's omni-present baseball cap and sunglasses did nothing to hide the irrepressible aura of a star. I could see no furtive high-end Nikons, but a woman in a red scarf was juggling a toddler with one hand and a camera phone with the other. Conner tipped his hat toward her, posing for the flash.

"Excuse me." Someone's elbow brushed me as she giggled, phone at the ready, searching for a clean shot. "Do you know who that is?"

"No."

"It's . . ." But a gasp cut her off. I looked up, and her eyes like lasers bored straight into mine.

My body temperature spiked so fast, I shook in every cell. She pointed the phone at me, then took off at a dead run.

I flew after her, not caring whom I might knock down, not caring who might see. I channeled every ounce of my demonic strength into my legs, but the sonic velocity that had been my best weapon, my alibi, failed me. My frayed body would go no faster than the pace of an ordinary girl.

I lost my quarry at the taxi stand. She shoved herself into a yellow car and drove away.

Conner found me sobbing, crumpled on the cement. He bent over me, his body obscuring my face from the crowds — and their cameras — which had followed. "Hey, are you okay?"

"No," I cried into my useless mortal legs, the dream of a lifetime realized at the moment Fate tore it away.

"What happened?"

"She recognized me."

"How do you know?"

My mouth filled with the taste of reprisal. "Because that was the real Stacy Higginbotham."

❖

I followed, numb, as Conner lead me to the back seat of a waiting hired car. Only my fingers remembered to function, madly texting Jeremy in the hope that he might find Stacy before she got through to the FBI. I hit send and then Conner gripped my hand in his, the veins in his temples throbbing in the silence we dared not break in the hearing of the driver. My phone beeped, but Jeremy's reply held only four letters: *Fuck.*

"Explain," Conner demanded as the door to my apartment finally banged shut behind us.

The moment of truth was finally here, but with the FBI almost certainly on its way, only lies could save him from being accused of harboring a fugitive. "I can't. The more you know, the worse this will go for you. I think it's called 'plausible deniability.'"

He blanched. "Is it really that bad?"

"Whatever you're imagining, I promise, the truth is worse."

"I'm imagining that the people you're hiding from are the police. And I'm imagining there's more to it than identity theft. Am I warm?"

"Scalding."

"Is it murder?"

I looked at the floor and whispered, "Yes."

He made a noise like a wounded puppy and gripped his baseball cap with both hands.

"Conner, you have to get out of here."

"Am I really never going to see you again?"

"Would you even want to?"

He crushed me against himself as his body wracked with sobs. "Always. It was an accident, or self-defense, or whatever, I know you . . ."

I held the solid wonder of the best man I had ever known, aching with the finality of his touch while his words pierced my heart like poison arrows. *Self-defense*. Helen had put the gun to my head: Kill these innocent people or you will die. I had to do it. It had always been them or me.

I only had to picture Carter and his dad, their mouths pressed greedily against each other's necks, to know it was a lie.

"Conner, it wasn't an accident. It wasn't self-defense. I made the choice, and now, I can't ever take it back." I wiped my thumb along the ridge of his cheek, tracing away the tears. "I love you. The only thing in my life I don't regret is the time I've spent with you."

He held my gaze, those eyes as deep as the ocean swollen now with red, like a crimson tide. "Tell me your real name," he said.

"Jennifer Carshaw." Five dilapidated syllables, letting in the drafts of home.

"Jennifer," he said, "I love you, too."

Conner laid his lips on mine, an ardor of sorrow infused in his embrace, but his words rang bright with trumpet strains, the single note I had heard before in the depths of my stone tomb. Gabriel's dirge pealed out anew, blown full of strident joy. The love I had yearned for all my life wrapped me in its arms, the love that resounded inside me because it knew the truth yet lived, unswayed.

"Jennifer, I love you, too."

Here, at last, I heard the answer to my damning question, singing from the shepherd's lips louder than my screams of vanity. Here, at last, a gentle goodness shoved aside the arrogance that named my darkness greater than God's light. *I love you, too*, He said, and I surrendered to the blindness of unknowing everything that I had ever known because here, at last, I could see my soul.

Crushed and broken, bruised and torn, I found it lurking where it had always lived, inside myself, shadowed by my pride.

Too soon, the song of heaven grew soft, the taste of beauty parting from my tongue. "Find me," Conner breathed. "Someday, when it's all died down. I'll wait."

I thought of all the reasons why that would never happen. Conner would hate me the minute he turned on the news; nothing would ever die down. "I will," I said. Everything was possible. Jennifer Carshaw had a soul.

Conner took my hand — I squeezed his tight — then he walked to open the door.

Helen was standing on the other side.

14

She carried a large blue duffel bag, bumping it against the frozen Conner as she strode in. Her cut ruby lips refracted the sunlight pouring through the open door; her polished emerald eyes taunted even as they charmed. "Hello, Jennifer," her sugared voice dripped across my ears. "I believe you've been looking for me." She threw her duffel bag unceremoniously onto my couch.

Terror surged like a geyser through my gut, but I had enough sense to look at Conner and say, "Run."

He tried, but Helen was faster. With the speed I could no longer match, she blocked his exit, pushed him back, and barred the door. He staggered back across the open floor into the kitchen, cowering against the stove as her eyes devoured him. "I must say, my daughter may be stupid, but at least she has good taste."

"You are not my mother." The word was sawdust stripped from truth. "You're the fiend who killed her."

She pursed her lips with disappointment. "I should never have put you in school with those nuns. Every time I brought you up to see beyond the confines of the human mind, they always dragged you right back down."

"They loved me."

"Love is weakness." She moved towards me and cupped my chin in her porcelain hands, as slippery-smooth as the slope toward hell. "I made you immortal, and you want to give it away for something as common as love."

"Immortal?" Conner croaked.

I tore my gaze from Helen to meet his. "Conner, listen to me. You have to surrender. The only way she will not kill you is if you're willing to die."

"Very astute of you, Jennifer." She let me go and moved toward Conner. "You see, my daughter is a vampire, as I created her to be. To me, you are nothing more than a glass of fine wine I can hardly wait to savor." He panted as the power of her smile pillaged his free will. I dredged the rubble of my arsenal for any way to save him. I sneaked around the kitchen island to draw her gaze, praying something remained of my charms.

She looked up, unafraid. "I have been watching you, Jennifer. Keeping tabs, you might say. Eight years is not very long to wait when you have lived as long as I have. I told myself, I made mistakes in the beginning, too. Give her time. She will learn. But all you wanted was to kill the gift I had given you." She turned to Conner, smiled, and crooked her finger to signal him, "Come here." In a trance, he took a step toward her. I sobbed as she traced her finger across his cheek.

"You have what you want now, Jennifer. Love has made you mortal. And the only thing of value a mortal can ever do is die." She tilted Conner's head back, baring his veins.

Conner's right hand flicked out from his side and grabbed the closest object: the lighter I kept for the sake of show next to my old-fashioned gas stove. With a click, he lit the flame, then pushed it into Helen's eyes. Surprised, she raised her hands long enough for Conner to leap across the room. He stared her down, brandishing the lighter like a torch.

She walked calmly toward him, blew it out with one cool breath, and then drew him into her arms. "How about it, Jennifer? Do you think your precious love will help him now?"

I sobbed and fell to my knees. "No."

"Yes." Conner held Helen Carshaw's fiery glare, his every breath redolent with the perfume of the green valley, the Lamb's wool like a breastplate covering his heart. "Yes," he said again. "I love her enough to die."

Helen spat, her revulsion battling his splendor as she dropped him on the ground. Her lip curled as she advanced toward me. "Of course you would be with someone as stupid as you. I never could get anything to penetrate that thick skull. I thought, at least, when you had to teach Jeremy, you would see the truth, but instead you only tried to make a mess of him too."

Questions raced across my mind, ramming against my vocal cords so that not a single one could escape. The mysteries of my life crept ever closer, the answers poised just on the edge of my mother's lethal smile, but with every step she took, my fascination faded. My fledgling soul could learn to soar without probing her psychosis. All that mattered was her destruction. *God, send an angel to help me*, I prayed.

"Fuck, seriously?"

He sent me Jeremy instead.

"Long time no see," he said to Helen, while to the amazement of my puffy eyes he leaned towards Conner and put out his hand. Conner took it, still shaking as he stood. To Helen, Jeremy said, "I've wanted to kill him a thousand times, too, but now's not a good time. I take it you're up to speed about us?" he asked Conner.

Conner swallowed. "More or less."

"Then how about we drop whatever bullshit y'all are fighting about and hit the road? I can't find Stacy, and by now it doesn't matter."

A malicious grin spread across Helen's face. "I believe that problem has already been solved." Her eyes twinkled as she nodded toward the duffel bag on my couch.

Color fled from Jeremy's face, the lights inside him bent by the gravity of grief. He took the zipper in his fingers, pulled it back, wincing at each groove as if the metal teeth had bitten through his skin. A shock of dull blonde hair spilled out, and Jeremy spun, the smoke of wrath spilling from his glare. "You." He took one step toward me. "This was just the excuse you needed."

The floor shook under his approaching feet. "No. Jeremy, it was Helen."

"Helen never threatened her. Helen's not the one who stole her name."

"I couldn't kill Stacy. I'm not the same anymore."

Uncertainty flickered in those russet-green eyes, but his fist flicked out into my jaw. My body left the floor and hit the fridge, bones cracking as my mind split into stars. "Get up," he ordered, but I could not move, could barely hear the sound of Conner crying, "Stop!" I could only imagine the gruesome glee of Helen's smile.

"Get up," Jeremy ordered me again, prodding the lump of my body with his toe. Blood gushed from my head and trickled towards my mouth, a soured font of salted gall. His foot descended on my ribs with words as splintered as my bones. "That's for Carter." He kicked my skull. "That's for his dad." He stuffed his fist into my stomach. "That's for Stacy."

The slimmest threads of consciousness still bound my gaze to his, the savage ache we always shared stretched taut across the air. Hope lay trampled in my broken flesh, but there was witness in my pain. "Get up," Jeremy said again, but now, it was a plea.

"She cannot." Helen's voice slithered calmly through the fray. "She is not one of us anymore."

"Is she human?"

"No. She is the most pathetic of all creatures: a mortal vampire." Helen crouched beside me. With motherly tenderness she had never shown before, she stroked my hair. "She is dead but still dying, alive but without life. My Jennifer . . ." She kissed me, and her touch was nectar, sweetness strong enough to lift me back into my doom.

"Finish her." I smelled the wooden stake I could not see as Helen laid it in Jeremy's hand.

"You killed my sister," he panted, with reverence and awe.

"I killed a mortal girl who stood between us and the future." She stood, but her radiance still warmed me as she caressed her other child. "It's what we always wanted, Jeremy: to be together, invincible, forever." Her promise shimmered, phosphorescent, drawing dreams in sparkled flame.

Conner slinked to the floor beside me, guarding my body with his. "You wouldn't," he dared.

Jeremy growled, "Get out of the way, Boy-Toy. She's killed more people than you've slept with. This is justice."

"No, it's jealousy. She had the courage to change."

Jeremy ground his stony teeth and stepped toward me. His angry fingers notched the stake as he drew it back to strike the blow. "Jeremy," I murmured from my deathbed on the floor. "Stop. Smell."

He stared at me, his nostrils twitching, flared. I knew he could not miss the faint but glorious perfume that spilled so improbably from my wounds.

Jeremy shook his golden head. "Fuck," he said, and swung the stake toward Helen.

She caught his hand, and the stake rolled out, the two immortals flailing limbs like rapiers as they fought to grab it from the floor. "Jennifer, get up," Conner pleaded. I groaned and tried to rise, but the pain in every broken bone crescendoed with the first inch I raised my head. *Get up. Save Conner.* But good intentions could not heal me. Only blood could manage that.

"Coward!" Helen pinned Jeremy's arms behind his back while her eyes like hellfire burned through me. "You know how to save yourself. Are you too craven to live?"

"Why do you care?" I choked.

"Because it's not too late."

Jeremy writhed and tried to speak, but she threw him to the ground. She stamped her foot against his throat and held it there. "I will not leave here alone. One of you will come with me, or I will kill you both and start again – with him." She nodded toward Conner, transforming him with her eyes.

Hatred coated my senses, a blanket of crimson rancor heavier than my pain. Nothing but death could have kept me on that floor, yet when I tried to rise, the world stumbled, capricious earth toppling me down. "That's right, Jen. Get up. You can save him from me and be healed."

The flash of Jeremy's eyes caught mine, shining with the fear that was all we ever truly shared. Conner upended my kitchen table, trying to break off a leg for a stake, pounding fruitlessly while he cried. Stacy Higginbotham's hair still spilled out from the bag, the specter of death we would all soon share.

Helen loured over me, her majesty tinged by my scarlet glare. "The choice is yours, Jennifer." She put the stake into my hand. "Kill them both and come with me, or put it through your own breast and end your pain."

Splinters sawed my skin as I gripped the weapon I would never let go until someone named Carshaw lay dead, but the pulse of every brutalized vein predicted it would be me. *God, I could use that angel right about now.*

"Last chance, Jennifer." Helen stomped on Jeremy's windpipe harder, then darted into the kitchen, to where Conner stood pounding on the table. Quick as lightning, she picked him up and threw him into the air. He landed and bounced like a tennis ball, his head crunching against the checkered tile floor. An ominous trickle of red spilled out near his ear.

Helen replaced her foot on Jeremy's throat before he could even groan, pinning him out of her way. She breathed, inhaling the sublimity that dribbled from my lover's open veins. "Mmm . . . so beautiful! Take it, Jennifer, or I will."

So beautiful. The soul that had saved me, the soul that had found mine, drip-drip-dripping out, the medicine of immortality. *Take it, or she will. He will die; let it be with your kiss. Let it be so that Helen dies, too.* I gripped the stake harder and inched across the floor. "That's right," Helen whispered. "Come back to me, Jen."

Jeremy coughed, an attempt to speak, but I did not catch any words. Lightning flashed through my skull as I lifted myself to my elbows. Conner's chest rattled as it rose, and I knew he did not have long. My aching body cried to drink, to save us both from pain. "I love you," I wept. "It should not have ended this way."

Something cold and wet dripped down my chin. I reached to wipe the tear, but my fingers came away red. Through all the grief and agony, an idea blossomed, so simple, so obvious, so complete. Conner Brazel was not the only bleeding mortal in this room. *Here goes nothing.* I touched the golden crucifix at my throat, then lifted my bloodstained finger to my lips.

One drop, and the crucible of my suffering shattered. One drop, and I ascended from the flames of all my trials, a sword of steel and heartache quenched in grace. I leaped to my feet, and with one clean squish, the stake hit home. The demon collapsed, her hands at her heart, red rain pouring from her open wound.

Jeremy scampered out and took his turn, ramming the rod of judgment home. She choked. She stumbled. She fell.

She did not rise.

The sickle of death sliced through her, leaving only dust and broken dreams behind. I breathed deeply, wanting freedom, wanting jubilance and relief, but the ashes of my enemy swept me with her woe. *Why?* I had cried to the universe so long, and at last, the creature who had called herself my mother answered. Within her swirling ashes flurried echoes of a desire so familiar, it might have been my own. She had wanted what I wanted, though she denied its name. She had made me, made Jeremy, hoping one of us would choose to share her blackened effigy of love.

I made the sign of the cross in the air. "Have mercy on us and on the whole world."

Jeremy murmured, "Amen."

I met his russet eyes. "Thank you."

"Yeah, well." He ground his toe into the floor. "She had us both fooled, didn't she?" He reached out and touched my still-bleeding face. He brought the blood toward his nose and breathed. "There's nothing quite like the scent of soul."

I blushed and fell to my knees beside Conner. "Can you run?"

Jeremy flexed his battered neck and answered, "Yes."

I stroked Conner's hair away from his fluttering eyelids, knowing our paths were unlikely ever to cross again. I would long for him forever, with every breath I breathed, but at least I left him better than I had found him: no longer a playboy but a man who would give up his life for love.

"Take him to the hospital. Tell them who he is. Tell them when he wakes up to give him this." I grabbed a piece of paper and scrawled: *I love you. God loves you. You will never be alone.*

Jeremy tucked it into his pocket and hefted Conner from the floor. "I'll come back for Stacy." He bit back his tears.

"I'm sorry. For everything."

"Me, too." He kissed my cheek, and then I was alone.

I looked toward the dingy residue of evil, all that now remained of four thousand years of terror. "I forgive you, Mother," I whispered. Then I took my suitcase, still packed, and I went home.

15

The train glided along as if cushioned by air, devoid of the rumbling clickety-clack I had learned to expect from the movies. For two days, across five states, I sat with my laptop, typing. First, my resignation letter to Amos, filled with apologies that could never suffice. Then I scoured my brain, leaving no stone of memory unturned. Dates. Locations. Descriptions. Names, if I knew them, though I had tried so hard not to learn them. Every murder I had ever committed, set down in black and white. I wrote where to find the bodies, the few whose bodies were available to find. Their families deserved answers. My victims deserved to be mourned.

At every station, I searched for news. Conner had been hospitalized with "undisclosed injuries," but every report listed him as stable. I found nothing about Jeremy or Stacy. Their schools were still out for Christmas vacation. No one had yet noticed they were gone.

The layer of dust on my abandoned apartment floor drew nary a word.

The *Sunset Limited* chugged into New Orleans around 10 p.m. the second day. I scrambled my computer's signal with a software Jeremy had installed during our roommate days and sent my list to the FBI. I gave no explanations, no excuses. Only the list and my word, however feeble it might seem, that I was done.

I found a cheap hotel for the night, where a box of drugstore dye restored my hair to its original mousy brown. I took out my green contacts, and, for the first time in more than four years, I washed off all my makeup and did not re-apply it. A tiny white blemish in the crevice along my nose confirmed what I already suspected: mortality had remembered me. Sixteen-year-old Jennifer Carshaw peered out from the grimy glass — sixteen plus two days. I lay down in the cigarette-scented sheets and dreamed of nothing more than day number three.

It dawned cold and foggy while the city still slept, the torpid week between Christmas and New Year's drawing few people out into the haze. I pulled my jacket tight and walked alone through the potholed streets. My fingers shook as I pressed the intercom outside the great Neoclassical façade of my destination.

"May I help you?"

"Delivery for Diane Patterson. I need her to sign."

"Just a moment. I'll send her down."

The December wind bit through me, but it did not cause the palsied quiver in my limbs. I touched her note, the brittle paper splitting along the creases as it nestled inside my bra, where I carried it close to my heart. The latch of the door handle clicked, and there she stood, my own personal St. Peter keeping watch at heaven's gate.

"I'm sorry," I said.

Sister Diane gasped and clutched her chest, the whole gamut of human emotions gushing from her radiant heart, but fear surpassed the rest. Her hand reached for the pocket where she always kept her phone.

"Please. Not yet."

"Jennifer." She breathed my name as if speaking it could make me real.

"I don't expect you to forgive me, but I had to come . . ."

She crushed me into her arms, weeping into my hair. "Jennifer. My Jennifer. You're home."

She hustled me away from the convent, into a classroom inside the empty school, denying my request to bring Mother Lily along. "She's Sister Lily now that we've lost our convent, thanks to you. She ate nothing but bread and water for two years. She still cries herself to sleep at night, and we just got her back into a classroom this past August. You are not going to hurt her again, no matter why you're here." She shut the door behind us, wiping her eyes on her sleeve. "All right. If you're planning to kill me, do it now. Otherwise, you better give me a pretty darn good reason not to call the police."

"Call them if you have to, only baptize me first. Please."

She took a deep breath, then lifted my chin, forcing me to meet those kind, pugnacious eyes that had believed in me every single day of my life. "Don't you give me any feel-good, born-again nonsense, Jennifer. You don't get to write off murders with 'I'm sorry.' Tell me the truth, or I'll make the call."

"Get a priest," I begged. "I'll tell you both."

I confessed to the archbishop for two hours with Sister Diane sitting by my side. I told them everything, from my ghastly birth through the oppression of my childhood, from the ecstasy of blood through the bewilderment of change. From Martin Reed to Malibu, nihilism to new life, no horror did I dare omit or gloss over. No eye was dry by the time my story brought me to New Orleans and the convent door.

The archbishop took off his glasses and polished them on his sleeve. "Jennifer, I have been a priest for forty-three years. I thought I had heard everything there was to hear in a confessional, but a *vampire* . . ."

"I know. I wake up every morning thinking the same thing."

"I wish I could withhold absolution on the grounds that you are clinically insane."

I held out my phone. "Call Conner. I don't know if he's conscious, but you can try."

"That will not be necessary." He returned his glasses to his face and stared intently through them. "Jennifer, there is only one penance I can give. If you truly want forgiveness, you have to face justice — and that might mean Death Row."

Sister Diane's vise-like grip tightened around my hand. "It won't come to that. It can't."

"Yes, it could." I pictured the executioner wielding a stake as we waited for the governor's twelfth-hour call. "Your Excellency, death and I are old friends. If that is truly your last word, I will go. But until then, I need blood."

He turned a sallow shade of green. "Yes, well, I suppose the blood bank can arrange . . ."

"No. *His.*" I touched my crucifix, its delicate threads as toilsome as the original old rugged tree. "You can't save me, Your Excellency. But He can."

His flinty eyes narrowed under their wrinkles. "Wait . . . are you saying . . . ?"

"Yes. Food for my body also feeds my soul."

"The food of angels," he whispered.

"I'm not an angel. Just a sinner like everyone else."

"Bow your head, child." He laid his hands upon me. "God, the Father of mercies, through the death and resurrection of his Son has reconciled the world to himself and sent the Holy Spirit among us for the forgiveness of sins; through the ministry of the Church may God give you pardon and peace, and I absolve you from your sins in the name of the Father, and of the Son, and of the Holy Spirit." The archbishop took my hand. "Now come with me."

He led me down the path of bridges yet to build, through halls where Jeremy still hunted and Mother Lily's tears flowed free. He unlocked the stained-glass door of innocence and drowned my shadowed past, the future dripping shamelessly from every strand of mousy hair. Crowned with oil and fire, I fell to my knees, and the Word translated the fruits of earth into a banquet of living joy. Eternity dawned, the red Sun that never sets, rising above the cares of every tomorrow. *Thank you*, I sighed into the fragrance of resurrection.

Then I drank.

AUTHOR'S NOTE

The Sisters of Prompt Succor and Our Lady of Prompt
Succor Academy, Baton Rouge, are completely fictional. There
are several schools of the same name in other parts of
Louisiana, and devotion to the Blessed Mother as Our Lady of
Prompt Succor originated at the Ursuline convent in New
Orleans. No resemblance to any real persons or institutions is
intended.

34154567R00210

Made in the USA
Middletown, DE
23 January 2019